Acclaim for the authors of

THE CHRISTMAS VISIT

MARGARET MOORE

"Ms. Moore is a master
of the medieval time period."
—*Romantic Times*

TERRI BRISBIN

"A welcome new voice…you won't want to miss."
—*USA TODAY* bestselling author Susan Wiggs

GAIL RANSTROM

"Gail Ranstrom certainly has
both writing talent and original ideas."
—*The Romance Reader*

DON'T MISS THESE OTHER TITLES AVAILABLE NOW:

#728 WYOMING WOMAN
Elizabeth Lane

#729 THE UNEXPECTED BRIDE
Elizabeth Rolls

#730 THE WEDDING CAKE WAR
Lynna Banning

MARGARET MOORE

Unknowingly pursuing her destiny, award-winning author Margaret Moore graduated with distinction from the University of Toronto with a bachelor of arts degree. She has been a Leading Wren in the Royal Canadian Naval Reserve, an award-winning public speaker, a member of an archery team and a student of fencing and ballroom dancing. She has also worked for every major department-store chain in Canada. Margaret sold her first historical romance, *A Warrior's Heart,* to Harlequin Historicals in 1991. She has recently completed her eighteenth novel for Harlequin. Margaret lives in Toronto with her husband, two children and two cats. Readers may contact her through her Web site, www.margaretmoore.com.

TERRI BRISBIN

is a wife to one, mom of three and dental hygienist to hundreds when not living the life of a glamorous romance author. Born, raised and still living in the southern New Jersey suburbs, Terri is active in several romance writers organizations, including the RWA and NJRW. Terri's love of history, especially Great Britain's, led her to write time-travel romances and historicals set in Scotland and England. Readers are invited to contact Terri by e-mail at TerriBrisbin@aol.com or by mail at P.O. Box 41, Berlin, NJ 08009-0041. You can visit her Web site at www.terribrisbin.com.

GAIL RANSTROM

was born and raised in Missoula, Montana, and grew up spending the long winters lost in the pages of books that took her to exotic locales and interesting times. That love of the "inner voyage" eventually led to her writing. She has three children, Natalie, Jay and Katie, who are her proudest accomplishments. Part of a truly bicoastal family, she resides in Florida with her two terriers, Piper and Ally, and has family spread from Alaska to Florida.

THE CHRISTMAS VISIT

MARGARET MOORE
TERRI BRISBIN
GAIL RANSTROM

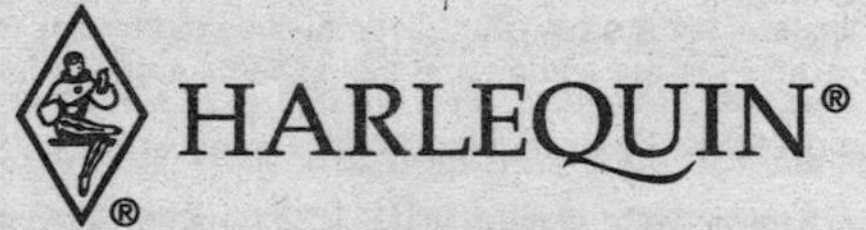

TORONTO • NEW YORK • LONDON
AMSTERDAM • PARIS • SYDNEY • HAMBURG
STOCKHOLM • ATHENS • TOKYO • MILAN • MADRID
PRAGUE • WARSAW • BUDAPEST • AUCKLAND

ISBN 0-373-29327-5

THE CHRISTMAS VISIT

This edition published by arrangement with Harlequin Books S.A.

www.eHarlequin.com

Printed in U.S.A.

CONTENTS

Dear Reader,

One thing that always makes Christmas merry for me is the music. Nothing gets me more in the Christmas spirit than my favorite carols, "Deck the Halls" and "Joy to the World."

During my research for this novella, I learned that "Deck the Halls" is based on an old Welsh folk melody, possibly dating from medieval days, and was likely what was known as a "dance carol," or *canu penillion*. The dancers would sing a line, and the "answer" would be played on a harp. That explains why the alternate lines of "Deck the Halls" have no lyrics.

I also discovered that the standard Welsh version wasn't published until 1873. I simply couldn't resist revealing that the music to this popular carol is of Welsh origin, so I confess I had the song appear somewhat earlier than is historically accurate.

Why didn't I just set the story after 1873? Because I also wanted to write about a character who's been in my head for a long time. Griffin Branwynne first appeared in *The Dark Duke,* published in 1997. When I was asked to do a Christmas novella, he immediately came to mind. He had already banished himself from his friends, so it was easy to imagine how he would feel when a young lady determined to provide a Christmas for "her children" came barging into his house seeking his help.

I hope you, too, enjoy the music of this festive season, and the company of friends and family.
Merry Christmas!

Margaret Moore

COMFORT AND JOY

Margaret Moore

With many thanks to Amy, for her critiquing, and Steven, for the wonderful Sunday dinners.

Chapter One

December 20, 1860
Llanwyllan, Wales

The young maidservant clasped her work-worn hands to her black worsted bodice as she watched her mistress prepare to depart. "Oh, Miss Davies, I think you're taking an awful chance! I'd be scared to death to go up there alone!"

"Nonsense," Gwen said briskly as she adjusted her untrimmed dark brown bonnet. "There's nothing to be afraid of. I'm sure the Earl of Cwm Rhyss can't be as bad as they say."

"But he is! Mean and wicked and terrible!" Molly cried. "Why, he never sees nobody, nor comes out of his castle, not since the accident. And he's scarred something horrible, they say."

Gwen turned to the anxious young woman and gave her a reassuring smile. "He comes out. He goes riding, or so I've heard. And he has a housekeeper who comes to the village every Saturday, as well as a man-of-all-work. I hardly call that living like a hermit."

"But nobody 'cept them ever sees him!"

"It doesn't seem so strange to me that a man horribly scarred would hide himself away from those who might stare or ask questions."

"Don't you remember what he did the last time anybody went up there to ask him to contribute to a charity? He threatened to shoot them on the spot!"

Gwen had been trying not to remember the tales that had spread through the valley about that incident three years ago. "I'm sure that was an exaggeration."

Molly rapidly shook her head. "I was working at the inn then. They said he got his shotgun and told them he'd use it if they didn't clear off."

"If I see any sign that he's about to start shooting, I'll run," Gwen assured her, only half joking, for in truth, the stories told about the reclusive Earl of Cwm Rhyss weren't encouraging, especially considering her purpose for visiting him.

Molly pointed to the window. "It looks like snow, Miss Davies. You don't want to get caught out in a storm, do you?"

Gwen followed the younger woman's gaze over the small yard between the gray stone orphanage and the wall surrounding it, a remnant from when it had been a House of Correction. Beyond lay the rough, rocky Welsh mountains. The slate-gray clouds above did not look promising, but she wouldn't let the threat of a little snow dissuade her.

"It's only four days until Christmas, and if I don't go to Rhyss Hall today, I might not get another chance before the holiday arrives," she said, voicing aloud the reason she simply couldn't defer her visit.

She gave Molly a smile. "I don't think it's going to snow for a while yet and, given that I don't expect to be asked to stay for tea, I should be safely back before the first flakes start to fall."

"Won't you at least let me call for Williams-the-Trap? He can take you there in his pony cart."

Gwendolyn shook her head as she pulled on her woolen gloves, mended at the thumb. "We've no money for that, and it's not far. I've walked plenty of miles up the mountains in my day. If I find myself in difficulty, I'll take refuge at Denhallows' farm. It's on the way."

"Look you, there's another thing," Molly declared. "It's no easy walk up to the hall. He's never had work done on the road since the river flooded in the spring."

"I'm sure I'll manage," Gwen said firmly.

"The earl's always had a fierce temper, they say, and since he was hurt—" Molly persisted.

"I was in the Crimea," Gwen interrupted, determined to get on her way with no more lamentations and dire warnings from Molly. "If I can withstand the horror of Balaclava, I think I can manage a reclusive nobleman. And if he's rude…well, it won't be the first time a man's been rude to me. Nor, I suspect, will it be the last. And if it should start to snow, I'll be safe and sound in the Denhallows' kitchen."

With that, Gwen took one final look at herself in her small, cracked mirror to make sure she was neat and presentable, ignored Molly's dismayed countenance and hurried on her way.

Picking her way carefully along the rough, muddy track that would have been a decent road except for the earl's neglect, Gwen raised her eyes to look at the massive stone wall looming in the distance. It was like something out of a fairy story, and it was easy to believe an evil sorcerer or ogre lived behind it. The wrought-iron gates, adorned with the earl's coat of arms—a Welsh dragon and a lion rampant—creaked as the wind began to increase. The few sparse trees along the way bent and moaned, and the sky was even darker than before.

Hardly a good day to go visiting, even if it was necessary.

She looked back the way she had come. The Denhallows' farm was two miles back down the valley. She could probably get there quickly enough if the weather worsened. And how long would she be at the earl's? She didn't think he'd really draw a gun on her, but she was also sure her visit would be a brief one.

Therefore, she decided, as her toes felt progressively more numb and she wrapped her thin gray cloak about herself, she would carry on to the hall, make her request and leave as quickly as possible. By the time she reached the Denhallows', the weather would either be improving or getting worse, and she could decide what to do then.

Her choice made, she walked as fast as she could to the gate, trying not to stumble over the ruts. She would hardly help her cause if she fell and arrived at the hall disheveled and covered in mud.

The way soon leveled out, for the manor house of the earls of Cwm Rhyss had been built on a plateau that overlooked the valley below. She'd heard that in the days of the Normans, there had been a castle there, although nothing of it remained. Beyond the plateau was a small valley, then the land rose again, more stark and rugged. A few farmers lived higher up on the mountain, but most of the local inhabitants lived below the isolated estate.

When Gwen reached the iron gates, she looked through the bars at the drive leading up to the huge house that dated from the days of Elizabeth and the Welsh-descended Tudors. Its front was grim gray stone, with tall windows that were all dark, making it look as if the house were abandoned. A massive portico sheltered the front door.

Not the most welcoming aspect, but she hadn't come this far to turn away now.

And she was desperate. She had only two pounds to spend for Christmas. That wouldn't buy many presents, or much in the way of a celebratory feast, and her children, who had so little, surely deserved a few Christmas treats. She wouldn't be able to excuse herself if she let the disquieting aspect of a building or rumors of a harsh temper dissuade her.

She looked about for some sort of gatehouse or a way to

alert those in the house that they had a visitor. Seeing none, she tried the gate. To her surprise, it opened easily.

That was more auspicious, although the gust of wind that caught her cloak seemed colder than before. Perhaps that was only because she was standing still.

Walking briskly up the drive, she was soon warmer, if not feeling much more confident of a pleasant reception. A light flared in one of the lower windows. Another hopeful sign.

Then a man appeared, silhouetted in the window—a tall man, with broad shoulders. She lifted her hand to wave a greeting, and the man abruptly drew the curtains closed.

"Well, merry Christmas to you, too," she muttered under her breath. If that was the earl, this was not a good sign, and she hoped he hadn't gone to fetch his gun.

On the other hand, as she'd told Molly, she'd survived the Crimea, and other things before that, without succumbing to fear. If she had, she would never have become a nurse, and she would have turned back at the first sight of the blood-soaked wharf at Balaclava. The wounded had needed her then, and her orphans needed her now.

She marched up to the enormous oaken front door, which bore a large cast-iron knocker in the shape of a horse's head, lifted it and knocked.

She cringed as the sound echoed through the house like the barrage of a cannon. She hadn't meant to make *quite* so much noise.

The door swung open to reveal not an irate nobleman with a shotgun—to her relief—but an elderly woman with a face much wrinkled, and dark, snapping eyes. She wore a cap and apron so clean they rivaled new-fallen snow for whiteness.

"I'm sorry to intrude," Gwen began with a smile. "I'm Miss Gwendolyn Davies, from Saint Bridget's Orphanage in Llanwyllan, and I've come to see the earl, if you please."

The woman smiled, then frowned and looked anxiously

over her shoulder. "The earl says he isn't receiving visitors today."

"Oh?" Gwen replied, her tone poised between concern and sympathy as she angled her way through the front door. "I do hope the earl's not ill. Perhaps I can be of assistance. I've trained as a nurse."

"It's, um, not that," the woman said with another glance over her shoulder. "He doesn't like visitors."

"I'm not here to visit," Gwen replied, still moving inexorably into the foyer. It had a spotlessly clean marble floor and was paneled in age-darkened oak. Several medieval pikes, swords and shields hung on the walls, and there was a complete suit of armor by the wide stairs that led to the second floor. Two corridors led off from the foyer, one to the right, the other to the left.

"It's a charitable matter," she continued, "and since it's nearly Christmas, I'm sure he won't mind—"

"Mrs. Jones!" a deep, powerful voice rumbled from down the corridor on her right, where the momentarily illuminated window had been. "Get that damned creature out of my house! She's not getting a ha'penny out of me!"

Any niggling doubt Gwen felt about intruding on the earl's privacy completely disappeared.

The old woman flushed and looked contrite. "I'm sorry, Miss, but I think you really ought to go. He's in a right foul mood today. It's the time of year, you see. He used to love Christmas, and then...well, it reminds him of all the things he used to like so much. A one for the parties and games and singing, he was. And he's busy, you see, trying to finish the history he's writing."

The fact that the earl had literary pretensions was news to Gwen, and she was sorry he'd been hurt, but even so, that didn't give him the right to be rude.

"Perhaps if you could tell him that I've come from Saint Bridget's?"

A door opened down the corridor to her right, sending a shaft of light into the dim hall. A tall, broad-shouldered figure with shaggy hair to his shoulders loomed into view, hands on his hips. "Miss-*sus* Jones! Will you *please* get rid of that woman, or must I?"

Gwen noted he didn't have a gun of any kind, so she marched toward her objective like a soldier going over the top, ignoring the housekeeper, who trotted after her, bleating like an agitated sheep. "Oh, dear. I don't think…miss…you'd better not…he's…"

"My lord, if you please, just a moment of your time," Gwen said, determined that he at least hear her proposal. "I don't wish to disturb you, but it's nearly Christmas and I've come—"

"I bloody well know why you've come, and the answer is no!" the man roared before disappearing into the room to his right and slamming the door behind him.

For a moment, Gwen hesitated—but only for a moment. He might be an earl, but she was at least deserving of basic courtesy and, in her mind's eye, she kept picturing the disappointed looks on several small faces come Christmas morning.

She reached the door with light showing beneath it, shoved it open—and entered the messiest room she'd ever seen in her life. Books and papers were scattered about as if someone had left the windows open on a windy day. A single lamp stood lit on a desk that was covered with handwritten pages that had lines crossed out and notations in the margins. Helmets of various metals and descriptions rested on top of the bookshelves that lined the room, and an enormous broadsword leaned against the desk that had sizable chips out of one edge, as if the someone had taken a few swings at it with the weapon.

Most disconcerting of all, the Earl of Cwm Rhyss stood in front of the glowing hearth, his expression fierce, feet planted, arms crossed, the very image of enraged authority, although he was dressed as simply as one of the local farmers, in a pair of woolen straight-cut trousers, white shirt open at the neck, a worsted vest and dark jacket. A plain gold watch chain and fob gleamed in the light.

Also visible in the light was a terrible scar that left the left side of his face permanently red and mottled.

She'd seen worse ruin done to a human face. Much worse. The scar skirted the eye socket, and she surmised that his long hair was intended to hide most of the scarring and likely a damaged ear.

"I'm sorry, my lord!" Mrs. Jones exclaimed, panting, as she followed Gwen inside. "I couldn't—"

"I heard," the earl growled. "You can leave, Mrs. Jones. I'll deal with this *person.*"

Instead of scurrying away, as Gwen expected, Mrs. Jones gave the earl the same sort of look one might give a recalcitrant child. Then she dipped a curtsy. "I'll go get some tea."

"We don't need any tea," he retorted. "I'll ring the bell when this insolent woman is ready to leave. *Shortly.*"

Mrs. Jones nodded, gave the earl another chastising look, then departed.

"My lord, I'm sorry to intrude—"

"The hell you are."

Supplicant or not, there was a limit to what Gwen would endure, and she was fast losing her temper. "If you think to dissuade me by such coarse language, my lord, I must tell you that I've heard far worse in my time."

She subdued a smirk of satisfaction when she saw that she had taken him aback with that remark. "My name is Miss Gwendolyn Davies, and I've come—"

"To ask me for money." He looked her up and down. "I *thought* you must be another charlatan out to rob me with some story about good works, or one of those ladies who turn themselves into Lady Bountiful at Christmastime, helping the poor unfortunates. But I can tell by your exceedingly ugly wardrobe that you're neither. I suppose, then, you're the sort of woman who, failing to get a husband, throws herself into charitable works. That would explain your incredible gall. And you probably want to preach the necessity of saving my eternal soul at this joyous season of rebirth, too. You may spare yourself the effort." He pointed at the door. "I think heathens are better off left alone, and so am I."

She very calmly and resolutely continued to face him. "My lord, I'm afraid you misunderstand. I don't give a damn about your eternal soul and you may happily go to hell for all I care."

His brown eyes flared, but she ignored his reaction and carried on just as matter-of-factly. "However, my lord, you can't take your money with you when you go. Before that melancholy day, and since it's nearly Christmas, a time when *most* people are inclined to be grateful for their good fortune and pleased to share with those less fortunate than themselves, I was hoping you'd make a contribution for some presents and special treats for several Welsh children who live in the orphanage of which I'm the matron down in Llanwyllan."

He limped around his desk. She hadn't noticed that he had difficulty walking before. He'd probably been trying to hide that, the way he grew his hair to hide his scar and what was left of his ear.

"By God, you're the most aggravating, presumptuous woman I've ever met."

"I simply refuse to be intimidated, especially considering the reason that I've intruded upon your—" she surveyed over his messy study "—interesting existence."

"I prefer that my *interesting existence* not include unwelcome visitations by people who want my money."

"And I would prefer not to trouble you, but it's only four days until Christmas and we have almost nothing for the children."

He sniffed as he sat in the chair behind the desk. "Christmas comes the same day every year. You should have planned for it, and not waited until you were forced to ask a stranger to come to your aid at the last minute."

"I did plan for it. What I did *not* plan for was the need for a new chimney when the old one collapsed. Or the addition of four children to our ranks. Or the sudden loss of one of our principal benefactors. What I had put by for Christmas had to go elsewhere."

"So you gathered your courage and came to beg of the Earl of Cwm Rhyss?"

"So I decided to ask a rich man if he'll consider helping us. We don't require much, my lord. Just something to get a treat for each child and a goose for Christmas dinner."

"How many children are you talking about?"

"Fifty."

His eyebrows shot up. "Only fifty?" he asked sarcastically.

"They don't expect much from Father Christmas, my lord. Perhaps an orange, or a bit of candy. The sum I require is likely almost nothing to you, but it would mean so much to them. I would hate to have them find nothing Christmas Day."

The earl's full lips twisted into a smirk. "You're very good at trying to wring a man's heart with thoughts of pathetic children, their big eyes moist with disappointed tears. Perhaps you should consider a career upon the stage, Miss Gwendolyn Davies."

"Perhaps I shall, if I've succeeded. Have I?"

"If I tell you you haven't, what will you do then? Go down on your knees?"

"If I must."

She made as if to do so, until he snarled, "Good God, woman, I wasn't serious."

"Oh?" she replied evenly. "You must forgive me for not realizing you possess a sense of humor. Or not comprehending that you wouldn't require a suitably humiliating display before you agreed to part with a small sum of money."

He gave her a sour look. "If giving you some money gets you out of my study and lets me get on with my work, I'll contribute to the orphans, the infirm, the aged and anybody else you'd care to name."

Not the most gracious of replies, but she smiled nonetheless. "In that case, my lord—"

"I was joking."

"Again, you must forgive me for not appreciating your wry sense of humor."

With something that sounded like a muttered curse, the earl yanked open a draw and started rifling through its contents. "As it happens, Miss Davies, I contribute to a number of charities through my solicitor. I simply don't advertise the fact, although perhaps I should consider posting a list on my door to keep shrewish harridans from marching into my house like irate sarjeant-majors and demanding I help them."

"You may insult me all you like, my lord, if it gives you pleasure," she replied. "I'll consider it the price I must pay for troubling you. But if it's any consolation to you, the children will be most grateful. Take it from one who knows, it's the one time of the year they find it easy to believe people care about them. It is the one time of year many do."

"You've been in the orphan business some time, then."

"Both before the war, and after."

He didn't reply, and as he continued to rummage, she pushed away her memories of Christmases past and surveyed the room again. It was clear the man enjoyed collecting medieval artifacts. Or perhaps they helped with his writing.

The books crowding the shelves, the pedestal table and even piled on the floor were many and various. The titles she could read were all histories and biographies. The titles she could not were in Latin.

"I'm so glad you're still here, miss!"

Mrs. Jones had returned, carrying a large tray with a teapot, cream, sugar, two Wedgwood china cups, scones and strawberry jam. "I'll just set this down over—"

She made an exasperated noise as she shoved the pile of books out of the way on the pedestal table. "For the love of God, Griffin, must you pile your dusty old books everywhere?"

If the earl's eyes could have shot arrows, the dear woman would be dead. "I told you, Mrs. Jones, that we don't need tea. Miss Davies will be leaving as soon as I find my damned cheques."

Mrs. Jones beamed, clearly not a whit disturbed by the earl's propensity to curse. Then she frowned. "You didn't even invite her to sit down—and after walking all that way!" she chided as she hurried toward Gwen. "She'll think you've got no manners at all. Give me your bonnet and cloak and sit you there by the fire, Miss Davies. I'll bring your tea to you. Do you take sugar?"

"No, thank you. I prefer mine clear."

"This isn't a damn tea party!" the earl muttered.

"No need to be rude, Griffin," Mrs. Jones said. "You've already growled at the poor dear quite enough. You ought to respect her, considering what she's done."

Gwen couldn't make out what he mumbled, but the gist of it was he didn't think she was a *poor dear,* and only barely deserving of a cup of tea or a chair.

"She was a nurse in the Crimea."

The earl shot Gwen a questioning glance. "You were in that mess?"

"Yes, I was," she replied, realizing that his eyes were not like any other brown eyes she'd seen before. They were flecked with green and gold, yet not green enough to be hazel.

He was fortunate his left eye hadn't been blinded in the fire.

He went back to the search.

"I do hope you can find a cheque, my lord," Gwen said as she regarded the top of his head and his thick, curling hair.

Many a woman would weep to have such hair. And such thick lashes, which should look ridiculous on a man but, somehow, seemed perfectly suitable to him.

"They're here. Somewhere."

"Perhaps I could help."

"No!" he snapped, darting an annoyed look at her. "Sit down, drink your tea and don't touch anything!"

"He's got a *system,* he says, so his notes won't get out of order. For his book, you see," Mrs. Jones explained in a loud, conspiratorial whisper as she handed Gwen a cup of fragrant Earl Grey. "*I* think he's just too lazy to tidy up."

Mrs. Jones's confidential revelations elicited another scowl and mumble from the earl, and a stifled smile from Gwen as she sipped her tea.

"Aha!" the earl cried triumphantly after rustling in the very back of the bottommost drawer. He straightened and brandished a book of cheques. "I found them. Don't get too comfortable, Miss Gwendolyn Davies. You'll be leaving very soon."

"No, she won't," Mrs. Jones declared. "She can't."

She frowned at their puzzled faces. "She can't go anywhere in a snowstorm."

Chapter Two

As Gwen looked at the window in dismay, another gust of wind rattled the panes. She could barely see beyond them because of the blowing, heavily falling snow.

She should have turned back at the gate. "I was sure it was going to hold off," she murmured, more to herself than anyone else in the room.

The earl came around the desk to stand beside her. "Unfortunately for you, Mother Nature doesn't seem to take much heed of your desires. Or maybe coming here in inclement weather was a clever scheme. Perhaps you thought you might need considerable time to soften my hard heart and being trapped here would give you the opportunity. I may live in relative isolation now, Miss Davies, but I spent plenty of time in society, and I know the wiles women are capable of."

"I thought nothing of the kind!" she indignantly replied. "I thought that if it was going to snow, it wouldn't be until I was safely home. And it was either venture forth now, or have nothing for the children. If you don't believe me—"

The earl held up his scarred hand to silence her. "As it happens, I do believe you. Only a fool would try such a tactic with me, and I don't think you're a fool. Headstrong, determined, stubborn and you can curse like a navvy, but not a fool."

He turned away from the window. "You can go home in my carriage. Jones can spend the night in the inn and return in the morning, or whenever the snow stops."

Mrs. Jones regarded him as if his suggestion was utterly ludicrous. "Daniel can't take the barouche out in a blizzard! They might get stuck. And it's not been used these four years or more—a wheel might fall off."

"It's not a blizzard," Gwen protested with more hope than conviction.

The earl snorted. "What else would you call it? A bit of bad weather?"

"Whatever you call it," Mrs. Jones said, "she can't go home tonight, or while this snow keeps up. I'll go get the blue bedroom ready," she finished, bustling off before Gwen, or the earl, could protest.

Gwen looked at her obviously disgruntled host, who couldn't be any more unhappy than she about the situation. "I *must* get back to the orphanage."

The irate nobleman limped back around his desk. "Will the children riot without you there to oversee them?"

Gwen stiffened. "I'm sure my staff can keep order."

"Then you fear your family will worry about you?"

"I don't have any family, and I said I'd take refuge at the Denhallows' farm if the weather changed."

"Aha!" the earl cried triumphantly, splaying his hands on his desk and leaning toward her. "Then you *did* realize the weather was likely to turn bad and you came anyway!"

"I truly did think it would hold off, at least long enough to get to the Denhallows' farm," she answered with all the dignity she could muster. "I didn't plan to impose on you, I don't want to impose on you, and I'm sorry I must."

"It's a little late for regrets," the earl growled as he lowered himself into his chair.

She'd had enough of his rudeness. "I may be nothing more than the matron of an orphanage in need of funds, my lord, but I deserve to be treated with courtesy and respect, regardless of how I came to be here, or what the weather's done. I'd rather risk trying to get to Denhallows' farm than put up with your incivility. Good day, my lord." She turned on her heel to leave.

Proving he was more agile than she suspected, he reached the door before her. "Don't be an idiot, Miss Davies. You're not going anywhere."

"I'm not an idiot, and that sort of comment is precisely why I'm leaving," she said as she attempted to go past him.

He moved so that he was blocking the door. "I won't allow you to martyr yourself in a snowstorm."

"I won't stay where I'm treated with such disrespect."

His eyes narrowed and his frown deepened. "Very well, I shall endeavor to refrain, since I don't want to be held responsible for your death—which means I'd best keep my distance from you entirely."

She met his glare with her own. "I believe that would be best, and I assure you, my lord, I'll cease imposing upon your *generosity* the moment I can."

The nobleman's expression shifted, to one slyly curious. "It's only my insolence that upsets you, Miss Davies? Or is there another reason you don't wish to stay here? Are you worried about your reputation? What will the neighbors say? The villagers? The clergy? A young, unmarried female staying with the reclusive Earl of Cwm Rhyss?"

Sure he was trying to use his powerful physical presence to intimidate her, she regarded him with contempt. "They'll say that I had no choice."

His lips curled up into the most wicked, devilish smile

Gwen had ever seen. "You don't fear that I'll come creeping into your bedchamber and try to have my way with you?"

"You could try, my lord, but I've been taking care of myself for a very long time, and I daresay you'd regret it."

"That sounds like a challenge, Miss Davies."

"Only if *you* are a fool."

He limped to the pedestal table and picked up one of the teacups, which looked ridiculously small and delicate in his large, powerful hands, as if he could shatter it simply by holding it. "There was a time, Miss Davies, when I could have made you fear for your virtue." He cut her a glance. "Or gladly give it up."

Her throat suddenly seemed very dry. But she'd been propositioned before, by soldiers and their officers, so she quickly mustered a response. "Boasting of past seductions and your ability to make a woman throw away her virtue is hardly the behavior of a gentleman."

He came toward her, his movements slow but seemingly inexorable. "The gentlemanly eldest son of the Earl of Cwm Rhyss died when that beam fell across me and left me a ruin."

Still she stood her ground. "Are you planning to continue this rather unusual method of seduction, my lord? Because if so, it won't work. I've spent many years around men, several of whom thought a woman who is neither pretty nor well-to-do should be only too willing to share their bed and be thankful for the opportunity. They didn't succeed, and neither will you, because my virtue is the one thing I can call my own. Still, I must admit the notion of portraying yourself as a scoundrel and reprobate in an attempt to make yourself more attractive is a novel one."

He set down the china cup with such swift force she was surprised it didn't break. "And no man who looks like me would ever succeed with any woman."

"Am I now to feel sorry for you, my lord, because your scars have ruined your ability to seduce women?"

"They ruined a lot more than that," he muttered as he went to the door. He shot her another look. "But you can't possibly understand that. Where the devil is Mrs. Jones?"

As if his question had immediately summoned her, the elderly woman appeared in the doorway, holding a candle that flickered in the draft.

"I'm right here, my lord," she said, giving him a chastising frown. "Come along now, my dear. I've got a nice fire going and some water to wash."

As Gwen joined her, the earl turned on his heel and limped back to his desk. "I'll have my supper in my study tonight. *Alone.*"

Mrs. Jones looked as if she wasn't pleased, but said, "If you say so."

Then, holding the candle aloft to light the way, she led Gwen toward the staircase. "Please don't mind him, miss. He can be a bit rude when his work's interrupted and the cold makes his leg ache."

A *bit* rude? Gwen had never met anybody so rude in her life. Coarse, perhaps, and unrefined, but not so breathtakingly, deliberately insolent. And dismaying. And disturbing.

As for the idea of trying to seduce her…it was ridiculous.

"He's got his book to finish, you see, and he always gets a bit testy when he's running out of time."

Then he should have been able to appreciate her immediate need for funds before Christmas.

"It's a history of Wales," the woman went on without prompting, and with obvious pride. "Starting from before the Romans up to Queen Elizabeth."

At the top of the shallow steps, they came to a long gallery, paneled in rich mahogany, the walls covered with portraits. They were the earl's family, Gwen assumed as she walked past the oil paintings of men and women wearing clothes from eras past that proclaimed their wealth and power.

She could practically feel them looking down their aristocratic noses at the orphaned daughter of paupers.

She wouldn't let the portraits intimidate her any more than she would their descendant. So she stared at them all as she passed, her steps slowing when she came to the last. It was the earl, in formal dress, probably painted when he was in his early twenties. Despite his attire, he was posed casually in front of a marble fireplace, one elbow on the mantel, with a sort of careless ease that matched the smile and expression in the eyes that seemed to suggest the world was his to enjoy.

And why not? Judging by the portrait, not only was he wealthy and titled, he'd been breathtakingly handsome.

The passage of time and the scars had certainly altered the earl's features, but there was much yet of the handsome young man in the man in the study below: the dark curling hair, the strong jaw, the straight nose, and those knowing, mocking brown eyes. The body was the same, too—broad shoulders, long limbs, narrow waist and hips, muscular thighs. Indeed, despite the scars, the earl was still a very attractive man.

Which made his self-imposed isolation that much more self-indulgent, and she would waste no pity on him.

"This was done during his last year at Oxford," Mrs. Jones offered, coming back to join her, "when he took a first in history."

So he was intelligent—another reason not to feel sorry for him.

"That was about five years before…."

Mrs. Jones's voice trailed off, but she didn't have to finish. Gwen could guess to what she was referring.

"The young women used to flock about him like so many birds," Mrs. Jones said with a sigh as she turned and started forward again. "And all the young noblemen wanted to be his friend. Oh, he was a merry fellow in those days, before the fire—and that woman—broke his heart. Ended their engagement right after the accident, she did. But he was well rid of her, and I told him so at the time."

Gwen suspected he hadn't been delighted to hear Mrs. Jones's comments, for she'd seen men face similar situations in the hospital—a body permanently injured or scarred, followed by an engagement broken. One, a man could hope to cope with, but both? She'd known at least two who'd killed themselves rather than go back to England.

"As for his supposed friends, there might have been one or two stood by him, but only because he was rich. My poor boy figured that out soon enough."

Perhaps there was more to the earl's self-imposed isolation than vanity, after all. He must have felt as if his whole world had come crashing down with that beam.

"Then at Christmas—you never saw a man put his soul into celebrating the day like he did. The whole house would ring with his singing. He comes by it honest, for his parents—bless their memory!—was just the same. There'd be gifts for everyone and anyone, and food! Oh, my, we had an army of cooks during the holiday. Wassail and pudding, tarts and pies and all sorts of fruit. Even the scullery would be full of pine boughs and mistletoe and holly." She wiped her eye with the corner of her apron. "I miss the singing most of all. Such a voice he has—like an angel."

"Did the smoke from the fire damage his lungs?"

"No. He says he has no heart for singing now." Mrs. Jones came to a halt outside a door. "Here we are. The blue bedroom, and as pretty a chamber as ever I saw."

They entered the largest and prettiest bedroom Gwen had ever seen, the corners shrouded in shadow until Mrs. Jones lit more candles. The walls were papered, the pattern one of delicate blue blossoms. The furniture was rosewood, of a simple light design, and really quite dusty. The bed was large, with a canopy and royal-blue velvet curtains. A thick blue satin coverlet was drawn back, and there were the signs the bed had been hastily made.

Clearly, this room hadn't been used in years.

"Why don't you make yourself comfortable while I fetch everything else you need to make you feel at home?"

As if she could ever feel "at home" in such a place! "If you don't mind, I'd rather go with you. I'm used to working, and I'd prefer the company."

"But you're the earl's guest and it wouldn't be right."

"I'm not his guest, strictly speaking," Gwen replied. "I'm a refugee from inclement weather."

Mrs. Jones cocked her head and studied the young woman. "Well, it's still chilly here, and that's a fact. The kitchen'll be warmer. All right, come with me. What Griffin doesn't know won't hurt him. When he's in this sort of mood, he'll stay in his study until the Lord only knows when."

Later that night, after convincing Mrs. Jones to let her eat in the kitchen and help clean up, Gwen sat in the large bed in the blue bedroom, her arms wrapped around her knees. She wore a voluminous nightgown that Mrs. Jones had loaned her. The kindhearted woman had also provided plenty of coal for the fire, a bed warmer, three candles, two more blankets and a shawl.

Outside, the snow continued to fall steadily, whipped by the howling wind. She could almost feel the drifts piling up against the house, blocking the road. What if she couldn't leave tomorrow? Or the next day?

There was still so much to do for Christmas. Her children had little enough at the best of times, beyond clean clothing and full bellies. She wanted to give them a happy Christmas, to assure them all that they were as deserving as any child of a treat or a toy. To make the day special.

She should have kept that in mind, and not let the earl annoy or upset her. What was a little personal humiliation when the children's happiness was at stake? What if he changed his mind and declined to give anything to the children? Why, oh why hadn't she held her tongue?

She threw back the covers and got out of bed. She sucked in her breath when the soles of her feet met the cold wooden floor. Grabbing the shawl, she wrapped it about her as she went to the window and peered out. She couldn't see a thing except blowing snow.

Looking around the huge room, she shivered—and it wasn't just from the cold.

She wouldn't stay here in this chamber. She'd dress and go to the kitchen, to wait for morning and Mrs. Jones. That was better than being here by herself.

After dressing, she took one of the candles and left the bedroom, tiptoeing down the corridor, and then the long gallery. She paused to look again at the picture of the earl in the flower of his youth.

If she had been a beauty, then been horribly scarred, rejected by the man who was to marry her and deserted by her friends, might she not retreat and hide herself away? Might she not be bitter and angry at the world?

She raised the candle a little higher and studied the portrait more. What would it be like to possess looks and property and rank? No wonder he'd enjoyed Christmas so. For him, it must have been a celebration of bounty, a joyous occasion to relish all that he possessed.

For her, Christmas had always been a time more of hope than celebration. Hope that people would think of needy children. Hope that they would be generous. Hope that she would get a gift—any gift. A ball. A pair of warm stockings.

"Is the accommodation not to your liking, Miss Davies?"

She whirled around to find the earl right behind her, looming out of the dark like a ghost.

A very solid, muscular ghost.

He grabbed her wrist. "If you don't mind," he said, taking the candle from her, "I've narrowly avoided death in one fire. I'm not anxious to tempt fate again."

Flustered and flummoxed, she didn't reply as he let go of her wrist.

His face lit from below by the candle, he raised a questioning brow. "Was the blue bedroom not warm enough?"

"It was most comfortable." That wasn't exactly a lie; it would be very comfortable, to most people.

"Why, then, are you prowling about my house in the middle of the night?"

He made her sound like a burglar. "I'm not going to steal anything!"

"That's a relief. Were you planning on staring at my family's portraits all night?"

"I was going to the kitchen."

"Was dinner not satisfactory?"

She tried not to betray any frustration with his persistence in thinking she'd found something to criticize. "It was delicious, and the Joneses are very hospitable."

"Unlike your host."

Ignoring that comment, she said, "I thought I'd go to the kitchen and help with breakfast."

His brow rose. "In the middle of the night?"

"It must be nearly dawn," she replied, hoping she was right.

He took a gold watch out of his vest pocket and opened it. "Three in the morning." He snapped it closed. "You'll have a long, chilly wait. Mrs. Jones banks the fires before she goes to bed. I suggest you retire, Miss Davies. Mrs. Jones will come for you when breakfast is ready."

He turned to go, taking the candle with him.

"My lord!"

He half turned, then realized what he'd done and offered it to her.

She hesitated, then instinctively clasped her hands together, as she'd always done when she was a girl and asking forgiveness for a transgression of the rules. "My lord, I regret what I said to you after you generously offered to donate something for the children's Christmas and I hope you won't change your mind about doing so."

The earl's lips curved up. In the flickering light of the candle, that made him look demonic. "Calm yourself, Miss Davies. I told you I would, so I will, for the children's sake."

She sighed with relief. "Thank you, my lord."

"I'm not really an ogre, although my looks may give that impression."

"I don't think you look like an ogre. I've seen worse scars many times, my lord."

"Because you were a nurse, of course. You are the exception then, and not the rule."

She could think of nothing to say to that, because she had seen more wounds than most people.

"Well, Miss Davies, since my face doesn't repel you and I can't sleep, either, perhaps you'll join me for a brandy in my study."

When she didn't immediately reply, he frowned. "I promise you'll be quite safe with me. You're not the sort of woman I'm attracted to, anyway."

As if she'd ever think she was! "I don't doubt that, my lord."

"Or are you, despite all you've said, afraid of me?"

"No, my lord."

"Then come along, Miss Davies, and have a brandy."

Determined to show him that she wasn't afraid of him in any way, she followed him to his study. He held open the door and gestured for her to enter. "Sit down."

She did, by the hearth where a cheery fire cast out its warmth. The bronze glow from an Argand oil lamp illuminated the messy papers on his desk. The windows of the room were etched with frost. The untidiness, the scattered books, the fire and dull, glow of the lamp, made it seem very cozy and comfortable, and not like a nobleman's room at all.

The earl took out two snifters and a crystal decanter from behind some books piled on the bookshelf nearest the door. "The glasses are clean. Mrs. Jones brought them this morning," he said as he poured the brandy.

Perhaps she should refuse the drink. "Thank you, my lord, but—"

"But?" he inquired as he walked toward her carrying the glasses. "As there's nothing to fear from me, there's nothing to fear from a little brandy." His eyes twinkling with amusement, he smiled that mockingly devilish smile. "Think of it as medicinal, Miss Davies."

As she accepted it, being alone with him suddenly seemed like a very dangerous place to be. But she wouldn't flee like a coward or risk offending him when he'd done nothing except hand her a brandy.

The earl settled himself in the chair opposite and regarded her over the top of his glass. "How much will you require to make this Christmas a merry one for your orphans?"

"Ten pounds."

He took a drink. "That doesn't sound like much for that many children."

"They don't require much to be happy. And perhaps I fear that if I name a larger sum, you'll never contribute again."

He laughed, a low rumble of merriment that was surprisingly pleasant. "A wise answer. And since you seem a wise and intelligent woman, I think I can do better than that."

She smiled. "Thank you, my lord."

"So your efforts were worth it, after all, Miss Davies." He rose and set his glass on the mantel. "If there was nothing else robbing you of sleep tonight, you should have no trouble now. There are still a few hours before dawn."

He casually leaned against the mantelpiece, in a pose very similar to the one in his portrait, reminding her that he was still very handsome, even if he didn't think so. "Or were there more than Christmas worries keeping you awake?"

"No," she lied.

"Then I wonder what compelled you to leave the room—or were you uncomfortable for some reason and you didn't want to tell me before because you feared I'd rescind my pledge?"

She had been extremely uncomfortable, but not for the reason he suggested. "The room was perfectly comfortable, my lord."

"Then why did you leave it?"

"You wouldn't understand."

"I might."

She shook her head. "I don't think so."

"I'll try."

What harm could it do to tell him? Her weakness wasn't anything to do with him.

"You may desire solitude, my lord," she said slowly, "but I don't. It…unnerves me."

Having started, she decided to continue. "My parents died of a fever one night, within hours of each other, when I was four years old. We weren't discovered until nearly noon the next day."

She stared at the flames, remembering her panic and desperate horror as she tried to rouse her parents. Then being carried away by the beadle, kicking and screaming and crying.

The earl wordlessly rose and poured her another brandy.

She accepted the drink, holding it in her hands and looking at the slowly shifting liquid without really seeing it. "I was taken to an orphanage."

She took a sip as the earl returned to his chair.

"I know many people, especially those who read the works

of Charles Dickens, think such institutions are all horrible places," she continued, more relaxed now that the worst of her story was over. "Many of them are. I was fortunate to be in one of the good ones. Food was meager, but enough, and the clothes they gave me were clean and better than the filthy, torn garments I'd had before.

"But I was terrified of being alone at night."

She tried to sound matter-of-fact, as if there was nothing unusual about revealing this aspect of her past and its effect on her. "I still hate to be alone, especially in the dark. I have my own room at the orphanage, of course, but I know I'm not more than a raised voice away from another person."

"You've not had an easy life, Miss Davies," the earl said after a moment.

"No," she agreed, thinking that a mild way to put it. "But I survived."

"I'd say you've done considerably more than merely survive. How did you become a nurse?"

"I was very fortunate. The vicar thought I was clever and when he heard I wanted to be a nurse, he offered to pay for my education." She saw no need to tell him how she'd had to struggle to achieve that goal even with the Reverend Mr. Johnston's help. "When I learned about the situation in the Crimea, I asked to be sent."

"Paying back the reverend with good works, or following a sweetheart?"

She frowned. "Neither. Reverend Mr. Johnston asked nothing in return for my education. And if I followed anybody, it was Mary Seacole."

"Not Florence Nightingale and her famous lamp?"

The sardonic earl was back, and it was not a transformation Gwen welcomed, especially given the subject. "She, and her methods, saved many lives. But I spent more of my time with Mary Seacole in Balaclava than at the hospital in Sebastopol. Perhaps you've heard of her, although she's not so famous as Miss Nightingale."

Gwen smiled as she remembered the determined Creole. "She's a marvelous woman, and so inspiring! Refused by the War Office, she went anyway and spent all her money setting up her own hospital close to the front. She didn't let anybody stop her. You should have heard her speak of the officers she knew when they were in the West Indies. 'My boys,' she always called them. She simply had to help them, and she made me want to help them, too." Her voice dropped as she thought of all the young men who had died. "As many as I could, anyway."

"She clearly made an impression on you, Miss Davies," the earl said as he leaned back in his chair, his features in shadow. "Was Balaclava as bad as they said in the newspapers?"

"Worse. No written account can possibly convey what it was like."

She'd never forget the sights, sounds and smells of the wounded being crammed onto ships to be taken to Miss Nightingale's hospital. Or the feeling of overwhelming helplessness in the face of so much suffering and pain.

"Is that why you aren't nursing now?"

She finished her brandy and nodded her head. "I've seen enough death and blood and mutilation to last me a lifetime. I like children, and I know the difference a good matron can make to an orphanage, having been so blessed to have such a woman in charge of the one where I was sent. When I heard about the opening for a matron for Saint Bridget's, I applied, and here I am."

The corners of his mouth lifted. "Yes, here you are—trapped with the Earl of Cwm Rhyss."

Chapter Three

Suddenly very aware she was alone in a room with an attractive, virile man while a blizzard raged outside and only two servants elsewhere in the huge house, as well as no neighbors for miles, Gwen swallowed hard.

Yet what she felt wasn't fear. It was something completely different—and completely wrong.

The earl rose and added more coal to the fire. "Rather like a heroine of a gothic story, or a fairy tale. The virtuous Miss Gwendolyn Davies has blundered into an enchanted castle, presided over by a handsome prince disfigured by an evil witch's spell." He straightened and looked at her. "Perhaps if you kiss me, the spell will be broken. My scars will disappear and I'll be as I was—young, handsome and happy."

Her heartbeat quickened. Her fingers trembled as she set down her glass.

Determined not to betray how his words and that look—especially that look—affected her, she answered bluntly. "The past is what it is, my lord. There are things I would change about mine, but I can't. We must accept that."

He grabbed the poker and jabbed at the fire, sending sparks

rising into the chimney. “I don’t need you to tell me the past can’t be changed. I see that every time I look in a mirror.”

She got up and grabbed the poker before he put a hole in the bricks. “You’ve got some terrible scars and you limp, but otherwise you’re sound of wind and limb. You’re rich, and you have a title. You have much to be grateful for.”

“That makes what happened to me nothing at all?” he demanded, glowering at her as he crossed his arms over his broad chest. “Easy enough for you to say, Miss Davies. Get yourself scarred so badly that people turn away in revulsion when they see you and then you may preach to me about how fortunate I am.”

She put the poker back in its place and met his glare steadily. “Do you know how many men would gladly trade places with you, my lord?”

“Do you know how many I would?”

“People will soon forget to see the scars.”

“The way you have, I suppose?”

“Yes. If people shun you because of your scars, that shows their weakness and lack of character. I can appreciate that your heart was broken—”

“What do you know of the state of my heart?”

She flushed as she continued. “I know you were jilted by the woman you were to marry.”

He laughed a cold, bitter laugh as he leaned back against his desk. “Not that it’s any of your business, but if there was one good thing about my accident, it was that it rid me of the lovely Letitia. If I’d married her, she would have made me a cuckold in a month. So I’m not pining for my lost love.”

She was relieved, for his sake. “I’m glad to hear it. But you’re still pining for the life you’ve lost and no good can come of that, except bitterness and discontent.”

“How simple you make it sound.” He swept the air with his hand. “Just march out into the world and reclaim your place in it." He gripped the edge of his desk, his knuckles whitening. "*You've* not witnessed the horror in people's eyes when they look at you. Or realized your entire future has been torn from you because of a brawl you didn't start, over a woman who proved to be no better than a whore."

"I'm not saying it will be easy. Do you think it was easy for me, an impoverished orphan, to make my way in a world that has few opportunities for women, especially poor ones with no family? I assure you, my lord, it wasn't. Perhaps your future isn't what you planned when you were young, but that doesn't mean you have nothing left to hope for, to strive for. Indeed, I think you already know that, or you wouldn't be writing a book. What is that but a hopeful venture?"

"It's an amusing pastime. Something to keep me from going mad."

"Then you won't mind if I throw a few pages of it into the fire." She reached around him.

With a cry, he lunged and grabbed her hand before she could pick any up. Then he tugged her close. "Don't touch my work!"

"Your *work,* is it?" she said, aware that she was but inches from his body and that her heart was beating with an excitement different from anything she'd ever felt in her life. "Not your idle pastime?"

His gaze seemed to bore into her. "I understand my own motivations quite well enough without you explaining them to me. I seek to shun my fellow man before they can shun me, while you do what you do because you crave the opposite. You want people to like you and you think that if you make yourself useful and necessary, they will. You'll be valued. *That's* what brought you here today—the longing to be loved, a need at least as selfish as my desire to be left alone."

As she stared at him, aghast, his mouth twisted into another smile. "Not so pleasant when the shoe is on the other foot, is it, Miss Davies? How does it feel to have your barricades stormed?"

She wrenched herself free of his grasp. "How dare you twist my work into something self-centered and selfish? At least I'm trying to help people. What are you doing but sulking and brooding on your misfortunes? I may be trapped here by the weather, but you've chosen to hide here because of vanity."

"Vanity?" he growled her. "How can I be vain, with this face?"

He shoved his hands through his hair, pushing it back so she could see the angry red scar that marred his face and neck and the remains of his ear. "Is it vanity to want to spare the world the sight of this?"

"It's vanity and pride. I've seen it before, especially among the officers who'd been handsome before they were wounded or crippled. A few even killed themselves rather than return home less than whole or with scars. You haven't done that literally, but you've buried yourself here.

"As for wanting to be loved, everybody wants that—including you, my lord. It's the fear that you're unlovable that keeps you here. Better to hide yourself away than risk rejection."

"I'm not the only one hiding, Miss Gwendolyn Davies, with her shapeless black gown and drab gray cloak and ugly brown bonnet and hair done up so severely it's a wonder her head doesn't ache."

She started for the door. "I wear what I can afford to wear, my lord, and my hair is this way because I have not the time, nor the maid, to do it differently."

He moved to block her path, so that she nearly collided with him. "Dressed like some sort of nun, you surround yourself with people dependent upon you, so they don't dare reject you."

"I won't listen to another word!" she cried, trying to go past him.

"How dare *you* come to my house and upbraid me? What sort of gall do you possess that you think you have the right to make presumptuous pronouncements about my character or my situation?"

"The same right you have to insult me and make fun of me and make presumptuous pronouncements about *me.*"

He grabbed her shoulders. His chest heaving, he stared down at her.

Panting with rage and indignation, her eyes full of angry tears and her heart with anguish at his insults, she glared back.

And then suddenly, everything seemed to shift, as if the room had tilted. A look of surprise flared in his eyes, while something within her leapt and kindled and surged, an emotion, an excitement, different from anything she'd ever experienced before.

A loud banging echoed through the corridor.

The earl let go of her and reached for the oil lamp on his desk. Limping from the room, he disappeared down the corridor.

As she hurried after the earl, Gwen struggled to regain her self-possession. Only an emergency would have sent someone out on such a night.

Encircled by the glow of the lamp, the earl threw open the door under the portico. A short, stocky man, his hat, black beard and woolen jacket thick with snow, stumbled into the foyer. He clutched a lantern containing the stub of a weakly flickering candle.

"Good God! It's Mervyn!" the earl cried as he caught the man and hauled him upright. "What the devil are you doing out in the storm?"

"Your lordship? Thank God," the man rasped, his breath coming in hoarse heaves as he leaned on the earl as if he was half-dead.

Gwen ran to help. Bill Mervyn had a small farm farther up the mountain. He sometimes helped around the orphanage when they needed some repairs done, accompanied by his two young sons.

Gwen got her shoulder under the farmer's and took the lantern before it fell from his grasp. "Where are the boys?"

"Still up at the farm," he answered. "I had to leave them. I need to get the doctor. For Teddy. He fell. His leg's broken bad. I've come to see if I can borrow a horse to get to the doctor."

"It's a damn good thing you didn't get lost or fall down and break your leg, too," the earl said as they half carried Bill to the study.

After they got him in a chair by the fire, Bill looked at the nobleman, his eyes pleading. "Can you give me the loan of a horse, my lord? I've got to get to the doctor down in Llanwyllan. I had to wait for the storm to let up, and it did a bit at last, thank God, but I've got to fetch him, and quick. I had to leave my boys all alone, and Teddy's bad off."

The earl examined Bill, and in the nobleman's expression, Gwen could see a mirror of her own thoughts: even if the weather was perfect, Bill was too wet and exhausted and distressed to go anywhere else that night.

As Gwen stirred the fire, the earl poured the man a large snifter of brandy and forced the glass into his mittened hand. "Drink that."

Bill started up. "I've got to go for the doctor."

"Sit down," the earl ordered, his voice as stern and commanding as any she'd ever heard from an officer in the British army. "You're half-frozen. You can't go back out into such weather."

"But—!"

"*I'll* go for the doctor." The earl strode to the door. "*Jones!*" he bellowed.

Both surprised and relieved by the earl's offer, Gwen knelt at Bill's feet and started to remove one of his wet boots. "Let's get these off."

"You don't have to do that," Bill said as he set aside the brandy and bent to help.

"It's all right, Bill. Take off your gloves, if you can," Gwen ordered in a voice that had proved effective with generals and orderlies and every rank in between. "You've got to get warm and dry, or you'll get sick."

Mrs. Jones, in a flannel robe, pushed past the earl and entered the room. "Mercy on us," she cried. "Is that Bill Mervyn?"

The white-haired, cherry-cheeked Mr. Jones appeared, with his shirt half-tucked into his trousers, one arm in the sleeve of his jacket, and his boots in his other hand. He silently gaped at the scene before him.

"His son's had an accident," the earl explained. "Jones, saddle my horse. I'm going for the doctor."

The Joneses exchanged anxious, uncertain glances.

"Mervyn tells me the snow's letting up, and his son cannot wait," the earl said. "Get going, man. We haven't any time to waste. Mrs. Jones, I think Bill could use a good strong cup of tea and something to eat."

Still struggling with his clothes, Mr. Jones hurried out of the room, followed by his wife.

"Bill," Gwen asked gently, "did the broken bone pierce Teddy's skin?"

The distraught man nodded, his eyes agonized. "Aye. It looks terrible. I cut off his trousers and got a bandage on it. I didn't know what else to do."

"You did the right thing, Bill," Gwen assured him, although she desperately hoped he hadn't done any more damage, and that the bandage was clean.

She rose and addressed the earl. "May I have a word with you, my lord? In private?"

Bill started up again. "What is it? What's the matter?"

Gwen thought fast. "I just wanted to ask the earl how long it might take him to get to the doctor."

"It's an easy road," the nobleman replied. "I shouldn't be long, provided the snow doesn't get worse and hasn't drifted."

Bill groaned and put his head in his hands.

"I've ridden through snow before, Mervyn," the earl said, as if insulted by the man's fears. "Now if you'll excuse us, I need to speak with Miss Davies." He hesitated for the briefest of moments. "About my knee."

Gwen hurried after him into the corridor. "Is your knee—?"

The earl grabbed her arm to pull her further from the door, then loosened his hold. But he didn't remove his hand from her forearm.

"It's fine. That was an excuse. The boy's in a bad way, isn't he?" he demanded quietly, his grip tightening again. "That's why you wanted to talk to me alone."

"Yes. Have you another horse, my lord? We're closer than the doctor, and Teddy's leg must be tended to at once. I can set it and clean it, well enough to prevent more serious damage until the doctor can see to him. Otherwise…well, he could lose his leg. Or worse, if the wound's already infected."

"Of course you can have a horse. I nearly lost my leg, and I wouldn't wish that fate on the boy. I know a shortcut to Mervyn's farm. Jones will go for the doctor and I'll show you the way."

Anything that could get them to Teddy quickly.

"It's not an easy track. How expert a rider are you?"

"I can manage to sit on one long enough to get to Bill Mervyn's farm, and it'll be faster than trying to walk through the snow."

The earl muttered another curse. "Then we have no choice."

"I'll run and fetch my cloak."

"I'll get it. You stay with Bill. He could use some comfort." The earl turned to go, then hesitated. "I've got laudanum, if you think that'll help."

"Yes, and any bandages you can spare."

With a nod, the earl limped off while Gwen went back into the study and helped a shivering Bill remove his coat and scarf and woolen cap. She rubbed his hands and his feet, trying to get the blood flowing. With relief, she saw that he wasn't frostbitten; his greatest trouble was sheer exhaustion.

"How did Teddy break his leg?" she asked as she worked to get him warmer.

"He fell on some ice in the yard," Bill replied. "Twisted his leg. I heard the bone snap. I carried the poor lad to his bed and tended him as best I could, but I knew he needed the doctor.

"All night I kept thinking it was going to stop snowing. Any minute, I'd say to myself. Any time now, until I couldn't wait anymore."

"I understand," Gwen said softly. "And it's good you came here."

Bill grasped Gwen's hand. "It's God's doing, that's what, having you here."

"I'll do my best to help Teddy, Bill." She made herself smile and covered his hands with hers. "I can set a broken bone."

"Wear that."

They both jumped as a ladies' cloak of scarlet velvet, lined with ermine and with a tasseled hood, landed on the desk. Blushing, Gwen gently pulled her hands free, although there really was no reason she shouldn't have been holding Bill's hands to comfort him.

She turned to look at the earl, standing on the threshold, wearing a long, indigo greatcoat and a beaver hat. His black riding boots gleamed in the firelight. He carried a bag that clinked dully as he shifted his feet, and she recognized the sound of bottles wrapped in cloth. The laudanum, no doubt.

"It's a little fine for riding about the countryside, but it'll be warmer than that gray thing you had on," the earl muttered before swiveling on his heel. "I'll be waiting for you in the stables, Miss Davies."

His tone was gruff and harsh again. She wouldn't wonder about the reason for the change; she would concentrate on helping Teddy Mervyn.

The earl had no sooner departed than Mrs. Jones returned with a tray bearing tea, toast, ham and eggs. As she set down the tray, she gave Bill a sympathetic look and said, "I'll just leave these things for you here, Bill. I'm to fetch Miss Davies's gloves and a good pair of stout boots I have, and a thick scarf. I won't be minute and then she can be on her way."

She spotted the cloak and sucked in her breath. "I thought he'd burned that," she murmured before she hurried from the room.

Because it had been the lovely Letitia's? Gwen wondered. If the woman could reject a man like the earl because of a few scars, she didn't deserve such fine apparel, either, although destroying the cloak would have been a waste.

Bill had barely started to eat when Mrs. Jones returned with the boots, gloves and scarf.

Gwen quickly changed her shoes for the heavier boots. They were at least two sizes too big, but that was of no consequence. She wrapped the scarf around her head and put on the velvet cloak.

"I think I ought to go with—" Bill began, half-rising.

"No, you stay here and get dry," Gwen ordered. "We can't have you falling ill, too."

Bill reluctantly returned to his seat.

"Mrs. Jones, can I count on you to get him into a bed?"

The kindly woman nodded and gave her a smile. "Leave him to me, deary. I know a wee bit about nursing myself."

"I thought you might," she said, suspecting Mrs. Jones had been entrusted with the earl's care since his childhood, which would explain her familiar relationship with the nobleman.

"Don't worry, Bill," she said gently. "I'll take good care of Teddy."

She hurried out of the study and into the yard. The snow on the ground was at least a foot deep, two or more where it had drifted. It was still falling, but the wind had died down, and the sun had obviously risen, for the sky was lighter to the east. Someone had already opened the gate. From the footprints in the snow, she guessed it was the earl.

She pushed open the door to the stable, which was welcomely warm. Three horses stood ready.

The earl was beside a huge black beast that snorted and stamped impatiently, reminding her of its master. The other horses were brown, and smaller. Even so, only an emergency would have compelled her to attempt riding either of them.

Mr. Jones started leading one of the brown horses outside.

"Stay to the road," the earl called out. "Don't put yourself in harm's way. If it starts snowing harder, you'll have to seek shelter at one of the farms. The boy will be in good hands until the doctor gets there."

Gwen hoped his compliment would prove justified and that Teddy's injury was less severe than she feared.

Mr. Jones nodded and, after touching his cap to her, continued on his way, while the earl led the big black gelding and the other horse, which had a dark muzzle, mane and tail, toward her.

"Hold on to the saddle and step into my hands," the earl ordered, lacing his gloved fingers.

She did as he commanded and was hoisted high enough to get on the saddle. It took her a moment to get in position, and she had to force herself not to be afraid, for her perch was precarious and she seemed so very high. She hadn't felt this way since she first set foot on the ship taking her to the Mediterranean.

"You have *sat* on a horse before, haven't you?" the earl demanded.

"Yes," she answered. "Once or twice. Well, once. At a fair. But the important thing is to get to Teddy."

"And all in one piece," the earl muttered as he led her outside, where he mounted the huge black horse in one fast, fluid motion.

Then, as the snow swirled around them, they rode out of the iron gates and headed up the mountain.

Chapter Four

The snow continued to fall heavily from lead-gray skies, but mercifully, the wind ceased gusting about the stone outcroppings. Every so often, there would be a break in the ground, where rivulets of water tumbled over rocks, moving too quickly to freeze. Otherwise, all around was silent save for the sound of the horses' hooves on the snow, and Gwen's own breathing. No other animal or bird stirred.

She had no idea where she was, for they hadn't taken the road. They were on a small path that ran parallel to the road, then veered to the right.

It was a good thing she had the velvet cloak. Without it, she'd be much colder, wetter and more miserable.

"Is it much farther?" Gwen called out to her guide as they continued up the narrow, rocky track through a small wood.

"No," the earl replied, his broad shoulders and beaver hat white with snow. His hips swayed from side to side with the gait of his horse, which sometimes pranced as if impatient with their slow pace.

The beast couldn't be any more impatient than she.

She hoped she was in time to save Teddy from serious complications. She tried to remember everything she knew about compound fractures and their treatment. She should have asked Bill what medicines he had in the house, although she doubted, given his poverty, that he had any. It was fortunate that the earl had laudanum. The boy was probably in a great deal of pain.

"There's the farmhouse," the earl announced after several more minutes had passed. He pointed to his left.

She could barely make out the stone walls and slate-roofed cottage and small outbuildings through the snow-laden branches before the earl turned his horse and led hers toward a rickety wooden gate. He dismounted and undid the flimsy latch, then they proceeded into the small yard.

The earl came beside her horse and, without a word, held out his arms to help her down. She put her hands on his shoulders and eased herself off the animal, while he seized her about the waist.

Very aware of the pressure of his two strong hands and the proximity of his body, she slipped to the icy ground.

She had hardly landed before he let go and turned away to rummage in his saddlebags. "Here's the laudanum," he said, handing her a bottle wrapped in a thick cloth. He gave her another bottle. "I brought some whiskey, too."

"Whiskey?"

"For cleaning the wound." He pulled out another small bundle of cloth.

"What's that?"

"Bandages," he said as he started to lead the horses toward the small stone barn to the right of the cottage.

"Hurry."

The earl came to a halt, then turned on his heel to regard her. "I'm not going inside the house."

She frowned. "You can't stay out in the cold. Nobody's going to come through the snow and steal your horses."

"I'm not worried about a thief, and I'll be warm enough in the barn."

She churned her way through the snow toward him, the large boots and the depth of the snow making it difficult to walk.

"I can guess why you want to stay in the barn—the same reason you've imprisoned yourself in your manor. But this is no time to indulge your vanity, my lord. Even if you were as hideous as a gargoyle—which you're not—I need your help with Teddy. He'll have to be held down while I set his leg. Bill Mervyn's younger son is only eight. He can't do it alone."

The earl's expression didn't change and, for a moment, she feared he was going to refuse, until he gave a slight nod of his head. "Just let me get the horses inside."

"Good." Turning her back to him, she struggled through the snow toward the door of the farmhouse. It flew open before she got to it, revealing the sturdy form of little William Mervyn.

Like his father, he had curly black hair and a round, full face. He had obviously spent a sleepless night, for his cheeks were pale and he had dark circles under his bright blue eyes.

"You remember me, don't you, William?" she said as she reached him. "I'm Miss Davies from Saint Bridget's. You and your father and brother come and help me sometimes."

"Where's Da?" the lad asked anxiously, looking past her. "Did he fall and hurt himself, too?"

With a reassuring smile, Gwen steered the boy inside and closed the door. "No, he's fine. But he was very tired and wet, and I ordered him to stay at the earl's. We don't want him getting sick, and just before Christmas, do we?"

The boy shook his head as she removed her wet cloak and hung it on a peg near the door that sported caps, a scarf and bits of harness.

"Fortunately, I was at the earl's, and so I was able to come. I've set lots of broken bones before."

"Who's that other man?"

"The Earl of Cwm Rhyss," she answered as she quickly scanned the small interior. The whole lower floor of the cottage was only slightly larger than the earl's kitchen. There was a loft above, where she supposed the boys slept. The mantel and the massive, ancient oak sideboard were decorated with pine and holly branches. Dirty dishes sat on the table.

The injured Teddy lay on a small bed in a corner by the hearth, very pale, his eyes closed, among the pillows and threadbare woolen blankets. With his tousled black hair and long lashes fanning his flushed cheeks, he looked younger than his twelve years.

Gwen quickly set down the laudanum and other items, then hurried to Teddy and put her hand on his forehead.

As she'd feared, he was feverish.

She gently lifted the blanket and started to remove the rough but clean bandage his father had put just below the boy's knee.

Teddy yelped and his eyes flew open, to stare at her with horror, his face twisting with pain.

"I'm sorry if I'm hurting you, Teddy," she said soothingly. "You remember me, don't you? I'm Miss Davies, from Saint Bridget's."

Gritting his teeth, the boy nodded.

"I've got to look at the break, and then I'll fix it."

It was indeed a bad break, one that would take all her skill and experience to deal with.

She put her hand on the boy's forehead again. This time, it wasn't to feel for fever; it was to brush back his hair and offer a little comfort. "Close your eyes and rest a moment while I get you something that's going to take away most of the pain."

He nodded.

"That's a brave boy," she said as she rose.

William watched her with wide, anxious eyes as she unwrapped the laudanum and whiskey.

"Is there water to wash?" Gwen asked.

William pointed at a bucket near the fire. "Da got that from the well yesterday."

The door to the kitchen opened, letting in a gust of frigid air, and the earl. William started, then stared when the nobleman entered, his head grazing the lintel of the door.

He didn't come further inside, but stood uncertainly on the threshold, his face half-turned in an attempt to hide the scarred side of his face.

He looked so vulnerable, as if the stares of a child could physically hurt him.

She thought it was the rejection of his noble friends or people who had known him in his handsome youth that had embittered him and that he sought to avoid; now she realized he feared the rejection of anyone who saw him. For a moment, she regretted speaking harshly to him before.

But pity was not the answer to his pain. Hiding himself away would only prolong and increase his dread. She would treat him like the vital, worthwhile man he still was.

"Come in and close the door," she said briskly. "You're letting in the cold air. William, will you put some wood on the fire, please?"

Both did as she asked, although William kept glancing at the earl as he shrugged off his coat.

"I see you've noticed the earl's scars," Gwen remarked. "He was very badly hurt a few years ago."

"You're really an earl?" William asked, his fear giving way to awed curiosity.

"Yes, I really am," the nobleman answered gravely.

"Were you hurt in a battle?"

"No," he said gruffly. Then he went on, his tone less abrupt. "There was a fire and I was injured."

"Oh." William sounded disappointed.

Gwen picked up the bottle of laudanum. "Is there a spoon, William?"

He nodded and went to fetch a handmade wooden spoon.

"I'm going to give Teddy some medicine to help him sleep," she explained to the boy. "Then I'm going to need your help and the earl's, too."

She sat on Teddy's cot and helped him to sit up. "Drink this, Teddy, the whole thing."

She tipped the spoon. The boy gasped and spluttered when he tasted the liquid, but he managed to swallow most of it. After she wiped his chin with the edge of a blanket, she gently laid him back down.

"We'll have to pull the bed away from the wall," she said to the earl. "Then if you'll hold Teddy's shoulders, William can hold his other leg for me." She looked down at the injured boy. "They're going to help you, Teddy, because you must stay perfectly still."

Although his eyes were already taking on the faraway look laudanum produced, Teddy nodded his understanding.

Gwen went to the head of the bed, and the earl went to the foot. "Gently now," she said, nodding, and together they eased the cot far enough away that William could get between it and the wall, on the side of Teddy's uninjured leg.

"All right, now, take your positions," Gwen ordered as she rolled up her sleeves and prepared to do her job.

The earl pulled something that looked like a pockmarked wooden spindle out of his jacket pocket and gave it to Teddy. "Put this between your teeth and bite down hard."

The nobleman met her questioning gaze. "It was given to me by the doctor who first tended me when I was hurt," he said as he prepared to help.

Shaking and pale, Teddy put the spindle in his mouth. Looking white as the snow outside, William took his place. The earl placed his large, strong hands on Teddy's shoulders and nodded that he was ready.

And then Gwen did what she had to do, gently but inexorably easing the bone beneath the torn skin and back into place.

"Scream if you want, boy," the earl said softly. "Nobody can hear you but us, and we won't tell. God knows I did often enough when the doctors worked on me, and I was years older than you."

His advice came too late, for Teddy had fainted. The spindle fell from his slack lips.

"Just as well," the earl muttered.

"Teddy's asleep now—that's good, isn't it?" William asked anxiously.

"He needs to rest," Gwen assured him as she felt to see if she'd succeeded getting the bone back into position. "You can let go of him."

"You must be strong as a bull, you held him so still," the earl said to William as he let go of Teddy. "I myself had a terrible time."

The boy gave him a shy smile as he moved away from the bed, followed by the earl.

"Now, is there tea?" the nobleman asked. "And bread? I'm sure Miss Davies needs something to eat."

"Da left some soup," the boy said, nodding at a pot far back in the fire. "He's a good cook," he added proudly.

"I've not had a lot of practice making tea. Do you know how to do it?"

"I've watched my Da."

"And I've watched my housekeeper. Well, let's hope between the two of us, we don't disgrace ourselves. Surely if girls can make tea, two clever fellows like us should be able to manage."

The little boy giggled. "My Da makes good tea."

Satisfied that she had done the best she could, her dress sticking to her back with perspiration, Gwen drew in a deep, shuddering breath and slowly straightened.

To find the earl at her elbow, holding out a damp cloth. "Here."

She gratefully took it and wiped her sweat-slicked face. "Thank you."

"Tea?"

"Not yet. I have to clean the wound first, then bandage it."

"It'll be ready when you are," he said.

She got the whiskey and a clean cloth William found in the drawer of the sideboard and began.

As she worked, she heard the sound of water being poured into the kettle. Then the earl's deep voice. "I see somebody's been getting ready for Christmas."

"Teddy and me did that. We always bring in the boughs and the holly and the mistletoe. My Da does the cooking. He was going to…" The boy's voice caught, but he continued. "He was going to start the Christmas pudding today, but then Teddy hurt himself."

"I'll see to it that you have your Christmas pudding. What else do you have at Christmas?"

"Last year, I had an orange!"

"Really? A whole one, all to yourself?"

"Yes, and oh, it was good! Have you ever had an orange?"

"One or two."

"What did you get for a present last Christmas?"

"I think we should be quiet, William, so Miss Davies can concentrate on her task and your brother can rest."

Gwen finished wrapping a clean bandage around Teddy's leg. She'd done everything she knew to do, as well as she could. Only time, and the doctor, would tell if she'd been successful.

Her hand on the small of her back, she rose and stretched. Her back ached and so did her neck. Her legs were sore, too, from the riding, she suspected.

She turned around to find a brown teapot and heavy white mugs on the table, William seated and the earl cutting thick pieces from a loaf of brown bread.

"How long before the doctor arrives?" she asked.

The earl glanced out the small window near the door. Then he set down the knife and went to the door. He opened it and peered outside. "I don't think the doctor will be getting here today. Nor will we be leaving. It's snowing worse than before."

Dismayed, Gwen hurried to stand beside him and discovered the earl was right. She could barely see three feet beyond the door. The wind had risen again.

Wrapping her arms about herself and shivering, she chewed her lip as he shoved the door closed. They looked at each other, and she saw that he was as worried as she. "How bad is this for the boy?" he asked in a low whisper.

"I've seen worse breaks," she answered, "and I've set several broken bones when the doctors were busy with more serious wounds, but I really don't know."

"You looked to me like you knew exactly what you were doing, and doing it better than some doctors I could name," the earl replied.

"I'm not a doctor."

"You should have been," he said as he limped back to the table and cut another piece of bread for William.

How many times had she thought that she and some of her fellow nurses could tend to wounds better than some of the doctors sent out with the troops? More than she could count, but the one time she'd mentioned it to a doctor, he'd regarded her as if she'd uttered heresy and condemned her to washing bedpans for a week.

She sat at the table and gave both William and the earl a smile. "Let's see if you two gentlemen can make a decent cup of tea."

It turned out they could, and if she hadn't been so anxious about Teddy, she might even have enjoyed herself. William was clearly excited to have visitors, especially one as exalted as an earl. He asked all sorts of questions that indicated he thought British peers spent all day every day in chain mail and armor, saving damsels in distress, or hunting with hawks. It took some effort on the part of the earl to make it clear that he didn't.

Unfortunately, his cause wasn't helped by his admission that he actually owned armor, several swords and shields, and a mace or two.

Nevertheless, he was unexpectedly patient with the boy's barrage of questions and, by the end of the discussion, seemed quite at ease, especially when the conversation turned to famous Welsh victories in the Middle Ages. Here was the earl's obvious area of expertise.

"You make it sound as if you were there," Gwen remarked, making no secret of her admiration, for he didn't describe those days in the dry, unfeeling tones of the academic. "Doesn't he, William?"

"I wish *I'd* been there," the boy said, hopping down from the bench and pretending to slash the air with his sword.

"Real battles are far from pleasant," the earl said gravely. He nodded at Gwen. "Just ask Miss Davies about that."

The boy frowned. "Girls don't fight in battles."

"No, girls have to take care of the wounded afterward, which is more difficult," the earl replied as he hoisted himself to his feet. "Now, how would you like to help me check on the horses and see that they've got water and something to eat?"

"You're going to go out?" Gwen asked, glancing at the window, which was so frost-covered she couldn't see outside.

"I must. We'll be careful, won't we, William?"

The boy nodded eagerly.

"Good." He rose from the table. "Get your coat and hat and gloves while I put on my coat."

Gwen stood up as William hurried to obey.

"Do you need any help with those?" the earl said, nodding at the dishes.

"No. I can manage," Gwen said as she went to check Teddy. His forehead was still hot and his cheeks flushed.

The earl came up behind her. "Any better?"

"It's early yet," she said, trying to offer comfort to herself as well as to him.

"I'm ready!" William cried.

"Good," the earl said, going to put on his greatcoat. "But we should be quiet in the house, or we'll wake your brother and then Miss Davies will be cross with us."

After they went out, Gwen hurriedly cleaned up the table, leaving some soup warming in the pot for when Teddy woke up. Then she set about binding four smaller pieces of kindling into two braces to hold the blankets off Teddy's leg, thinking that would help to ease the pain when he woke up.

She was just finishing when the earl and William returned. She saw at once that the earl's limp was worse, and that William, now full of soup and bread and fresh air, looked completely exhausted, as did the earl.

"Why don't the two of you lie down and rest?" she suggested as the earl brushed the snow off William's coat and then his own.

"I don't want to lie down," William petulantly replied. "The earl said he'd play checkers with me."

"And I will—after you've had a nap. You had a long night here with Teddy, and you worked hard helping Miss Davies and me."

"You need to rest, too, my lord," Gwen said.

He regarded her steadily. "So do you."

"I'm used to long nights tending patients. You're not."

"I'm used to long rides, and you're not. I'll wake you the moment the lad stirs."

"I'll sleep later," she said, hands on hips. "For now, the two of you should lie down."

The earl gave her a disgruntled look, then addressed William. "I think she's serious."

The little boy yawned and rubbed his eyes. "I'm not tired. I want to play checkers."

"Later," the earl said. "Where's your bed?"

"In the loft," he said, pointing.

The earl frowned, and she suspected climbing a ladder was not something he was anxious to attempt, at least at present.

Gwen walked past him to a curtained alcove. As she'd assumed, this was where Bill slept, for there was an iron bedstead and small washstand. "Since it's just a nap, why don't you both lie down here? That way, if I need help, you can come quickly."

William looked up at the earl. He looked down at William. "I don't think Miss Davies is going to take no for an answer, do you?" the earl inquired.

William yawned again and shook his head.

The nobleman stepped closer to Gwen and whispered, "Only for a little while, and then *you're* going to rest."

She didn't want an argument, so she nodded as if she agreed.

"My Da always sings to me before I go to sleep. Will you?" the little boy asked as the nobleman escorted him around the curtain. "I like 'Deck the Halls.' Because it's Welsh and so am I."

"It's been a long time since I've sung anything. Perhaps Miss Davies—"

"But *Da* sings to me. Please. Just one."

The earl sighed heavily. "All right. Just one carol."

She heard the bed ropes creak a bit as William climbed up and lay down. "Sit here beside me," he said.

After a moment, she heard the ropes creak from a heavier person sitting on the bed. "I'll stretch my leg out, if you don't mind."

"No, I don't mind. Now first 'Deck the Halls,' and then 'All Through the Night.' Those are my favorites."

"You said just one."

"But 'All Through the Night' is Welsh, too. You're Welsh, aren't you?"

"Yes."

"Then we should have both."

As Gwen bustled about preparing to wash the dishes and checking Teddy again, she wondered if the earl was going to acquiesce or refuse, although she wished he'd sing "All Through the Night." She loved that song. When she'd been in the Crimea, several Welsh soldiers had sung it for her one Christmas Eve, reminding her of home. Even a poor orphan could have fond memories of Christmases when joy was an unexpected apple, or something warm to wear.

Then the Earl of Cwm Rhyss started to sing the merry "Deck the Halls." What a fine baritone voice he had—one that would stand out even in Wales. He was immediately joined by William's wavering soprano.

When that was finished, he began "All Through the Night," singing it as gently and soft as a lullaby. William started singing with him, but in a very short time, his voice drifted off, leaving the earl singing alone. He got quieter and quieter, too, until the last line seemed more a sigh than singing.

She tiptoed around the curtain to see if her suspicions were correct. They were. The earl was sitting on top of the covers, leaning against the simple headboard, his eyes closed, his chest moving slowly as he slept. William lay under the covers beside him, nestled by his side.

Relaxed, the earl's stern features softened and he looked very much like the handsome young man in the portrait.

With those looks and that magnificent body, he must have been irresistible to women then. He was irresistible now, and not just for his looks or his form. He had a kind and generous heart, too, and if people could see him with William, they'd know—as she did—that much of his gruff exterior was just that: an exterior, designed to send people away before they could hurt him with their revulsion.

If other women could see him now, they'd want to creep up beside him and brush that dangling lock of hair from his brow, and perhaps press their lips to his forehead. Just as she did.

She chided herself for a fool as she backed away and let the curtain fall. Even scarred, he was a wealthy nobleman, and she was a pauper's daughter who ran an orphanage. To even imagine anything else was silly and foolish and…

Irresistible.

The shuffling sound startled her. Turning, she beheld the Earl of Cwm Rhyss coming drowsily around the curtain. He'd slept for nearly four hours, she guessed, during which Teddy had shifted and cried out once or twice, keeping her alert.

The earl glanced at the window. "Still snowing?"

"Worse than ever."

She sighed, then rubbed the back of her neck. It hadn't been as terrible a vigil as she'd ever had, but given that she hadn't slept the night before—

She froze when she felt the earl's strong hands on her shoulders. Before she could move or speak, he started to knead the tension from her aching back and neck.

She should protest or make him stop, except that it felt so very good….

"How's the boy?" the earl asked, his deep voice low and soft.

"Still feverish," she admitted.

"Will he need more laudanum?"

"He may."

"Use as much as necessary. I have no need of it."

"It doesn't ease your pain?" she asked, afraid his injuries were more severe than she'd assumed.

"It's supposed to help keep…to help me sleep, but it doesn't."

She made a guess based on experience. "You have bad dreams?"

"Yes."

"That's not unexpected, after what happened to you."

"I haven't had a decent night's sleep since my accident." His hands paused a moment, then continued. "Although I slept like a lump of rock just now."

She tried to ignore the warmth and slight pressure of his hands on her. "I'd hate to think helping the boys and me did you harm."

"You didn't. In fact, Miss Davies, I'd say that, in your own unique and inimitable way, you've done me a lot of good."

He stopped kneading and she had a moment's genuine regret, until she felt him pull a pin from her hair.

"What are you doing?" she cried softly, putting her hand to her head to hold her hair in place.

"That knot looks so tight, it can't be comfortable," he said as he pulled out two more pins on the other side.

She slapped her other hand there. "Stop! It'll fall down."

"That's the general idea. You have beautiful hair, Miss Davies."

"I have very ordinary hair," she snapped, rising and turning to face him, her anger hiding her very real dismay.

She used to dream of having hair as golden as ripe wheat, or dark as a raven's wing, like his, but hers was brown as a mouse's fur, and no flattery was going to make it anything but ordinary.

No flattery, no kind, softly spoken words were ever going to make *her* anything but ordinary.

He shook his head. "You have remarkable hair. When it's loose about your face like that, it makes all the difference in the world. And when your green eyes flash with that indomitable spirit of yours, you could rival the finest beauty in London."

"Now I know you're lying, although I have no idea why you think you have to flatter me," she said, trying not to let him see how much he'd upset her.

"I'm merely telling you what I honestly think. I don't have any ulterior motives. I conclude, Miss Davies, you don't get many compliments about your hair or your looks."

"No, I don't."

"You should."

She flushed hotly and told herself to pay no heed to him. "May I have my pins, please?"

His lips curved up in a smile as he held out the pins in his upturned palm. "Come and get them."

"Oh, of all the silly—"

She reached for them, and he curled his hand around hers, then brought it to his lips for a kiss. "I think you're very attractive, Miss Davies."

She should pull her hand away. This should be an unwelcome familiarity. Who could say what he might do next, or what *she* might do? The most outrageous ideas were churning through her mind.

Yet she couldn't move, until a weak voice came from the cot by the hearth. "Is it Christmas? Did I miss it?"

More flustered than she'd ever been—even during the worst of the Crimea—and trying not to show it, Gwen quickly wound her hair in a knot at the nape of her neck and stuck the pins in to hold it as she hurried over to Teddy.

She could tell by his eyes and his voice that the laudanum was still in effect, although not much, to judge by the pain etched in his features.

"It's not Christmas yet," she assured him. "You haven't missed it."

Teddy struggled to sit up. "Where's Da?"

"You must stay still," Gwen urged, gently pushing him down. "Your father can't get here yet. It's still snowing very hard. I promise I'll wake you when he comes and until then, you should try to sleep."

Teddy's gaze floated around the room, before coming to rest on the earl. "He's still here," he murmured as Gwen hurried to prepare another dose. "I thought maybe I'd dreamed him."

"He's been most helpful," she replied.

"I remember the stick he gave me to bite on."

"You didn't really need it. You were very brave," the earl said, coming to stand beside the cot. "I'm sure you impressed the pretty Miss Davies with your courage."

She flushed and told herself he was only trying to amuse Teddy. His words did bring a weak smile to Teddy's pale lips before his eyelids fluttered closed.

As for what he'd said before, he couldn't seriously find her attractive. Perhaps he was merely trying to amuse himself, since they were almost alone.

Gwen tried not to think about that and was very glad when the earl went to the hearth and added more wood to the fire.

She also tried not to notice how he moved, or the way his jacket stretched across his broad shoulders before he straightened. "I'll go see to the horses before William wakes up. His heart's in the right place, but I'm used to tending to Warlord by myself. And Warlord isn't used to an inquisitive little fellow, either."

She nodded, relieved that he was leaving.

After giving Teddy a bit more laudanum, she sat by his side until she was sure he was asleep, then she went back to the hearth to add more water to the simmering soup.

Focusing on something other than the earl, she considered the food situation. It didn't look like there'd be enough soup for the four of them later.

The earl returned, softly stamping his boots to rid them of the snow clinging to them as he took off his coat and hat and hung them back up to the pegs.

"Now that I've had my rest, and your patient's sleeping again, you should lie down," he said to her. "I'll keep watch over Teddy and fetch you if anything changes."

Although Gwen felt bone weary, Teddy was her responsibility. "I can't. He might require my help. And I shouldn't sleep until the fever's broken."

"If he gets worse and you're exhausted, you won't be much good."

"William will be waking soon," she replied. "He'll be hungry, and Teddy needs to eat, too. I should have more than the soup."

She ran her hand over her forehead and tried to think of something she could cook. "Stew, perhaps. Or maybe I could use that ham hanging from the ceiling."

"I think you need to sleep before you swoon from sheer exhaustion. You lie down and I'll make something."

"You can't cook."

He raised a brow. "How do you know *what* I'm capable of, Miss Davies?"

She started to sigh with exasperation and wound up yawning prodigiously. "You're an earl."

"I'm an earl who doesn't spend all his time in his study writing a book. Sometimes I go to the kitchen and watch Mrs. Jones. I believe I can manage the rudimentaries, at least."

The earl grabbed her hands and started to tug her toward the curtain. "I told you, I won't have a martyr's death on my hands."

She planted her feet and tried to tug her hands from his strong grasp. "You're not in command here, you know, my lord. This isn't your manor house."

"But it *is* my property. Bill Mervyn is one of my tenants. Now stop arguing—or do I have to pick you up and carry you to bed?"

What a host of images that brought to her mind! "Take your hands off me, if you please."

He tugged her closer, and when he looked into her eyes, she saw an expression that made her breathing quicken and her heart race. "Maybe I don't please," he whispered, bringing her clasped hands to his lips. "There was a time you'd have been the envy of a ballroom full of giggling, foolish girls, Miss Davies, because the Earl of Cwm Rhyss was holding you this way." He slowly leaned closer. "And if the Earl of Cwm Rhyss kissed you…"

"Are you dancing?" a little voice piped up. "Has my Da come?"

William was standing by the curtain.

With a nervous smile, Gwen swiftly moved away from the earl. "No, laddie, your Da hasn't come yet because it's still snowing. The earl was just, um…"

"Trying to get Miss Davies to have a nap. Now go along, Miss Davies, and leave me to make William some tea and toast, to start."

She still wasn't quite willing to relinquish her responsibility. "But Teddy—"

"If Teddy wakes or I see the slightest change in the boy, I'll fetch you at once. You must sleep, Miss Davies, or your judgment will surely be impaired."

If she was entertaining the notion that a nobleman could be truly attracted to her, if she was envisioning a life by his side, her judgment was already impaired. "You promise to wake me at the first sign of change?"

He put his hand over his heart and bowed as elegantly as if they were in Buckingham Palace. "My dear Miss Davies, you have the word of the Earl of Cwm Rhyss."

Chapter Five

Gwen awoke to the sounds of quiet voices talking, one soft and deep, one high pitched and excited—thc earl and William, and she was in a Bill Mervyn's cottage, tending to the injured Teddy.

Wondering how long she'd slept, she glanced at the small window near the bed. It was too dark to tell the time of day, or if it was still snowing.

Whatever time it was, she'd napped too long. She quickly got to her feet and hurried around the curtained partition, to discover the reclusive Earl of Cwm Rhyss wearing a patched apron, flour on his cheek, stirring something in a big bowl. William was beside him at the table, seated on the top, his legs dangling over the side. Something cooking in the iron pot over the fire was sending the most delicious smell wafting through the cottage.

"Good evening, Miss Davies," the earl said quietly. "I trust you slept well."

She had, especially considering the circumstances, but her first concern was for her patient. "How's Teddy?" she asked as she crossed the room to the cot by the hearth.

"Still fast asleep, as you can see." The earl frowned. "I would have called you otherwise."

She hadn't meant that for a criticism, but she said nothing. Keeping her distance, as much as possible under the circumstances, was her best weapon against foolish flights of fancy concerning a handsome, virile nobleman.

Noting that Teddy's breathing seemed easier and his cheeks were less flushed, she placed her hand on his forehead.

It wasn't burning hot.

Holding her breath, she leaned closed and kissed his brow to confirm the prognosis of her hand. "Oh, thank God," she murmured fervently.

She straightened and regarded her companions with relief and happiness. "The fever's broken."

The earl smiled. She smiled. William grinned, then crowed, "Teddy's all better!"

He immediately clapped his hand over his mouth, eyes wide. "I'm supposed to whisper," he said, the words muffled behind his hand.

"Not *all* better. Not yet," Gwen said as she approached the table. "But he should be well soon."

"Before Christmas?"

"It takes longer than that for bones to mend, I'm afraid," she replied. "However, he should be feeling better before Easter." She nodded at the bowl. "What's that? Bread?"

William grinned widely. "We're making the Christmas pudding!"

The earl gave her a look that was a delightful mixture of sheepishness and pride. "I always helped Mrs. Jones make the Christmas pudding." Then his pleasure faded. "Until recently."

"I'm hungry," Teddy murmured from his cot.

"Teddy!" William cried, scrambling down from the table. "We're making Christmas pudding, the earl and me."

Grateful for this other sign that Teddy was improving, and thinking she might need to protect him from his little brother's enthusiasm, Gwen hurried to the cot.

"I'll get him some stew," the earl offered.

That explained the delicious aroma, and if the stew tasted as good as it smelled, the earl had indeed learned something watching Mrs. Jones.

"He puts lots more nuts in the pudding than Father does," William said as he skidded to a stop beside Teddy's cot. "And he put in something else that he brought from the manor. Whissy, or something. It's going to be the best Christmas pudding *ever!*"

Gwen's brows rose. "Whiskey?" she asked as the earl ladled out a very rich, thick stew from the pot into a wooden bowl.

He gave a little shrug. "There was no brandy, so that had to do."

Teddy gave a little cry of pain and Gwen turned back to see William sitting on the end of the cot.

"Don't sit there, please, William," she cautioned the younger boy. "His leg should stay as still as possible."

William looked horrified as he carefully got down.

"It's all right. Can you please fetch the pillows from your father's bed? Teddy will have to be propped up to eat."

William eagerly did as he was asked.

The earl set the bowl on the table and, when William returned with the pillows, helped her raise Teddy to a sitting position and make him comfortable. He fetched the stew and a towel and, after handing her the bowl and spoon, laid the towel over Teddy's chest.

"I can do it myself," Teddy whispered, blushing.

"You're going to be a bit shaky from that medicine she gave you, and the bowl's hot," the earl said. "No man wants to be treated like a baby, I know, but no man wants to dribble all over his chin, either. And this man doesn't want his culinary efforts going to waste."

Teddy's blush deepened.

"Speaking for myself, I'd enjoy the opportunity of having a lovely young woman help you while you can."

Gwen flushed as she assisted Teddy. She'd had more flattery in the past two days than she'd had in years. No wonder truly pretty girls were vain, if they had such comments made to them often.

No wonder *he* was. And no wonder the loss of such attention was devastating. She might feel something similar if she was told she could no longer care for her children.

"What's 'culinary efforts'?" William demanded.

"My cooking," the earl replied. "Now, wee Willie Mervyn, this pudding is nearly ready and I haven't forgotten that you challenged me to checkers. Set it up and I'll be ready in a moment."

"I'm a good checker player, aren't I, Teddy?" William asked his brother.

The older lad nodded.

"I fear no opponent!" the earl cried, brandishing the wooden ladle like a rapier. "Make haste, young Mervyn, that I may defeat you and boast of it to all and sundry!"

Teddy grinned, William giggled and Gwen had to smile. Looking at the Earl of Cwm Rhyss now, she could almost forget that he lived in a manor house and was a peer of the realm. She could almost believe that this was their cottage, and they lived here together, sharing their days. And their nights.

She could almost believe that. But not quite.

"One more time, and then no more."

The earl, up in the sleeping loft with William, sounded adamant, but Gwen had already heard him say that before he began the previous rendition of "Deck the Halls." At least this time, William's request was said wearily, as if he was on the verge of sleep.

Teddy had fallen back to sleep after his stew, and was slumbering as peacefully as one could expect. So far, he was doing well, but that didn't stop her from praying that the doctor would be able to ride up the mountain tomorrow.

The earl's deep, beautiful voice drifted down to her. The spruce boughs on the mantel filled the air with their scent. The windows were still cloaked with frost, but inside it was warm and comfortable. The kettle sat on the hob, ready for another cup of tea. Teddy wasn't in serious danger and for the time being, she had fewer responsibilities than she'd had in years. This must be how it was for many happily married people with children.

Such domesticity was not likely to ever be her lot. Yet she had much to occupy her and give her joy. Her work was important, and she had a host of children who needed her love. If there could be no husband for her, she could accept that, because of all the other compensations she had. And yet…

The earl fell silent, and in the next moment, she heard him making his way to the ladder leading from the loft. Wiping her hands on the apron she was wearing, the same one he had, she watched him make his slow progress downward.

"Is your knee hurting you?" she asked when he reached the floor.

"A bit," he answered without looking at her. "I thought I'd never get that boy to sleep."

"You sing beautifully."

"I'm rather rusty. It's been a long time," he said, still not looking at her as he limped to the window. He reached out to clear a spot with the heel of his hand. "By God, I don't believe it. It's stopped snowing."

She came to stand beside him, rising on her toes to look outside. He was right. The night sky was like black velvet, and dotted with the small, twinkling lights of the stars. In the east, the moon rose, full and pale, gleaming on the snow.

"There's not a cloud left," Gwen murmured, amazed.

"If it stays clear, the doctor and Bill will be able to come here first thing in the morning."

For Teddy's sake, she was glad. "Yes, and you must be anxious to get back to your manor."

He cut her a glance. "As you are to get back to your orphanage."

"I've lots to do before Christmas, my lord, and now even less time in which to do it."

He faced her, and she was taken aback by his intensity when he spoke. "It seems ridiculous for you to call me by my title. My name's Griffin."

She was equally surprised by his request. "It would be presumptuous of me to call you by your first name, my lord."

It was also a necessary reminder that they were from two different worlds, and to two different worlds they would return.

"It was presumptuous of you to barge into my study, but that didn't stop you," he noted with a wistful smile. "Can't you call me Griffin while we're here? Not many people call me that anymore. Think of it as a Christmas present."

She couldn't resist that entreaty. "Then you must call me Gwen."

"All right, Gwen."

Never had her name sounded so lovely to her ears.

His smile drifted away as he nodded at the window and the sky beyond it. "I've always thought this must be the way it was the first Christmas, when the angel came to the shepherds. A cold, clear night, with the stars twinkling like little diamonds. And then the star, so bright that it could light their way to Bethlehem, and lead the wise men, too. It must have been a sight to see—that star. Like something God saved from the first days of creation."

He faced her again, and it was as if whatever intimacy had been between them just moments ago had disappeared. "I expect the doctor and Bill Mervyn will be making their way here first thing in the morning."

She wondered if she was only imagining the disappointment in his voice.

She returned to the hearth, putting some distance between

herself and the nobleman whose voice and presence seemed to weave such a dangerous spell around her, of need and desire and a foolish, wild, impossible hope.

"It's been dam—very odd weather," he said as he limped toward the chair on the opposite side of the fireplace and eased himself into it, keeping his left leg straight. "A storm prevented you from leaving my home, then let up enough that we could come here to help Teddy. Then the weather worsened so we couldn't leave, and now it's as fine as a winter's eve can be. You would almost think Mother Nature was playing tricks on us, or trying to keep us together."

Gwen shifted uneasily. That was a fanciful notion, and as ridiculous as the way she was feeling about the man seated opposite her. Such emotions would avail her nothing, and she should do her best to subdue them.

"Do you think Teddy will have lasting troubles with his leg?" Griffin asked.

"I'm not certain, but I hope not."

"He's lucky you were able to help him."

"He's fortunate his father braved the storm. If it had been much longer…"

"You seem to be very friendly with Bill Mervyn," Griffin observed as he toyed with a loose thread at his cuff.

"He's a very nice man."

"Perhaps you ought to set your cap at him."

That was not something she wanted to hear, especially from him. "I'm not looking for a husband."

"Not one with two children, at any rate."

"Not at all."

"You don't wish to marry? You've refused every man who's ever asked you?"

She laced her fingers in her lap. "I've never been asked."

"What, not at all?"

He sounded genuinely shocked.

"No," she confessed. "Never."

"Surely some wounded veteran of the Crimea must have fallen in love with his nurse."

"Sometimes that happened, but not to me."

The earl leaned back in his chair and regarded her steadily. "It must be your air of self-sufficiency," he mused aloud. "Most men want to feel a woman needs him when he falls in love. That she requires help and protection."

Mindful of what he'd said to her in his study, she raised an interrogative brow. "So it's all very well for a man to want to feel needed, but if I do, I must be desperate to be loved?"

He rose and leaned against the mantel, staring into the fire. "I was an idiot to say that. I was angry and wanted to upset you." He glanced at her, and in his expression, she saw genuine remorse. "I'm sorry."

She, too, got to her feet, facing him. "You did upset me—because I do want to feel that I'm necessary. I do want to be loved. But don't we all want to be needed? Don't we all want to be loved? Don't you?"

He kicked at a log and sent a flurry of sparks up the chimney. "Why else would I have got myself engaged to Letitia?" he muttered.

She'd forgotten about his former fiancée.

"Even I, the handsome, popular Earl of Cwm Rhyss wanted to be loved, and I thought Letitia loved me. What she loved was my title and my money. I suppose the fact that plenty of women were after me and I asked her to marry me flattered her vanity, too."

He sighed wearily. "One night, my friends and I were in a tavern and some of them tried to enlighten me about her mercenary motives. Others joined me in denying the accusations and defending Letitia. Then a lamp got knocked over. If it hadn't been for the landlord's bravery, I'd have died for a woman who abandoned me seemingly without a second thought."

Hearing his bitterness and his sorrow, Gwen yearned to put her arms around him, to offer him a comforting embrace, but she didn't dare, any more than she would admit that if she discovered she was being forced into permanent exile here, with him, she wouldn't feel it a punishment. Instead, she said, "I'm glad you didn't die."

"Then you wouldn't have had a way to get to Teddy, or a Christmas benefactor for your orphans."

That was not the only reason she was glad. Yet she didn't voice that thought, either. "I am truly thankful for your generosity, my lord."

"Sincerely spoken."

"Sincerely felt, from the bottom of my heart. And the children—"

"Have a most impassioned champion. I would that I had such a one, to upbraid the alleged friends who deserted me."

"If they would desert you, they weren't your friends."

"I know that better than you, Miss Davies," he said, turning back to stare at the fire. "I learned the hard way that the people I thought were my friends were mere acquaintances, or seeking to exploit my generous nature. They would flock to my parties and fêtes and musical evenings, and be wildly grateful for my gifts, but when I most had need of them, they wouldn't come near me."

"Did not one of them stand by you?" she asked.

"One, the Duke of Barroughby. But it was he who accidentally started the fire, so in my bitterness, I refused to see him. By the time I thought better of it, I was sure he wouldn't want to see me. Thus I am alone, except for my servants."

"You don't have to be."

He raised a brow and, afraid of revealing too much, she rushed on. "Teddy and William accept you as you are, and Bill, too. If you would try, others would as well."

He tilted his head to study her. "You think the world would come to see me as a man, not a scarred monstrosity?"

"Yes."

He shifted, inching closer. "You see me as a man?"

"I see a healthy, vital man with many years before him."

He smiled as he reached out and caressed her cheek. "Have a care, Miss Davies. I don't think you quite know what you're doing."

Perhaps she didn't, but she knew he was touching her cheek, and as he did, a host of contradicting emotions stirred within her—hope, joy, fear, desire.

"You're marvelous with the boys," he said softly. "I'm sure your wards at the orphanage receive the same excellent care. I'm sure they love you for it."

"I try to be more than a matron to the children who depend on me," she said, barely resisting the urge to turn her head and press her lips to the warm palm of his hand.

"I can well believe that you're much more than that," he replied, lowering his hand. "You remind me of my favorite teacher at Harrow. He was stern, but fair."

Stern? He thought her stern? Yet he meant those words as a compliment, and she would take them as such. "Children need rules and guidance."

"And a motherly woman to do both, so that the rules are not seen as prison and the guidance gentle prodding, not enforced conformity."

Again she should be flattered, and not feel…deflated…that he thought her so maternal.

"You'll make an excellent mother. An excellent wife."

He couldn't have any idea how those words hurt her. They were stabs to her very heart, because *he* would never want her for a wife. "I'm not likely to marry and I have plenty of children to mother already."

"But you do *want* to marry, do you not? What if some fine

young preacher fell in love with you? Or a charming schoolmaster asked for your hand?"

"I don't think either scenario is very likely. And there is a very serious drawback to your fanciful plans."

"What's that?"

"I'm neither young enough nor pretty enough to attract either. And then there is my headstrong, persistent, unfeminine nature, my lord. Those traits enabled me to get an education and stand me in good stead at Saint Bridget's, but they are hardly the qualities a man looks for in a wife. No, my lord, I shall gladly content myself with my orphaned children and entertain no such ridiculous fancies."

"A man can come to admire and respect persistence and stubbornness, when the goal that provokes them is a worthy one. As for the traits men are supposed to want in a wife, they might be suitable if a fellow wants nothing more than a boring, agreeable creature as obedient and lively as a doll."

He toyed with a piece of greenery on the mantel. "Or are you trying to say that you think hoping for love when the cards seem stacked against you is a foolish waste of time?"

"I'm a practical woman who has no time for silly, girlish dreams and desires."

"Not even at Christmas?"

She hesitated for the briefest of moments before answering. "No."

"Yet I am to have hope that people will accept me, despite my face."

"That's different. You still have much to offer the world."

"I think you have much to offer to the man who can win your heart." He held the greenery above her head, and she saw that it was mistletoe. "If your theory is correct, and I'm not as repulsive a fellow as I thought, you'll let me kiss you."

She flushed and glanced up at the mistletoe. Oh, God help her! What was happening? Why this? Why now, here, with this nobleman? Why couldn't she have had these feelings years ago, for a carpenter or a bricklayer or a foot soldier?

Her feelings for him were doomed to give her nothing but misery. They could never lead to anything lasting between them. No matter what he said, or the desire and emotions he aroused in her, she must never forget that. She must and would protect her heart as best she could. "That hardly seems fair, my lord. I could have several reasons for not wishing to kiss you."

"Name one, other than my ugly face."

"I hardly know you."

He dangled the mistletoe above her. "You know me better than many another person."

She would be blunt, because there seemed no other way. "You're an earl and I'm the daughter of paupers."

"I'm a man, and you're the most interesting woman I've ever met. You've intrigued me from the moment you charged into my study like a conquering general. I've had my fill of timid, simpering, giggling women. You're direct and forthright, intelligent and determined. Any man should consider himself fortunate to have your good regard."

She turned away. "Stop saying such things, my lord."

"I'm telling you the truth." He stepped closer and caught her around the waist, letting the mistletoe fall. "I'm also going to kiss you."

Chapter Six

And he did, capturing her lips and moving his with firm, deliberate, delicious leisure.

She'd never been kissed in her life, let alone by a man she found compelling and attractive. Anything she had ever felt before—happiness, contentment, a sense of belonging—paled compared to the wondrous emotions his kiss elicited.

Her arms encircled him, holding him close. Her breasts pressed against the strong wall of his chest as his hands slid up her back. Still kissing her, he undid her hair and let it tumble loose about her shoulders.

His tongue pressed against her lips, silently seeking an invitation. Instinctively she parted hers and, when he deepened the kiss, her limbs seemed to melt like ice in sunlight.

During the long nights on ward duty, watching over a patient or tending to a restless child, she had dreamed of being held in the arms of a man who loved her. Of being kissed with passion and desire. Of no longer feeling so alone and unwanted and unloved. That there was hope a man would care for her as she could only imagine.

This man was like the very embodiment of her dream lover. A hero of old come to life, just for her.

A fantasy.

Reality intruded and it was like a gust of wintry wind. This was no different from the fancies she used to harbor at Christmas in her childhood when, in spite of her situation and every previous Christmas, she would dream of waking to a host of presents and a Christmas feast of roast goose and gravy, sweets and pudding. Disappointment inevitably followed, until she'd learned to expect nothing.

She could expect nothing from him, either, except more disappointment and heartbreak. It was ridiculous to hope that the Earl of Cwm Rhyss could ever truly love the matron of an orphanage in Llanwyllan.

She broke the kiss and pulled away from his warm, exciting, passionate embrace.

"What's wrong?"

"*This* is wrong," she said, stepping back, summoning her determination to do not what she desired, but what was necessary. "We shouldn't be kissing."

His expression grew wary, and the look in his eyes…she wouldn't look at his eyes.

"Then I'm wrong to think that you like me?" he asked slowly.

"I do like you. You're everything—" She stopped herself before she betrayed too much. Her feelings couldn't change the fact that they were from two very different worlds, and always would be. "You're a kind, generous man."

"And I think you're an utterly amazing, desirable woman," he said as he reached out for her again.

She moved farther away from him, and the temptation he offered. "Here, in this place, under these rather extraordinary circumstances. But we barely know one another. We've only just met."

She straightened her shoulders and mustered her resolve. "You're a lonely man who thought no woman would ever want you again. I've proved you wrong. What you feel could be the result of that, and nothing more."

"You think what I feel for you is gratitude that you don't find me hideous?"

"I don't know *what* you're feeling."

"Except that you're certain of what it is not. So what *do* you feel for me?" He spit out the next word, as if it tainted his tongue to speak it. *"Pity?"*

"No, most definitely not pity."

He pulled her close. "I assure you, Gwen, what I feel for you is more than gratitude or lust or simple affection. It's more than I ever felt for Letitia, or any other woman. I want you in my life."

Oh, heaven help her, she wanted to believe him! She wanted to believe that he loved her, and that what she felt for him was the sort of love that could triumph over any difficulty and render the differences in their status and position meaningless. But she couldn't have such faith, not yet. "Loneliness and altered circumstances can make people believe their feelings are deeper than they are. When we return home, things will be different, and you might soon feel differently, too."

"You truly believe that?"

"I've known wounded officers who imagined themselves in love with their nurse. I've seen them marry and I've heard what happened after they returned home. Away from the battlefield and the hospital, they had nothing in common. More than one bitterly regretted what they'd done."

"Then they can't have been truly in love."

"And neither are we. You're an intelligent man who's lived in the world. You know I'm right to doubt that what's happening between us will last."

"You don't believe in love at first sight?"

"No, I don't. Lust at first sight, attraction and temptation at first sight, but not the kind of love that lasts a lifetime."

His intense, steadfast gaze finally faltered. She was both relieved and sorry to see that her words were finally having some effect.

"Sincerely spoken," he said softly, "and if you doubt it, I have no choice but to doubt it, too." He raised his questioning eyes. "Yet you do *like* me?"

She nodded.

"And I know you felt desire for me, as much as I feel for you."

She couldn't deny it, for that would be a lie. "I do, and therefore, I must ask that you refrain from trying to kiss me again."

The look he gave her! "I may not be the gentleman I was, Miss Davies, but I haven't become a lustful lout. Of course I'll respect your wishes, and keep my distance, too.

"Now you should go to bed. You're exhausted. I'll watch the boy and wake you if he stirs."

It was better that he be angry rather than looking at her with such longing and desire; otherwise, she might succumb to the desire she could scarcely subdue. "I'll agree only if you'll wake me in a few hours. You're exhausted, too."

"I don't think I'll be sleeping tonight—trying to control my base animal desires should keep me awake."

He sounded more bitter, more angry, more hurt, than he had when speaking of Letitia, and that realization increased her anguish. "My lord…Griffin…"

"Go to bed, Miss Davies. And leave me alone."

Gwen stood at the window as the sun rose in a glory of pink and orange, tinting a thin line of clouds high in the sky. The sunlight reflected off the snow outside seemed celestial in its brilliance. Everything looked clean and new-made, like hope hiding reality.

For the snow would melt, just as whatever happy dream she'd dreamed here in this cottage would disappear when life returned to normal.

The change was already beginning. When Griffin had awakened her in the night, he'd said not a word, and neither had she. It was her fault, of course, but there could be no other way. To believe anything else was to deny the reality of the world, to think that life could be like a fairy tale. She knew full well it was not.

The doctor would soon arrive, and Bill Mervyn, and then she and Griffin would part. At least she could have the satisfaction of knowing that she'd helped Teddy, and spared him from the fatal consequences of so bad a broken bone.

She heard Griffin stirring behind the curtain and moved to the hearth, ostensibly checking Teddy, who still slept.

"How's the boy this morning?" Griffin asked gruffly when he appeared.

She immediately noted Griffin's drawn features. She straightened at once, all resolutions to keep her distance disappearing in her concern.

"Are you ill?" she asked as she hurried to feel his forehead.

"No," he said, grabbing her hand before she could touch him. His brows lowered as he frowned. "Keep away, Miss Davies."

Frustration replaced concern. "Any man of sense would appreciate that what I said last night was right. Any man who truly cared for me wouldn't press me for a different answer. I told you I have only my virtue to call my own, and I won't give it up for a passion that may be as fleeting as snow on a warm rock."

"Miss Davies?" Teddy called weakly.

Gwen forced herself to put aside her frustration as she went to Teddy's side. It was immediately obvious he was still in pain. Ignoring Griffin, who was putting the kettle on the fire, she prepared a little more of the laudanum.

How she wished the doctor would get here soon! That *anybody* would get here soon and end this waiting for the inevitable.

"Da!" William shouted from the loft. "It's Da! He's come on a horse!"

For a moment, it was as if time itself stood still. Cradling Teddy, Gwen hesitated, the spoon halfway to his lips. The tea canister in his hands, Griffin stood motionless beside the table.

The spell broke when William clambered down the ladder and ran to the door. Gwen finished giving Teddy the medicine, while Griffin returned to making tea and cutting the last of the bread.

Bill Mervyn appeared in the doorway. "How's Teddy?" he anxiously asked as he scooped his younger son up in his arms, his attention focused on the boy in the cot.

"Doing well," Gwen answered. "Better than I'd hoped."

"Thank God!" Bill cried as he rushed to Teddy's bedside, not bothering to take off his boots or his coat or hat. He set William down, then knelt beside the cot.

Out of the corner of her eye, Gwen saw Griffin put on his greatcoat and hat. "I'll tend to the horse," he muttered as he slipped outside.

"I can't thank you enough, Miss Davies!" Bill said, gratitude lighting his face.

"I couldn't have come if the earl hadn't brought me," Gwen said, but Bill didn't hear. He was too busy brushing the tousled curls back from his injured son's forehead.

In spite of the laudanum, Teddy opened his eyes and smiled weakly. "Da?"

"Yes, my boy, my son," Bill said roughly, surreptitiously wiping his eyes, one hand on Teddy's arm, the other around William beside him. "Here I am, and here I will stay."

"Is it Christmas Day?"

"Not yet, my son."

Teddy clutched his father's mittened hand. "I don't want to miss it."

As Gwen watched them, an unbearable ache, a longing for something she had never missed before—had never *known* to miss before—overcame her.

She turned away—and nearly collided with Griffin, who had returned and was standing right behind her. Still in his greatcoat and hat, he caught hold of her shoulders to steady her, then looked into her eyes. In his, she saw a longing that matched her own, a yearning that made her heart turn over and the hope she'd tried to conquer since he'd kissed her struggle to break free.

Sleigh bells jingled in the yard.

"I think that's the doctor," Gwen whispered.

"Yes, it is," Griffin answered, not taking his gaze from her face. "I saw him coming up the road."

Very soon now, she would be back at the orphanage, back to the only sort of home she'd ever known. The only kind of home she would likely ever know.

Griffin let go of her and turned toward the door. "I'll see to his horses, too, while you confer about your patient."

Then he was gone, and in the next moment, the jovial middle-aged Dr. Morgan, black bag in his hand, his hair, mustache and muttonchop whiskers as white as bleached linen, bustled into the cottage.

"Now, where's this young lad who chose such an inconvenient time to break his leg?" he asked as he removed his overcoat and handed it to the waiting Gwen. "Jones nearly had apoplexy when it started to snow again. Mighty odd weather, I must say."

Bill got out of the way to allow the doctor to conduct his examination. Trying not to think about Griffin or returning to the orphanage, Gwen waited with bated breath, hoping she'd done everything right.

"Most competently set, Miss Davies," the doctor pronounced. "I couldn't have done it better myself. Rest, a fresh bandage and something for the pain is all Teddy should need."

"Then I can return to my children?"

"Yes, indeed," Dr. Morgan replied as he measured out a spoonful of liquid from a bottle he took from his bag.

The door opened and Griffin paused to knock the snow from his boots.

"I'll take you back to Llanwyllan in my sleigh," the doctor offered.

"Thank you," Gwen said. "That would be most kind."

"Since that's settled," the earl announced, "I'll be on my way. I'll send Jones with a cheque for the children's Christmas, Miss Davies, as I said I would."

She couldn't believe she'd forgotten about that.

He turned to leave. "Merry Christmas."

"Merry Christmas," said Bill, Teddy and the doctor simultaneously.

"And thank you," Bill added fervently.

"Goodbye and Merry Christmas!" William cried, running to the door and waving cheerily.

Gwen said nothing at all.

The dining hall at the orphanage was a vision of slightly supervised pandemonium. The initial rush of excitement had passed, and now, as the children and staff finished the Christmas feast, exhaustion was beginning to take over.

Gwen was exhausted, too, from the last-minute rush of preparations, then rousing all the staff and children for the *plygain,* a predawn candlelight procession to the church for singing, followed by the Christmas service. She'd tried not to hope that the earl would be there, that no matter how they'd parted, he'd no longer be a recluse.

He hadn't come. Her disappointment had been extreme, so much so, she was afraid she might never stop regretting being with the earl at Bill Mervyn's cottage, because of the foolish hopes that had inspired.

The earl's nonappearance was the confirmation that her

feelings for him were foolish and hopeless, and she had been right to tell him that once they returned to their respective homes, he would think differently.

The bell to the outer gate rang, loud and insistent above the children's voices.

"Who can that be?" Molly demanded. "Can't we have our Christmas supper in peace?"

Gwen had to smile at that last word. The happy din wasn't what anyone would call peaceful. "I'll go," she said, rising from the table. "It might be someone who needs our help."

It wouldn't be the first time a child had been left on their doorstep. Christmas could fill a heart with despair as easily as joy.

Once at the door to the main building, she put her shawl over her head and hurried across the cobblestone yard, taking care not to slip. Most of the snow that had trapped her with the earl had melted, but it was cold enough to make it icy in the shadows.

She opened the wicket in the door, and the first thing she saw was the familiar black muzzle of a horse.

He'd come. He'd come down from the mountain. Griffin…the Earl of Cwm Rhyss…had left his manor and come here.

Her heart soared, until she quickly yanked its leash and brought it back to earth. He couldn't have come here simply to see her, or he wouldn't have waited until today.

He hadn't even sent a note with the cheque for a hundred pounds that had been delivered by Mr. Jones, as if Mr. Jones was acting for Father Christmas, not a man who'd kissed her and claimed to care for her. She'd sent the earl a brief note of thanks, along with the velvet cloak, her words sounding formal and stiff even to her own ears.

Perhaps he wanted to witness for himself the happiness he'd brought to the children. And perhaps she *had* persuaded him to venture out into the world more, starting here, with grateful, happy children.

In spite of her silent vow to act as if he were any other benefactor coming to call, her hands shook as she opened the gate.

Sitting on Warlord, he wore his greatcoat and beaver hat, with his hair was drawn back in a tail. His mutilated ear was still covered, but the scar on his face was much more visible.

"Merry Christmas, my lord," she said, smiling and trying not to show how his unexpected arrival affected her.

He dismounted and stood before her, his expression difficult to read in the waning late-afternoon light. "It may be for you, but this is the most miserable Christmas I've had since my accident."

She didn't know what to say to that.

"May I come in, or shall we stand here?"

"Oh!" she cried, embarrassed. "Please, come in. You must meet the children. You've made them so happy with your generous gift." She softly added, "Me, too."

He didn't seem to hear her. Or perhaps he didn't care about her gratitude. "Where may I stable my horse?"

She led the way to the barn where they kept the three cows to provide fresh milk for the children. "You're well, I hope?"

"I've been better."

"Oh? You didn't suffer any ill effects from escorting me to Bill Mervyn's, I hope," she asked, doing her best to sound like a dispassionate nurse.

"I'm physically well," he replied as he led his horse to the empty stall. He ran a measuring gaze over her. "I gather you're not suffering any ill effects, either?"

"I'm perfectly fine," she assured him.

He reached into the saddlebag and produced a bundle wrapped in brown paper. She wondered if it was a Christmas present, and was upset that she had nothing to give him, then chided herself for a fool. He wouldn't be giving *her* presents.

"You shouldn't have sent the cloak back," he said gruffly, handing the bundle to her.

She quickly clasped her hands behind her back. "I couldn't keep it, and I shouldn't accept it now."

"Why not?" His dark brows lowered. "You should have a warm cloak as you go about your good works." He studied her again, in a way that made her blush from the roots of her hair to the soles of her feet. "I should have told you to use part of my money to get yourself a decent dress, too."

"My clothes are serviceable and practical. That cloak is too luxurious for me."

He wasn't pleased by her refusal. "If you don't take it, I'll burn it."

"I understand you've threatened to do so before, my lord."

His brows jerked up, then down. "I gather Mrs. Jones has been talking."

He closed the stall and moved closer. "Then sell it, if you don't want to wear it."

She wasn't so stubborn that she wouldn't accept it under those circumstances, so she nodded and took it from his grasp, being careful to avoid any contact with even his gloved hands. "Very well."

Turning away, she started for the main building. "I'm sorry I don't have anything to give you for a Christmas present."

"That remains to be seen," he said, in such a tone she forgot to pay attention to where she was going and slipped on a patch of ice.

Two strong hands caught her and held her up. "Careful, Miss Davies. I wouldn't want you to break your leg."

Blushing hotly, wondering if any curious eyes inside the building had seen her, she twisted out of his grasp.

"I'll be more careful," she said as she continued on her way, trying to sound matter-of-fact. "The children will be so pleased to see you. They've been asking all sorts of questions about you."

"Have they, indeed? Mrs. Jones has been asking all sorts of questions about *you.*"

And he'd answered…what? Her mind leapt with all sorts of possibilities—the good, the bad, the complimentary and the insulting.

They entered the main building, and as they walked down the whitewashed corridor, complete with water stains where rain and melting snow had leaked under the eaves, Gwen told herself it was just as well they hadn't yet had time to fix the plaster. He could see for himself how different their circumstances were.

The sound of the children got louder the closer they got to the dining hall. To a man like Griffin, unused to being around children, it must sound as if they were running amok. "That's happy noise," she said by way of explanation.

They were nearly there when Griffin came to a halt. "It won't do," he said with sudden fierce defiance. "I can't pretend I want to see anybody but you, at least until I've said what I've come to say. Is there somewhere we can talk alone?"

The nagging voice of her practical conscience warned her they shouldn't be alone. Her resolve was wearing too thin. "I really don't think that would be wise, my lord."

He took hold of her hands and gazed at her. "Please?"

If she ignored the fervent, pleading look in Griffin's eyes, it would haunt her for the rest of her life. "Come with me."

She led him past the dining hall to the small room that served as her office at the end of the corridor. Unlike his study, it was uncluttered and painfully neat.

She went around behind her desk, making it a barrier between them.

Griffin stood before her, his hands clenched into fists at his side, looking like a man about to go to his destruction. "You were right to doubt the strength and permanence of the feelings that grew between us when we were in Mervyn's cottage."

Why, oh why, had she allowed even the smallest hope to blossom?

Then he leaned forward and splayed his strong hands on the desk. "But you were *not* right to say it couldn't last. I think it can, and that what I feel for you is the beginning of love, if not love itself—although I think I *do* love you, and I believe that for a little while at least, you loved me, too. Perhaps you feel otherwise now that you're back among your charges, but I can't rid myself of the hope that if you let me into your life, we could be happy together. Will you give me—will you give *us*—that chance?"

It was Christmastime and she was a little girl again, staring into the shop windows at all the toys and treats inside, desperately craving, yet knowing that come Christmas morning, they wouldn't be there for her, because of what she was. What she still was. "I'm sure all things look possible to you, my lord. You have wealth and rank, power and influence. I'm not a part of that world, and I never can be. My work, my life, is here, with the orphaned children who need me."

Looking steadily at his face, she held out her work-hardened, callused hands. "No matter how much I wish it could be otherwise, these aren't the hands of a fine lady worthy of the Earl of Cwm Rhyss."

He strode around the desk. Before she could back away, he took hold of her hands and brought them to his lips, pressing a gentle kiss upon each palm before answering. "These are the hands of a woman who's known hard work and suffering, and made the world better with her efforts."

Her heart fluttered like the wings of a caged bird, but the cage could not simply be wished away. It was made of the strongest of conventions; she had seen what had happened to those who tried to bend the bars. "Society will condemn us both—you for lowering yourself, me for my presumption. They'll say you were desperate, and that I was after your wealth."

"Are you not the same woman who told me to ignore what people say? Why should we pay attention to the small-minded and ignorant?"

He put his hands lightly on her shoulders. "Oh, Gwen, please, don't deny us the chance to see if what we feel is true and lasting because you fear the world, as I did. You gave me hope—not that I could be what I was, but that I could be happier than I ever dared to dream, even before my accident, if you loved me. Please, don't take that hope away from me. Not yet."

It was Christmas, and she'd received the most wondrous present of all.

"I want to hope," she whispered. "I want to believe that we can be together."

"And the rest of the world be damned?"

She smiled through her joyful tears as she looked at his happy face. "The rest of the world be damned."

His arms tightened about her, and they kissed happily, tenderly, then with growing desire, until she gently pushed him back. "I think we'd better stop and rejoin the others. They must be wondering what happened to me."

"I think you're right," he said with a wry grin. "Or I fear there would be cause for scandal at Saint Bridget's." Then his grin became a glorious smile that seemed to light the dim room. "Suddenly, Miss Davies, my Christmas has become very merry."

"Suddenly, so has mine."

"I shall live in hope that next Christmas will be merrier still."

She nestled against his broad chest. "I don't see how I could be any happier."

"I know when I'll be happier," he whispered, holding her close. "The day you agree to be my wife."

She felt again that blast of wintry doubt. She drew back and looked up at him. "It's much too soon to talk about *that*."

He smiled that devilishly seductive smile of his. "But you don't discount the notion entirely?"

"No," she admitted, snuggling against him again and allowing herself to envision that wonderful possibility. "And I'm sure, my lord—"

"Griffin."

"My lord Griffin, that if I did discount it entirely, I wouldn't do this." She bussed his cheek. "Or this." She kissed his chin. "Or this," she finished in a low murmur before giving him a kiss of desire, longing and promise.

"By all the saints in heaven—Miss Davies!" Molly cried.

They jumped apart, to see the young woman standing on the threshold, her eyes nearly as big and round as the bowl of plum pudding in her hand "I was just…the pudding…and here you are…with…who's he?"

Gwen forgave Molly her incoherence and didn't even blush, although she was glad Molly had witnessed a relatively chaste kiss. "This is the Earl of Cwm Rhyss. My lord, this is Molly."

He bowed elegantly. "Charmed."

Molly's mouth moved, but no sound came out.

"It's my scars, isn't it?" Griffin remarked. "Ugly, I know. But if you're kind and leave the pudding, maybe I'll let you see the ones on my legs someday."

Molly yelped, dropped the pudding and disappeared.

"What on earth made you say that?" Gwen demanded as she bent down to pick up the broken pieces.

He pulled her up before she could. "I unrepentantly confess that I wanted to make her go away."

"I'm beginning to think people were right about you. You're a wicked man."

"Then you must continue in your reformation of my reclusive character. It will be an uphill battle, I expect. Indeed, I think you'll *have* to marry me to do it completely."

"If I marry you, it won't be to reform you. It will be because I love you." She reached up to kiss his scarred cheek. "Merry Christmas, Griffin."

His arms went around her. "A very merry Christmas to you, my darling, my love. And I pray God we share many more."

Dear reader, they did.

* * * * *

Dear Reader,

I have always been fascinated by the different ways in which the holidays were celebrated throughout history, and I especially like the Scottish custom of "First Footing." It began in medieval times, and it was said that the first person through your door on the first night of the New Year (Hogmanay) determined your luck and prosperity in the coming year. It was said to have begun as far back as the Viking raids on Scotland, so a tall blond man was not the person you hoped to see that night!

The hero and heroine of my story could both use a bit of good luck in their lives. But what will happen if the man Elizabeth loves is an older, stubborn, red-haired Scottish warrior and not the dark-haired young man needed to bring her luck? Can love prevail and grant them their wishes?

I wish you and yours a happy holiday season and I hope that your first-footer brings your household much health and prosperity in the New Year!

Terri Brisbin

LOVE AT FIRST STEP

Terri Brisbin

This story is dedicated to my sons, Matthew, Andrew and Michael, who are all dark-haired heroes in the making and who give me joy in the holiday season and throughout the year. I love you all!

Chapter One

"Let me send her to you this night."

"Are these shorter days making you daft, man?"

Gavin MacLeod glared at his host, lifted the goblet to his mouth and swallowed deeply. The heather ale slid smoothly over his tongue and kept his other retorts quiet. He needed no help in finding a woman to bed, if 'twas his wont to do so.

He'd been visiting Orrick of Silloth at the time of the winter solstice for years and did not remember Orrick ever expressing an interest in or notice of any of the women villeins or servants before this. Of course this was his first time here since Gavin's wife's death, so mayhap Orrick felt more at ease discussing women with him now. Or was it the festive season approaching that put him more in the mind to bring up the subject?

"Look you there, Gavin. She is a whore as much as I am king of England," Orrick said, under his breath.

"Are you my procurer as well as my foster brother?"

Gavin did watch the woman now. How could he not? Orrick's words forced his attention to her form and he noticed the attributes of most any woman were enhanced on her. Full, lush breasts, narrow waist and flaring hips, and long legs declared her attractive appearance. But instead of displaying them in an inviting way as a woman who made her living on her back usually did, this one hid them beneath a serviceable gown and veil and an almost modest demeanor.

"You are her lord, Orrick. Know you not how she makes her living?"

Orrick grunted and took a mouthful from his own goblet. For a few minutes Gavin observed this woman as she served the lower tables. She wore a ready smile on her face and spoke softly to all she served. No blatant enticement of the men was apparent in her manner and no hostility came in answer from any of the women at table. Orrick truly ran his lands and demesne differently than most English lords.

"I know how she makes a living, brother. I do not know how she came to be in that living."

Orrick's words surprised him. Orrick had a way of getting at the truth and yet this woman had kept her past a secret from him. Surprising. Intriguing. Something within him stirred for the first time in a very long time.

Curiosity.

He pushed himself into the tall-back chair on which he sat and studied her. He guessed she had about a score-and-five years. He noticed that she looked to have all of her teeth when she smiled and that her skin was clear of pox or blemish. Her back was straight as she stood; no deformity showed itself. Not the usual village harlot.

"Does it matter why she does it, Orrick? Is she causing trouble for you?"

Orrick leaned closer so his words would not be heard, most likely by Margaret, his wife, who sat on his other side. "I find an unanswered question unacceptable. Who knows what trouble she might bring if someone comes seeking her?"

Gavin felt the tug of a puppeteer's strings. He recognized

his foster brother's machinations for what they were and decided that he could play at it, as well.

"Then throw her out, as is your right as lord of these lands."

The grimace and dark glare told Gavin the truth. She had stymied Orrick's quest for her story, but he would never rid his lands of even one helpless soul who lacked sanctuary. And especially not as the feast of Our Lord's Birth and the celebration of the new year approached. 'Twas ever his weakness. Gavin laughed at Orrick's plight.

"Although you are wrong in your assessment of me and in your attempts to manipulate me, I will take pity on your plight and discover the information you seek about your village whore." He nodded in the woman's direction as he spoke and nearly missed the painful look that crossed Orrick's face. Nearly.

Did Orrick have some personal interest in this woman? He thought not, but what else could explain his behavior. Gavin tilted forward to check on Margaret's attention and found her in an animated conversation with the woman at her side. Now was as good a time as any to ask his question.

"Do you want her for your leman? Is that the object of all this?"

"Leman?" Orrick asked, choking on the word.

"Aye. I can find out if she is married or if there is another obstacle in your way, if 'tis your wont to claim her as your leman."

This was not such an unusual thing among nobles, but something did not feel right to him. He never would have believed that Orrick would take another to his bed while married to Margaret. It had been much too long between his visits if things between them had changed this much.

"I want no other woman but my Margaret, you thick-skulled arse," Orrick whispered furiously to him. "This is about a friend helping a friend in a task. I thought it would give you something to do while you visit with us until the new year arrives. That is all."

Relief flooded him that he would not be involved in deceiving Orrick's wife. She could be formidable in her fury and he did not want to be the one receiving such attention. And he was glad in his heart that Orrick was still as faithful to his Margaret as he had been to his wife Nessa while she lived.

"Fine, then. Send her to me and I will discover her secrets for you."

"Be discreet." Orrick whispered the warning. "The needs of a guest cannot be ignored, but even in these long, dark days of winter Margaret cares not for whoring in her keep."

"Do not get me in trouble with your wife, Orrick. And do not get the woman—" he nodded toward their quarry "—in trouble with the lady for your curiosity."

Orrick waved off his concerns. "She will be sent to your chambers to assist you in your bath. Even Margaret will accept that. What happens from there is between you and her," Orrick said, nodding in the same direction.

Gavin sat back and took another mouthful of ale from his cup, all the time watching the graceful movements of the woman under discussion.

"Her name? You never did tell me her name, Orrick."

"Elizabeth."

Elizabeth. It was high-sounding for a whore, but it fit her graceful ways and demeanor. Her customers probably called her "Lizzie" or "Betsy," a name more suited for a woman on her back.

Elizabeth.

There! He was eyeing her again. Elizabeth watched out of the corner of her eye as Lord Orrick's friend gazed intently at her. She purposely walked to the farthest end of the rows of tables to see if he turned his look upon someone else. He did not.

Nervousness bubbled up within her as she tried to ignore what his attention meant. Although Lady Margaret forbade her from plying her trade in the hall or keep, fulfilling the needs of an honored guest was expected. And one so high in the esteem of the lord would have every whim satisfied by anyone within the lands of Orrick.

She had done it before with others and would do it again, but she felt the uncertainty growing inside. Like some untried girl. She smiled at the miller's son as she filled his cup with ale and tried to ignore the lord's guest. Of course, with his size and his position next to Orrick at the high table it was nigh to impossible to do that. So Elizabeth decided to meet his challenge directly and raised her eyes to meet his.

His frown, even from this distance, was apparent. Had she done something to displease him already? She continued to look at him and was surprised to see the edges of his mouth begin to curl up in a smile. He was not nearly so fearsome when he smiled.

A shiver moved up her spine and she was certain that he had been discussing her with Lord Orrick. To what end? This man traveled alone, without even a squire or page or man-at-arms for his protection. The cook told her that Lord Gavin visited Lord Orrick each year at this time and usually stayed through the solstice and new year festivities before returning to his lands in Scotland.

Did he want her as a whore? Probably. She was able to recognize the intensity in his gaze as that of desire. She admitted to herself that she was not a good and practiced harlot. This was still somewhat new to her and she was still learning the art of enticing customers and recognizing what their looks meant. One day she would be better at this.

One day.

She sighed and turned her attentions back to the task she was carrying out now. The people here were kind to her, even the men who frequented her cottage were never rough or disrespectful to her in their actions or in the height of their passionate attentions. For that she was grateful. For many things she was grateful—especially for the day she had wandered into this village and into the demesne of Lord Orrick of Silloth. He had offered her a place and saved her life that day. If she needed to lie with his friends to pay back her debt to him, she would without complaint.

Lord Orrick's friend stood and nodded at him and took leave of Lady Margaret, as well. He was tall, taller than the lord, who stood at least four inches past six feet. It must be his Scots blood, for she had heard he was from the barbaric Highlands where the men were giants and known for their fierceness. In her thoughts she could see him swinging a massive sword in battle against his enemies. She shivered again, thankful that other than a glance in her direction, she would have nothing else to do with him.

When her jug of ale was empty, Elizabeth returned to the pantry to fill it again. Rounding the wooden partition that separated it from the rest of the hall, she found herself face-to-face with the man who had just filled her thoughts. She had to tilt her head back to meet his eyes at this closeness. His eyes, as dark a blue as she had ever seen, met hers and her mouth went dry.

She could not turn her eyes away as he smiled at her. The rugged angles of his face, the life-roughened expression in his eyes and his overwhelming size took her breath away. The jug tumbled from her grasp and landed with a thud on the floor at her feet. The steward's voice pierced her confused state as she stood staring into the Scot's icy-blue eyes.

"Lord Orrick wishes you to tend to his guest now, Elizabeth. Someone else will serve the ale."

Blinking, she looked at the steward and waited for his words to make sense. Before she could react, the man stepped back, leaned down and picked up the empty jug from the floor. Holding it out to the steward, he never moved his gaze from hers. Heat built within her and her stomach began to tighten.

"My thanks, Lord Gavin. Your bath will be ready in your chambers anon. Elizabeth? See to it now."

The orders of the steward broke her reverie. Lowering her head, she curtsied to the steward and to Lord Gavin.

"Yes, my lord."

She turned to go to the kitchens to arrange for the hot water needed for a bath. He would need the largest of their wooden tubs if there was any chance of him fitting those legs in it. Focusing her thoughts on the items needed kept her from thinking about what else this summons meant, what came after the bathing was done. When he was clean and relaxed from the heat of the water. When he was still naked.

She shuddered, part in fear and part in anticipation of what the night would hold for her. There was something different about this man and this service. Elizabeth feared not what would happen in the joining of their bodies, but what he might do to the heart she kept hidden so well. And she did not know why he felt like such a threat to her.

Chapter Two

She tested the steaming water with her elbow and nodded, pleased that it was hot enough but not too. Looking over the small bottles and jars on the tray, she chose several and added an amount of each to the water. Fresh and soothing scents filled the chamber as the oils mixed with the steaming water. Stirring them with her hand, she nodded again. The bath was ready, but where was Lord Gavin?

As if his name in her thoughts had conjured him from nothing, the door opened and he stood just within the frame. Silhouetted by the torches in the corridor, she could see nothing but the outline of his form.

"'Tis ready, my lord." She walked to the door as he stepped into the room. Trying to keep in as much heat as possible, she closed the door behind him. Beads of sweat, from both her exertions and from the heat, trickled down her neck and back. Using the back of her hand, she wiped it from her brow.

The man stood before the large tub and just stared at it. Was there a problem? What did he need?

"My lord?" she asked. "Is something wrong?"

"Did you pick out the scent yourself?"

"Aye, my lord. The oils are from Lady Margaret and will

soothe the roughness and dryness of your skin. If they are not pleasing to you, I could change them."

It would take four servants each carrying two large buckets of heated water to refill the tub, but it could be, would be, done if he so wished.

"I should have waited for you before adding them, my lord. I beg your pardon." She leaned her head down respectfully, awaiting his decision. In truth, she chose the scented oils that reminded her of the coming festivities—pine, holly berry, and Lady Margaret's precious balsam.

"I asked because 'twas an appealing combination, not because it displeased me."

Turning away, she busied herself organizing what she would need for his bath. Cloths, jars of soap, extra buckets of water, drying linens. She laid them out near the tub so she could reach them easily as she needed them. All in an effort to avoid watching him undress. When she could wait no longer, she looked across the room to where he remained…fully dressed and watching her every move.

"The water is cooling, my lord," She said as she held out her hand over the bath. "Do you need help with…your…?" She did not finish the words, but simply pointed to him.

"I am not such a bairn that I need help getting undressed," he answered in a voice so deep and smooth that it reminded her of warm honey, fresh from the hive on a summer's day.

"No, my lord. I did not mean that."

He seemed bothered by something. Was she not brazen enough toward him? Was he waiting for her to take charge of this? After all, everyone knew that a male guest asking for "a bath" was simply another way to speak of their desire to tup. Elizabeth stepped closer and reached for the ties on his tunic.

"Nay, lass," he said, stepping back. "I can take off my own clothing."

His words were not harsh, but she felt the rebuke. Mayhap

she had misread the situation? She would not overstep her place again with him. Turning her back to him, she walked to the side of the tub and waited there. Busying herself by checking the water, she did not watch his movements. Elizabeth could see him out of the corner of her eye and when he turned his back to her, she took advantage of the chance to take a closer look at him.

He was of the same age as Orrick, having just over two score of years, and his experience as a warrior showed on his body. The scars of old wounds covered parts of his back and even one thigh, but they did not detract from his physical beauty. His long, dark red hair was liberally sprinkled with gray and fell below his shoulders. Wide, brawny shoulders they were, as was his back. A narrow waist and hips led to strong, muscular legs. The perfect male body. She sighed, imagining what the front of him would look like. So deep in her thoughts was she that she did not notice him turn at the sound she made.

Aye, he was impressive. And he was watching her as she watched him! Now, he stood before her, naked as the day his mother birthed him.

Blinking quickly, Elizabeth turned her face to the tub and cleared her throat. How incredibly stupid to be attracted to such a man! He would bathe, take his pleasure on her and be gone from her life by the morn. Apparently the hard lessons of the past year of her life were not yet learned well enough.

"Watch your step, my lord. The oils make the tub a bit slippery when you step into it." She hoped that concentrating on the bath would lessen the tension she felt between them.

Without a word, Lord Gavin walked to the tub, stepped into the heated water, turned around and sat down. As she had suspected, his long legs did not fit so he drew them up, his knees now exposed above the tub's rim.

Without delay, she lifted one of the jars, scooped out a generous handful of the soft soap and shared it between her hands. Pushing his hair off his back with her hand, she spread the soap over his shoulders, down his back and around again. Taking a cloth, she dipped it into the water and lathered the soap until the thick foam covered his back.

Elizabeth moved to the side and lifted his arm to continue the washing. She noticed his eyes were closed, but she doubted that he was asleep. He allowed, even aided, her work as she moved around him, washing his limbs. He lifted one leg out of the tub and then the other as she spread the soap over him. It was as she began to scrub his chest and stomach that he stopped her with his larger hand over hers.

"I can do the rest, lass. If you would move the bucket of rinse water for me and leave it where I can reach it, you may go."

"My lord?" Elizabeth did not understand his dismissal. "Have I done something to displease you?"

"Nay, lass. The bath has been pleasant and well-done. 'Tis all I need from you."

Elizabeth nodded, still surprised that he did not want bedplay as other men would. She knew she was not the best-looking of women, but she had washed her face and tidied herself before coming here tonight. Was there something wrong with her? Mayhap he did not frequent whores?

She walked to the hearth in the chamber and moved one of the three buckets of clean water closer to the tub. The lord had dipped his head into the tub and was scrubbing his scalp as she moved the cloths and drying linens to where he could reach, always watching his movements in the tub. She also moved an empty bucket for rinsing his head nearer to him.

"Lass? It looks like I do need your help. Would you pour that water over my head?"

A nervous tension grew within her. Although his manner was straightforward, she felt as though he was toying with her. But, why?

"Aye, my lord," she answered as she lifted the bucket as high as she could.

Lord Gavin leaned his head back over the side of the tub so that the water would flow into the empty bucket. Elizabeth poured the warm, clean water over him and he rubbed to remove the soap from his hair. As she put down the bucket, he twisted the length of his hair, releasing most of the water it held.

Then he stood up.

She was trapped between the tub and the bed and had nowhere to look or move as he stretched to his full height and stepped out of the tub. Beads of water sluiced down his body, over every muscle from neck to chest to thighs and down. She was unable to look away as he used one of the drying cloths to press more water from his hair and then he wiped his body once. Their eyes met and Elizabeth found that her breath and voice had left her.

"What other tasks do you have this night, lass?"

His voice made her toes curl and a pool of heat formed in her belly. This was startling. She had been tupped by many men since her arrival here and this mix of fear and anticipation surprised her. Why did he not simply take his pleasure and be done?

"None, my lord, save you. Lord Orrick said I should tend to you only." How she had forced the words out, she knew not.

"The water is still warm and nigh to clean. Use it if you would like," he said, pointing to the tub, completely comfortable in his nakedness.

"A bath? Me?" The opportunity for a bath in a tub of warm water did not come often to her, and especially not in the dead of winter. Being second in would also be a treat. But she would need to undress here to take it.

He laughed and the sound of it echoed through the chamber. Lord Gavin was a handsome man and when he smiled, an attractive set of dimples formed in his rugged cheeks giving him a much younger appearance. She watched as he nodded at her.

"Aye, lass. For you, if you be wanting to enjoy it."

She worried her bottom lip as she thought on his offer. She was about to refuse when he laughed again.

"I am to bed now, lass. If you would put out the candles when you leave?"

Elizabeth nodded her head, still in disbelief, as he did just as he said. He tossed the cloths in a pile near the hearth and, after pulling several blankets off the rope-strung bed, he climbed in and made himself comfortable. He rearranged the pillows and then turned on his side facing away from her. Deciding that to pass up this chance was foolish, Elizabeth moved quietly to the side of the tub.

"May I, my lord? Truly?" Part of her wanted to tear off her soiled garments and jump in. Another part urged caution with this man who was unknown to her.

"'Twould be folly to waste good bathwater. 'Tis yours to use," he answered without moving.

"My thanks to you," she whispered as she tugged at the laces on her gown. If she moved quickly, she could wash, dry herself and be dressed in a few minutes. If she was quiet, he would fall to sleep and never even know she was still here.

She loosened her gown and pulled it over her head. Then her shift, stockings and shoes followed and she stepped into the tub and sat as soundlessly as she could. She could not, however, stop the sigh of pleasure that escaped as the heat soothed her tired body. The tub in which he barely fit gave her nearly enough room to lie back.

After unraveling her braided hair and dipping beneath the water, she lathered and washed and rinsed as quickly and silently as she could. Only a few minutes had passed when she twisted the length of her hair to squeeze out the water and prepared to stand. Elizabeth did not know what made her look up, but there he stood with a bucket of the clean water held up to rinse her free of the soap and dirt from the now twice-used bathwater.

And he was still naked.

She swallowed several times trying to think of what to say and trying not to look at his body. 'Twas a difficult task since he was so close and so…large.

She was being an empty-headed ninny. She was a whore and had been for several months now. Why did this one man cause such nervousness within her? They would tussle. They would tup. She would leave. Nothing different from the other men who had used her body before him.

With a renewed sense of her place in this, she stood and waited for him to pour the water over her. She did have to struggle with herself not to raise her arms to cover herself from his sight. Instead, she concentrated on the warmth of the water as it flowed over her head and down the rest of her. She had not been this clean…in months. When she wiped her eyes clear, she saw Lord Gavin standing with his hand outstretched to her, to help her step from the tub.

Elizabeth accepted it and found herself wrapped in a drying cloth and standing before the hearth, absorbing its heat. 'Twas pure luxury, she knew, but if this was the way he would pay her, she was tired and dirty enough to accept it. Of course, as Lord Orrick's guest, there was no fee to be paid. Without a word, he walked back to the bed and climbed in it.

"My lord," she said, turning to him. "My thanks for sharing your bath. Should I call the servants to remove the tub now?"

"Nay, lass. Leave it until morn."

She hesitated, not sure of what to do or where to go. He watched her every move. Finally she decided not to delay his pleasure any longer. This sense of unbalance in her that his nearness and his looks and his voice caused within her had to end. She unwrapped the cloths from around her and walked to the bed, not hiding from him. A woman's naked flesh seemed to get most men ready for tupping and she expected that he would grab her and take her now.

He did nothing but look at her. Slowly his gaze moved up and down over her, making her breasts tighten and sending waves of heat through her belly. Elizabeth did not recognize these feelings and was not certain if she wanted them to stay or go. Lord Gavin turned from her for a moment and she realized he was holding the covers out for her to enter the bed, but he offered her the side of the bed away from the door of the chambers. After a momentary hesitation, she walked around and climbed in next to him.

Elizabeth lay next to him, enjoying the comfort of the overstuffed mattress and the smell of the clean sheets on it. The thin pallet on which she slept here and the one in her cottage offered nothing close to the feeling of floating that this one did. She sighed and allowed herself a moment before turning her attentions to the naked man beside her.

He smiled when she looked at him. Were her small comforts humorous to him? Most likely since he was accustomed to such. She had been, as well…before. His expression turned serious and she expected that 'twas time to begin.

"Sleep well, lass."

Lord Gavin shifted on the mattress and arranged the bedcovers several times before seeming to find a comfortable position. He was going to sleep. Sleep?

"My lord? Is there something else?"

"Nay, lass. I asked for a bath and I had it. 'Tis all I wanted this night."

"But my lord…" She began to push the blankets off her. "I should go."

"And rest on a dusty pallet in the hall? Now that you are clean, why not rest here this night?" His hand on hers stayed her leaving.

His voice held compassion and caring in its deep, velvety tones and Elizabeth fought the tears that burned in her throat. No one, not even Lord Orrick, had treated her with this much concern in years and years and she felt herself weakening in the face of it. Did he know what he did to her? Did he know that he could destroy her with such consideration?

"If you wish, my lord." She would rest the blame on him.

"I wish it, lass." His thick burr curled around his words and she felt his heated breath next to her ear.

So be it then. Elizabeth sank into the mattress and the heat of his grasp on her hand spread through the rest of her. Tired from hours of serving meals and cleaning in the kitchens, she could feel sleep taking its hold of her.

"My name is Elizabeth," she whispered, for no reason she could think of.

"Sleep well, Elizabeth."

"Any success in our quest?"

Gavin glared at Orrick as he seated himself next to his host at the table in order to break his fast. Lady Margaret was nowhere to be seen this morn. A serving girl placed a tankard in front of him before he could ask for it.

"*Our* quest? I did not know you were working on this with me." He drank deeply of the ale.

"Do not quibble with me, Gavin. Did you find the answers I seek or not?"

Orrick was testy this morn. Good. Served him right to feel the frustration that he himself felt. Well, he was certain 'twas not the exact same frustration. He delayed answering by drinking again and then calling for food and waiting for its arrival.

The mealy porridge served here did not compare with the hearty one served at his keep, but 'twould have to do. The food here would not vary much in substance or amount until the feasting days of the anniversary of Our Lord's Birth and the twelve nights after it. For now, the serving girl familiar with his ways placed a bowl of porridge, a jar of honey and a jug of cream before him. The steward brought out a small skin of *uisge beatha,* whisky, to him and he mixed it into the steaming porridge. Soon it smelled much more appetizing than the original did. He ignored Orrick's glare and spooned several mouthfuls in before stopping.

"No answers yet."

"She spent the night in your chambers, Gavin. What did you do?"

"The usual things a man does with a woman in the night." He could not help himself. Orrick was such a pleasure to goad into a reaction and this one was not long in coming.

"Blast you," he whispered harshly. "Tell me what you learned."

Gavin smiled at Orrick's displeasure and could not resist drawing this out a bit more. "We bathed and we slept."

"Expect a challenge as soon as the weather clears, friend."

"Orrick, if your words did not say otherwise, I would swear I hear jealousy in your voice."

Orrick exhaled loudly and sat back in his chair. "Not jealousy, Gavin. Concern at a wrong done to an innocent."

Orrick had always been too soft when it came to his people. He coddled them and treated them as though they were much more than simply his property. Gavin had never quite understood it until Orrick had explained it as his application of the Scottish clan system on his English estate. Clan was about more than property and lands, it was about family and belonging. Orrick gave his villeins a sense of belonging, even though his authority was clear and never challenged.

"We bathed and slept and no more than that. Truly."

"Do not use her, Gavin. I did not ask you for help to play her falsely."

"She has proclaimed herself a whore. If she is not one, then, as her lord and master, forbid her to play that role."

"I tried that. It did not work." Orrick's tone was sullen.

"What did she do?" Gavin recognized the same stubborn streak in Elizabeth that had gotten him in trouble many, many times.

"She refused food. She told me quite boldly that she would earn her way and not be beholden to anyone."

"Did you not offer her work in your hall? Or in your laundry? Or your kitchens?"

Gavin thought that those places would be a good place if a woman could work but had no skills.

"She asked if we had a harlot in the village and when I said not, she said that was how she earned her living in the past."

"So, where is the problem, Orrick? I think you make too much of this." The tightening in his gut told Gavin that there was something more here. How did you help someone who did not want help?

"Discover her secrets so I can let this go."

"I told you I would. You act like an old woman instead of the Orrick I knew."

His friend said nothing, but clapped him on the back and left him to his food. Gavin turned back to his still-hot porridge and contemplated his methods.

He had had her off balance—she fully expected to be bedded when he called for a bath. And when she bent over him, spreading the soap on his flesh with a thorough but soft touch, his body had reacted as it should. 'Twould be no hardship to lay her on the bed and take her. And take her again.

'Twas more important to his task to build her trust and so he'd ignored his body's demands and forced himself to sleep next to her.

Although he did not admit it to Orrick, he was certain that she had not been raised a whore. There was a moment or two during the night when a look of fear or uncertainty entered her eyes and when she seemed to be convincing herself of what she needed to do. And it did not come easily to her.

So, why then did she force herself to do this when Orrick had offered her a different way? What loss had she suffered that made her seek her own way in this world, especially since the world was an unkind place for most everyone?

Gavin looked out over the hall to see if she was serving the tables. He'd awakened to find her still deeply asleep and he had hesitated to wake her. 'Twas obvious she had enjoyed the bath. The sound of her sigh as she slipped beneath the water had weakened his resolve not to touch her and he found the excuse he needed when he spied the bucket of rinse water. And the enjoyment in her eyes as he wrapped her in the drying cloth made his mouth water.

She was no whore, but she was an enticing woman who made him feel desires he had ignored for a very long time. That alone made her a danger to his well-established life.

So tonight he would summon her again and build more trust before asking his questions. He almost felt guilty over how easy this would be….

Almost.

Chapter Three

His chamber was ready. Servants had brought him a selection of foods, some hot, some cold, some plain and some more elaborate. They all had one thing in common—they were temptations for his use. In the middle of winter, food tended to become plain and monotonous. With the lord's permission and the cook's help, Gavin had planned a feast for Elizabeth. When all was ready, he sent a servant to summon her. Her knock came just a few minutes later.

"You called for me, my lord?"

Her voice was quiet and she stood just outside the door. He waved her in and walked over to close the door behind her. Her eyes resembled a deer surrounded in the forest by hunters with no escape route left to it. She surveyed the room, from corner to corner, past the bed and back to him.

"I asked for a meal and they sent up enough to feed several people. I know you served the meal in the hall and did not eat yet, so I thought you might join me."

"I could not, my lord," she said with a curtsy. "I take my meals in the kitchen after my duties are done." He could see she was gauging her distance to the door and his position there.

"Your duties are done for tonight, Elizabeth. Orrick said I could have you now."

He purposely chose the words to make her think his intent was physical. And from the way her breathing changed and her eyes widened, he had been successful. His own erection spoke of his success, too.

She lowered her head and curtsied once more. "As you wish, my lord."

"I am not your lord. Call me Gavin."

She looked up, startled by his familiarity and shook her head. "I could not do that, my lord."

"In Scotland, we do not fall back on such formality as you do here. My given name is what my retainers, my family and even my enemies call me. Surely, you are brave enough to use it."

Elizabeth looked torn over what to do, but then she nodded her answer. "I cannot join you for this meal. 'Twould be unseemly."

"Ah, you cannot join me to eat, but you could share my bed if 'twas my wish? Is that what you are telling me?"

She did not answer him and he wondered if she was thinking on the absurdity of it. Well, there was more than one way to get closer to her.

"'Tis a fine idea, lass. Get on the bed, then."

He pointed to the bed and watched as, with an air of resignation, she crossed the room to it. As she had done last night, she climbed on it from the side farthest from the door and waited. When he did not move, she began to loosen the ties on her gown.

"Nay, not yet," he said. "You may not be hungry, but I am."

Gavin saw the surprised look on her face, but ignored it to sit by the table. He thought about facing away from her for a moment, however he decided to face the hearth so he could still watch her expressions. Her reactions began as soon as he tore the leg off a capon and bit into it. The juicy meat was hot and seasoned and he ate it with gusto.

Her mouth tightened and a frown crossed her brow, but she said not a word. Gavin increased the pressure on her by choosing another chunk of meat from the platter before him and putting it in his mouth. Chewing for a moment, he washed it down with a mouthful of Margaret's special ale.

The silence was broken by the noisy rumbling of a stomach—and it wasn't his. His amused gaze met her embarrassed one and he fought to keep the threatening smile from his face. He lost the battle and broke out laughing.

"I told you to eat," he said, holding out a chunk of steaming bread. "There is plenty for both of us."

He watched the battle raging within her. Her hunger was obvious from the rumblings of her belly; the ravenous light in her eyes intensified as she followed his every move. When it looked as though she would continue to resist his efforts, he chose another piece of roasted beef and took it to her. Sitting down beside her on the rope-strung mattress, he held it out in front of her mouth, urging without words that she take it from his fingers.

Gavin knew the moment he had won this battle, for she tilted her head slightly and lifted her mouth to his hand. In spite of knowing it was only a way for him to gain control, he discovered that he was not immune to her after all. The touch of her lips on his fingers as she finally accepted the food jolted him from head to toe, mostly in between. He could not move his hand away even after she took the meat and began chewing it.

Shaking himself free of her spell, he returned to the table and brought his goblet back to her. As she finished chewing, he lifted it to her lips and tilted it for her to drink. In his inexcusable haste, he let some of the ale spill over. He watched as it trickled down from her mouth, onto her neck and then under the thin layer of the chemise under her gown. His mouth hungered to follow it, so he did.

He nipped and licked the path of the spill, his tongue feeling the pounding of her pulse under the delicate skin of her neck, the tense panting that began as he moved lower and the heat of her skin as he tasted his way down toward her breasts. He grew hard and he shifted to accommodate himself in his breeches. But when she drew back, he accepted the message and moved away.

She was afraid of him.

Did she fear him as a man, as a Scots warrior? Or was it something else? Did she fear that he would discover her secrets, her weaknesses, and use them against her? Gavin slid from the bed and went to the table, sitting and eating more from the platters of food before him. He would bide his time.

Mayhap not.

He took a few more bites of meat and mouthfuls of ale before speaking again. Elizabeth sat as still as stone on the bed where he'd left her. Only her eyes moved, fastened onto his every gesture. She was like no whore he'd ever met.

"Are you afeard of me, lass?"

The emotions flitted across her face—a fierce frown on her brow, a tightening of those lips he wanted to claim. Even her breathing had not slowed. He saw the struggle within her as she attempted to answer his question and the challenge within it.

"I know many Sassenachs that are afraid of us. Scots warriors are known for our ferocity and…"

Her laughter surprised and interrupted him. This was an unexpected turn.

"You must not know the true nature of the Scots if you can laugh at my words."

The sound of it echoed through the chamber and he wanted to drink it from her lips. Her face changed as she laughed and all the tension was released. She looked years younger when a smile graced her. How many years did she have?

"My grandmam told me the true nature of Scottish men, my lord. They like their whisky strong, their nights of drinking it long, and their women to ignore it." Elizabeth smiled again, but the way her eyes looked off in the distance told him she was remembering something…someone from her past. "Change the drink and that describes most men of any origin."

Something within him was insulted at first, but he realized that her lot in life had shown her only that part of men. The laughter burst out from him and he did not try to restrain it. She had spunk, when she wasn't trying to be so plain. Gavin looked at her once more and realized this truth—she was a beautiful woman hiding it in a work gown and kerchief.

"Is that all you know of men?" He probed for more than the knowledge he'd received already.

Elizabeth sat up straighter on the bed and rearranged her gown so she could sit cross-legged. He watched her struggle with an answer.

"I know much of men, my lord. Their actions, their desires." Her eyes flashed at the mention of desires, yet her look was not one of wanting but of loathing.

"And what of women's desires? What know you of them?"

Her chin lifted and regret and loss entered her expressive eyes. Did she know how much she gave away with simply a glance? "Women have no desires, my lord. At least not for more than a safe place to live."

Gavin was saddened by her words—they struck deeply within him, for in his experience women lived life to the fullest. He knew that his late wife met him match for match in her appetites for living and loving. How empty had Elizabeth's existence been that she believed this and would rather be a whore to men's desires than have her own? He watched her gather her control around herself and he knew that another direct question would be deflected. What had she told him? Her grandmam knew the Scots?

"Was your grandmam Scottish herself?"

"Aye, my lord. But from the Borders, not the Highlands like you."

"Did you live with her? Or she with you?" he probed, suspecting that her relative was a safe subject. Gavin chose to turn his attentions back to his food as though this were unimportant chatter.

"I was only a girl when she died, my lord," Elizabeth said. A soft smile crossed her face. "I remember many of her sayings."

"All about men?" He lifted a chunk of bread and tore off a piece with his teeth,

"Nay, she had wisdom about many things. Mostly I remember her songs."

"Come, lass. Share the food with me." He tried once more to get her to the table.

Her stomach betrayed her hunger again and Elizabeth decided that eating with him would be the least of the dangers he offered. She tugged on the laces of her chemise and slid off the bed, accepting his invitation. She had had no chance to eat an evening meal yet and, as he'd said, there was more than enough for both of them. She sat on a stool on the opposite side of the table from him and waited.

"Dinna be shy," he said with a brogue she had noticed only once before. He pushed a few of the platters closer to her and even poured her a mug of ale.

Making up her mind to enjoy the wondrous meal before her, she chose a variety of the dishes and went about eating them. Licking her lips, she marveled at the assortment, especially in the middle of winter when the food in the hall did not include such choices.

"You must have bribed the cook to get such a feast," she said.

"I did," he answered with no hint of guile or guilt.

"Why? Surely the meal in the hall was filling enough?" The gravy of a meat pasty leaked down her chin and when she looked for a napkin to catch it, she found his beneath her chin. With his hand wiping her lips. She must learn to let go of the past and simply use her sleeve. Elizabeth waited on his answer and was not certain he would give one. His eyes turned serious and then heated, and she began to fear his response.

"For you, lass. To entice you into my chambers."

With a sense of resolution, she understood this now. He was paying for her services. There was nothing else to it. Somehow it was easier now that she knew, and she began the process within her mind and soul to try to detach herself from the act that would happen soon.

"I will lie with you if you desire it, my lord," she said. Pointing to the table covered with food, she continued, "You do not need to go to this extent and effort. As my lord Orrick's guest, I could not accept payment from you anyway."

He surprised her then, pounding his fists on the table, making his goblet and her mug shake and wobble. His face flushed red and she saw his expression turn hard. How had she insulted him? What could she do to assuage his anger?

"I do desire it and I have been foolish to delay my pleasure. 'Tis past time to bed you."

His words were exactly the opposite of ones he'd spoken last night. 'Twas only a matter of time with men before taking their pleasure overcame any hesitation or other distractions. He was proving to be the same as the others who had come before him and would come after in her bed. Elizabeth could understand that, but she could not explain the deep sense of sadness within her at the realization.

He stood and came around the table toward her. As she rose to meet him, she worked to find the calm place inside her where she could hide until this was over. His kiss, when it came, was not the overpowering one she expected, but a soft touch on her lips. It was devastating.

He wrapped his arms around her and half-walked, half-carried her to the bed, and she found herself sinking into the softness of the mattress and covered with the hard planes of his body. His lips never lifted from her and the kiss deepened until she felt the heat of him pouring into her. He tasted and savored and touched. His mouth devoured hers and his hands began to explore her body.

As she had before, she pulled back and relaxed her body, letting him have his way. She was hardly aware of it when he lifted her skirts and loosened her chemise to gain access to her flesh. She focused on the roughness of the skin of his fingers and not on where they touched. She closed her eyes and let her thighs fall open, allowing him to enter her.

Elizabeth's thoughts wandered as she heard his moans and as he moved within her. 'Twould not be long now for he was nearing his climax. Soon, it would be over and she would clean herself of any signs of this joining and find her pallet for the night. His insistent voice broke into her reverie.

"Elizabeth? Look at me, lass." His voice was thick with his passion and she opened her eyes. She struggled to gather her thoughts and look at his face above hers. She realized he was still hard within her.

"My lord?" she asked, wondering why he called her name.

A stricken expression filled his face as she felt his seed spilling within her. She waited for him to finish and to withdraw, but he held himself still and simply stared at her as though waiting for something from her.

"My lord?" she asked again. "What have I done wrong?"

This attention unnerved her and she felt exposed before him. Usually, the man saw to his pleasure, finished and left before she had to do anything. This was so different.

Finally he lifted himself off her and stood next to the bed, pulling his breeches back around his waist and shoving his tunic over them. Elizabeth pushed her own skirts down over her legs and slid back against the headboard of the bed. Now he would not meet her gaze. He brushed his hair from his eyes and ran his hand through it, confusion clear on his face and in the frown on his brow. He looked around the room as though he had lost something. Then he looked directly at her and the pain in his eyes pierced her.

"Do not leave," he ordered even as he grabbed a long cloak from a peg on the wall near the door. His harshness was unlike anything else that had been spoken by him before and it scared her. Then he tugged open the door and, as it slammed behind him, he was gone.

For the first time since the early days of making her own way in the world, Elizabeth felt used…soiled. The calm acceptance of her situation that she had struggled to attain shattered around her and she did not know how to piece it back together.

His head pounded as he climbed the stairs that led to the roof of the keep. Gavin knew only that he needed to get away from the scene of his crime and consider how to go on from here. All his plans to entice and seduce had turned on him and in an instant when she offered herself so calmly to him, all he could think of was claiming her and taking that resolved expression from her eyes.

He reached the fourth floor and pushed through the door leading into the frigid wind that buffeted the top of Silloth Keep. The storm that had raged for days around them, forcing them to live inside, now began to abate. Still, the cloak he'd thrown around his shoulders was pulled and twisted as he moved from the doorway. The lone guard assigned to this location nodded at him from the small stone enclosure and he walked on into the dark and cold.

Making his way to the edge of the wall, Gavin peered into the darkness and tried to understand what had just happened. Never, never in his memory had he lost control of himself as he had with Elizabeth. Something in her air of resignation challenged him and for a moment he was determined to make it different for her. He would not be like the others who lay with her and took of her. He would not pay for her favors. He would make her want him and want to…

The stupidity of his thoughts shocked him. She had ceased to be a person to him and had become only a means to an end. Orrick's quest had become his own and he used any means, even her, to succeed in it. And he had become just one more man in her bed.

He pushed his hair back from his face and gathered it in a leather thong he kept in his cloak. He walked a few paces and rubbed his eyes, trying to see into the darkness around him. The winds swirled and he let them beat against him. It was nothing compared to the chaos of feelings within him.

He closed his eyes and saw in his thoughts the moment he realized what he was doing. They were already on the bed and he had filled her to her core. Ignoring the reality of her reaction, he had plunged in and was nearing his peak when he looked at her, really looked at her for the first time. She lay beneath him, unmoving, taking everything he gave and never responding. Oh, her woman's flesh was soft and wet as he moved within her, but she was not feeling him. She was not feeling anything at all. He thought her unconscious when she did not open her eyes at her name.

But it was far worse when she did look at him with cold, unseeing eyes. Her vacant stare forced him to think and to realize what he was doing. He was taking her. He was with a woman who was not even aware of what was happening between them. A woman who lay as one dead beneath him.

The shudder that tore through him had nothing to do with the bitter cold around him. It was about the coldness within him for his mindless tupping of a woman who had no choice in it. That was something that he had never done—not even from his earliest experiences with lust and the sins of the flesh.

Under his breath, he cursed his lapse in control and judgment, and wondered how it had happened at all and how he could correct this. The crunching steps signaling the approach of the guard drew his attention.

"My lord, Lady Margaret awaits you within and requests that you join her."

With a nod, he followed the man back across the roof to the doorway and pulled the door open. Orrick's wife stood just inside and stepped aside to allow him to enter. She said nothing but turned down the hallway and made her way to a small alcove. He pulled off his wet cloak and threw it over his shoulder.

"There is some trouble, my lord?" Margaret's words carried the soft accent of her youth.

"None that I know of, lady."

Her focus sharpened and she tilted her head, examining him closely. "My lord husband told me of your special arrangements for the evening and of the task he set for you regarding the young wh…woman Elizabeth. Now, you slam out of your chambers and stalk to the roof. Something is not right?"

Damn! Orrick should have kept this between them. Women had a strange way of looking at some things and the lady of the keep was not one to be told of arrangements between men.

"Worry not, my lady. All is well." He was not about to explain what had happened in his chambers. He shifted on his feet and prepared to end the conversation when her words shocked him.

"Will she need the services of our healer, my lord?"

Margaret thought he had hurt Elizabeth. The insult of it lashed him to his soul. He had not treated her well, but she had not been harmed. He had never taken a woman in anger. Never.

"Margaret! You know me better than that. How can you ask

such a thing?" But a niggling of guilt slid through him. Her words confirmed it.

"My lord, I have heard how well you treated your wife, but whores are a different matter, are they not?"

He met her steely regard and knew she spoke of many things in her own past. He knew the story of how Margaret moved from being the king's whore to being Orrick's wife. This was far too personal to continue.

"I assure you that Elizabeth is well, lady. And now that I am done my walk, I will seek my chambers for the night." He nodded a bow to her and began to turn when he realized that he had a question for her. "Do you worry about Orrick's attention to her?"

Margaret smiled and lowered her gaze for a moment. "You mean that he seeks her company or favors?" He nodded. "Nay, my lord. You see I know that, by his very nature, Orrick draws strays and wounded creatures to him. He gives them sanctuary while they mend and then they are loyal to him forever."

"You think that Elizabeth is one of these strays?"

"Just so, my lord. As are we all."

Then, with a nod of her own, Lady Margaret moved past him and left him standing in the corridor. Gavin heard her words and realized the truth in them, but his thoughts turned to the woman he'd left behind in his room.

Chapter Four

The door opened quietly and she would have missed it had she not been watching for it. He entered like someone not sure of what he would find inside. And since she was not certain of how he would react, she knew the feeling well. He looked around the room until he found her, sitting in the far corner, away from the food and the bed—the two temptations of the evening. Well, two of three if the truth be told, for he was as tempting to her as the others had been.

"Lass," he said as he pulled the chair away from the table and turned it. Straddling it backward, he faced her. "Did I hurt you?"

She sat up straighter on the stool and gathered the blanket around her shoulders. His words were soft and she could feel his concern for her well-being in them. Why did he do this to her? What was it about him that was so different from the others? And why did part of her yearn for the difference he offered?

"I am well, my lord. I waited as you ordered." Elizabeth watched him as he searched for words. Something had not gone correctly in their joining and he struggled with it, she could see. Unfortunately, she knew not what it was and so could offer him no help.

"I lied to you, Elizabeth." He shifted on his chair and

looked away from her. Glancing at the table still laden with uneaten foods, he continued, "I did arrange this to entice you here, but I had no intention of…of…bedding you this night."

She did not know what to make of his words. "My lord, I confess that I am confused. You know I am a whore and you invited me to your chambers. For what other purpose than your desire to have a woman would you ask me here?"

"For your company. To share a meal and some conversation."

No man had wanted her company since her husband in the early years of their marriage when he still kept up the pretense of interest. After that, he still desired her body, but only in an attempt to gain an heir. Gavin MacLeod made no sense. Then, she thought she understood what had happened.

"You are married, my lord?"

"Married?" He looked startled at her question.

"Aye, married and feeling some sense of guilt for lying with me? Did you make some vow to your wife that you believe broken by what we did?"

That stricken look was back in his eyes again and Elizabeth knew she had the right of it. That he was so upset at breaking a vow to his wife touched her somehow. 'Twas a good thing to know that some men actually believed in keeping their marriage vows and that he considered his lying with her, a whore, a violation of that vow. Most men did not.

"My wife is dead these last three years, lass. And lest you think differently, I never broke my promise of fidelity to her during our twenty years of marriage."

"I meant no insult to your honor or to her memory, my lord. 'Tis just that most men believe that lying with a whore does not mean anything to any vow they've taken."

His brow furrowed with a deep frown and she wondered what was wrong. He was a curious man, unlike any other she'd known. His explanation proved her right in that assessment.

"Hold now, lass. Let me begin again. When Orrick pointed

you out in the hall…" He paused and cursed under his breath. "When you helped me with my bath last evening, you seemed tired. I thought mayhap you would enjoy a few hours of leisure and a good meal. Since I wanted some simple companionship, this meal seemed like the way to accomplish something for both of us."

He stood then and moved his chair back near the table. Then he poked around the dishes there until he found something he was looking for and turned to her.

"There is still the cook's wondrous spiced cake to eat. From past years, I know we'll not see the likes of it again until he produces the mince pies for Twelfth Night. If you stay, I promise that I expect nothing more than conversation from you…and help in finishing the cake." He held out his hand to her and she knew he was offering her some apology for bedding her.

Elizabeth stood and accepted his offer, and something changed within her at that moment. Some lightening of her spirit for the first time in a very, very long time. The urge to smile won out and she felt one spread over her face. His eyes were alight with a mischievous look that promised an unforgettable meal, at the least.

Gavin felt his heart fill with hope when she smiled and stood, taking the hand he offered her and joining him at the table again. Torn now between fulfilling Orrick's request and learning more about her for some need of his own, he decided to simply let the rest of the evening happen. He was certain she would talk of personal things, of her family or her upbringing, so he could discover the information that Orrick sought.

He watched as she cleared away some of their uneaten food and moved the platters on the table aside. Once he took his seat, she served them, cutting slices of the cake he mentioned and placing it before him. Before she sat, she poured cider into two metal mugs and carried them over to the hearth. Lifting the poker from the side of the flames, she dipped it into each mug, heating the cider and releasing the fragrant aroma of apples into the air. Finally, although he knew but a few minutes had passed by, they were sitting at the table enjoying the cook's work.

"Tell me of your wife."

"My wife?" he asked, startled by her direct question.

"Aye, my lord. You mentioned that she passed away three years ago. Did she visit Lord Orrick's holding with you?"

He drank of the cider and smiled as he thought of Nessa. "Nay, she did not travel this far with me."

"Where did she travel with you?" Elizabeth maintained an even expression, nothing but honest curiosity there in her eyes. It could not hurt to talk of it, of her.

"Her family was a clan distant from mine and we traveled back to her home from time to time. Less after the children were born."

"You have children?" Her voice hinted of envy.

"I, we, have three, now all grown with bairns of their own. A daughter and two sons." Could it be this easy? "And you? Have you any bairns?"

She paled a bit at his question and shook her head rather than speaking the words. He watched as she lifted her mug to her mouth and drank deeply from it, all the time averting her eyes. The issue of children caused her some amount of pain and she tried to avoid it. Fine.

"Where…"she began, and paused when the trembling in her voice was so apparent. "Where is your village, my lord? I know only that you hail from the Highlands."

"My village is on the west coast of Scotland, about five days' ride north of the Firth."

"Is it a large place?" She broke off a piece of the cake and his gaze followed her hand as it moved to her mouth. His own mouth went dry when he saw the tip of her tongue reach out to claim the morsel. He swallowed before being able to reply.

"The entire holding is larger than Orrick's lands, but that includes all the lands held in the name of our clan. My nephew, the earl, is chief of the clan."

He thought he heard some measure of bitterness in his voice, but he did not begrudge his nephew the position he held. He supported the elders' decision to name Alaisdair as chief and laird of the clan. Hell, he was one of the elders who had voted for Alaisdair's claim.

"I apologize, my lord, for I cannot remember all the lessons taught by my grandmam. If your nephew rules the clan, what do you do?"

Nothing.

The word echoed through his thoughts, but he kept it within him. That was the root of his time spent here in England. Long the strongest warrior of the clan, Gavin knew he had been replaced by those younger and stronger, including his own sons. Now he served as one of the council of *elders*. That word was bitter on his tongue. Better to say the truth—he was unneeded.

He looked across and realized she was waiting for an answer, one that he did not want to say. Could not say without a further explanation he was unwilling to give. He would use her tactic.

"What did your grandmam say that you do remember?"

She looked away for a moment and then smiled. He was beginning to enjoy the light in her eyes when she allowed a smile to grace her features.

"She often spoke of 'First Footing'? Or am I saying that wrong? She had the Gaelic and her accent was so strong that I know I am mistaken in how I remember some of the words."

He laughed out then, enchanted by the way she named his language. "You have it right, lass. On the first night, it is the custom that foretells your luck in the coming year."

"Tell me more, for I remember not the details of it."

He leaned back in the chair and finished his cider. "The age and coloring of the person who takes the first step through your doorway when midnight has passed and the gifts they bring determine how lucky and how prosperous your household will be for the next year. Many will offer coin or rewards to make certain that the 'best' person takes that first step."

"And the best to enter first?" she asked.

"Tall, dark-haired men, young and strong enough to protect those inside from those would attack and pillage."

"My lord, who would attack your village?"

"Most likely be another Scots clan on the attack, since the Vikings keep to their isles off the coast. But the custom began long ago when they would still rampage on the mainland."

"I think my grandparents met through First Footing. He had dark hair in his youth, she said. But the memories are so hazy and long forgotten, I cannot be certain."

Their eyes met for a brief second and he was nearly knocked over by the desire for her that pulsed through him. He wanted her. And he wanted her to know it was him when he filled her. He grew hard as his body understood the feeling within him. Wanting. Needing. Hunger.

She flinched. He did not believe she even knew she had done so, but he saw it and recognized that it was a reaction to him and to the lust he knew showed on his face.

Gavin stood and she sat unmoving, as though waiting to see what his intentions were. He had no doubt that if he picked her up and dragged her to the bed again, she would allow it. Or if he ordered her to take off her clothes and get into the bed on her own volition, she would do that, too. Although his body urged him to that taking, he controlled himself, not wanting to lose the meager ground he had gained since he'd used her badly earlier.

"Will you stay the night, lass?" he asked, both hoping and fearing her answer.

She blinked several times and looked at the bed before answering. "Is it your wish, my lord?" He could see her losing color and becoming empty even as she asked.

"Elizabeth, I erred when I took you without thought. I promise it will not happen again between us." Surprise, fear, resignation and puzzlement filled her eyes as she took in his words. He reached up and touched her cheek with the back of his hand. "Stay or go, it is your decision."

She stood and stepped away from the table. "Will you have me punished if I choose to leave?" Fear overtook the other emotions clear in her expression. She had moved just out of his reach with the steps she took toward the door. A defensive move.

"Have you been punished before for refusing?" He knew that Orrick could not have mistreated her, but who had? He took a step toward her.

"Aye, my lord, but, pray, think not that I have suffered ill treatment by Lord Orrick or his people."

But someone else had. She gave him more clues to her history even though she said little.

"Fear not, Elizabeth. I know well that Orrick does not abuse his people. And your decision to leave tonight will not be met with anything save regret on my part."

She nodded and turned to the door. He had spoken her choice and so there was nothing else to say. He did not move as she tugged the door open and walked out, pulling it closed quietly behind her. He half expected her to come back, but when several minutes passed by, he gave up any hope of it.

Unable to waste food, he took a few minutes to wrap the food that remained and could be saved. Then Gavin banked the flames in the hearth and stripped off his clothes. It took a long time for sleep to claim him that night, for his mind was filled with thoughts of her and he realized, as he drifted off, that the expression that filled her eyes called to something within him. Her vulnerability could not be ignored.

Chapter Five

Like insects pouring out of their nests in the ground, the inhabitants of Silloth Keep scurried forth into the bright sunlight, anxious to take advantage of the break in the near-continuous winter storms that battered the area. Defenses were strengthened, repairs made to roofs and walls damaged by the recent strong winds, and everyone who'd been cooped up for too long enjoyed the freedom, treasuring it more for not knowing how long it would last.

And preparations must be made for the upcoming festivities. Although weeks away, holly and ivy needed to be gathered to decorate the hall and, to honor Lord Orrick's heritage, a large log would be cut, carved and burned from the day of the solstice until Twelfth Night. A yule log, she was told it would be called. Under Lady Margaret's direction, groups of servants went off into the forest to accomplish those tasks.

Elizabeth finished her temporary duties under the steward's watchful eye and made her escape, as well. Her small cottage was set some distance from the keep and she had left it with no chance to prepare it for any lengthy absence. Not that she had many possessions, but she knew she would feel better checking the cottage before she was trapped in the keep once more.

The cold air knocked the breath from her as she stepped into it, but she relished the freedom from the constant company of the others and did not allow it to chase her back. Pulling her cloak tighter around her, she stepped around the many icy puddles in the yard and trotted toward the gate. The raucous yelling caught her attention and she slowed her pace, curious about what could be causing such an uproar. A crowd grew around one of the practice yards and she walked closer trying to see what was happening.

Two men, no, two warriors, of a similar size and build, fought to the cheers of the spectators around them. In spite of the cold, they had thrown off their tunics and fought in breeches alone. Sweat covered them as they struck at each other with long, wooden staffs. They were equal in ability, as well, for each spent time on the ground after being upended by his opponent. She managed to make her way closer and then recognized the combatants.

Lord Orrick.

And Lord Gavin.

He was—they were—impressive.

Although she could tell this was a friendly competition, both men were serious in their efforts. Their muscles strained as they took blows meant to knock them to the ground. Their breathing labored from the temperature around them and from their efforts. Someone in front of her turned and saw her and then moved from her path and Elizabeth was able to approach the fence surrounding the yard.

'Twas as she had thought—he was magnificent in battle. He called out his battle cry as he attacked Lord Orrick and she shivered from the fierceness of it. This could not be the same man who met her resistance with little reaction. Then, as though he'd heard her thoughts, he turned and saw her. She could not breathe.

Lord Orrick used this momentary distraction to his advantage and, before Elizabeth could blink, he struck a blow that landed Lord Gavin in the freezing mud on the ground. Laughing, Lord Orrick declared himself the winner and held out a hand to his friend.

She had cost him this battle. She had caused a lapse in his focus. How would he react to this very public embarrassment? Surely he could not let it go unnoticed?

Not willing to wait for his reaction, Elizabeth backed away and turned toward the gate, escape the only thing on her mind. A few minutes at a quick pace took her through the gate and nearer to her cottage. Out of breath when she arrived, she lifted the latch and stepped inside. Unwilling to let the door slam against the wall, she struggled to pull it closed behind her.

The cottage was as she had left it, nothing looked out of place. First, she loosened the leather flap that covered the small cut window and then, with flint and tinder, she lit a small lamp and made a closer inspection. There were really only two things she needed to check and they were hidden in the wall near the small hearth. With an ease born of practice, she pried a stone free and reached behind it for the small box she kept within. It was still there. Elizabeth was about to take the box out when the pounding on the door came.

"Mistress Elizabeth?" a voice called out. A man's voice. "Are you within?"

Had someone followed her already? Elizabeth pushed the stone back in place. She knew that many were restless from the days and nights of inactivity within the keep, but she had no idea that someone would follow her this soon.

Going to the door, she held on to it as she opened it a crack to see who stood beyond. The miller's son. He must have seen her leave the keep and followed her. From his shifting stance and heated glances, she knew his intent. Sighing with resignation, she pushed the door open more to allow him entrance.

The loud cracking of dead branches behind him drew their attention. They both looked to see the cause of the noise.

Clean, but still damp from the hurried washing he must have taken, Lord Gavin wore his hair pulled back from his face and his tunic lay stuck to his wet skin. And he stared at her with a frightening intensity that she could do no more than meet. And barely that. The miller's son understood the message. The nobleman was staking his claim. Liam stumbled back, with a tug on his forelock and an excuse to leave, and in a moment they were alone.

"My lord," she said, stepping back for him to enter. Elizabeth watched his expression as he passed her, trying to decide if he was angry or not. He had promised last night that hc would not take her against her will, so why had he followed her here? Was he angry over her distraction that caused him to lose the battle with Lord Orrick?

Lord Gavin ducked to clear the low door and crossed the width of her cottage in three paces. It had never seemed as bare and mean as it did now with his presence. He filled the room and her meager possessions shrank next to him. He surveyed the room, taking it in and then turned to her.

"Did you enjoy the match?" He stood with his legs apart and his hands on his hips. She listened to his tone and could tell nothing from it. "'Twas good to get some action in with Orrick after so many days within the keep."

"You were even in skills, my lord. I have seen Lord Orrick fight before, but not with one who matched him so closely in size and ability."

He turned his head and stared out the window, apparently watching the continued retreat of Liam through the trees. "It felt good. 'Twould seem we are all restless." He looked back. "Orrick said the old ones are predicting the storm's return."

"'Tis the pattern of winters here, or so I've been told, my lord." She gripped her hands together, not certain of what to do. This casual conversation was difficult to maintain. Not that she was not trained to it. Not that she did not have experience in it. But she had put that as firmly away from her as she had the contents of the hidden box. Or, rather, it had been taken from her as so many other parts of her life had been.

He relaxed a bit in his stance and smiled. "Ah, I forget that this is your first winter in Silloth. How does this compare to your home?"

Although his probing was gently done, she felt the jab and sting of it. Swallowing to clear her throat, she needed to look away before she could answer. Would the pain be as evident in her voice as it would in her eyes?

"Silloth is my home, my lord." His questions were becoming more difficult to evade.

"'Tis now, but we each come from somewhere else. In my village," he said as he walked closer to her, "we have the same kinds of storms, but more often in winter 'tis snow instead of this rain."

"Is your village in the mountains?"

A smile tugged at the corners of his mouth and she fought the urge to touch his lips. Why was something as simple as a smile so attractive and dangerous on this man? In spite of not wearing a cloak and in spite of being wet, heat poured off him as he approached. Not until she felt the wall at her back did she realize she had backed away as he stepped closer. Now, 'twas no place left to move.

"My village sits in the valley, with mountains surrounding us. Their height protects us from many of the worst storms, but every season there are a few storms that sweep down on us." He reached out and brushed the hair that had been loosened by the winds from her face. "But we Scots do not coddle our villagers like they are wee bairns. We do not all run for cover as the weak English do." His voice trailed off to a whisper as he stroked her cheek and then her neck. "Aye, the English are too soft."

She knew he was going to kiss her. His hand crept around her neck and he steadied her for his touch. His mouth was hot, his lips firm against hers. He cupped her chin with his other hand and kissed her over and over, slanting his mouth on hers and then tasting her deeply. She thought he was done when he lifted his mouth from hers, but he simply angled it the other way and joined their mouths once more.

His presence, his body leaning against hers was overwhelming, yet she did not feel threatened. For a moment, a brief moment, she decided to simply let the sensations come. When she would have closed off her mind to what would follow, she stayed with him, staring into his eyes as he made her feel what she never permitted herself to feel.

An ache built within her at his gentle touch. Her breasts swelled as her body readied itself for what would happen next. Her hands, clenched at her sides, crept up to clasp his tunic and he pulled her closer, his arms moving down to embrace her. Still she did not let her mind run from him. He trailed hot, wet kisses down onto her neck and then to her ear where she could swear he used his teeth on the sensitive skin there. Shivers passed through her and when she felt the urge to surrender to the need within her, she knew it was over.

Finally, and almost with regret, Elizabeth began the pulling away from within. Her body became a separate thing that he could use without touching her soul. It had to be this way or she would never survive the life she had to face.

Almost immediately, he released her and stepped away. His expression was intense and his breathing labored. She could smell his maleness, his strength, his desire. He was completely dangerous to her and there was nothing she could do to resist him. His displeasure screamed to her although he said nothing for a few moments.

"Why did you do that, lass?"

Elizabeth shook her head, trying to clear her thoughts. "Do what, my lord?"

"Make yourself into that lifeless thing. Why do you bundle yourself up within yourself?"

Her eyes narrowed and the frown that marred her brow told him he had hit the mark. She drew everything she was inside and left only some lifeless shell there to suffer the touches she could do nothing to prevent.

"Is it just me or do you do this with every man you lie with?"

Fear filled her expression and was tinged with something like regret. So, 'twas done apurpose. "My lord, I cannot..."

"Cannot what, Elizabeth? Lie with a man and enjoy it? Give some measure of response to his efforts? Not allow yourself to be given, but only taken?"

"Please, my lord," she said, raising a hand to him in a plea to stop. "Please do not make me speak of this...I beg you..." Her voice now shook as her eyes filled with tears.

'Twas the first time he knew she felt something deeply. And the conniving, questing part within him knew she would talk to him of other things if he did not force this subject now. Cursing himself for even thinking of the tactic, he asked her the question she had ignored before.

"So, how does this weather compare with that of your home?"

She took a deep breath before she replied, and they both knew she would answer him now. Part of him was exultant as she spoke the words he wanted to hear.

"We have cold and snow in York, my lord, but not so much rain as here in Silloth."

He nodded as she revealed this truth about herself. Now he had some piece of her. Was there more? Dare he ask another? He would ask her nothing too personal that would scare her away.

"When were you last in York, Elizabeth?"

She looked away from him. "Nigh to two years have passed since I was last in York, my lord."

Defeat filled her voice and he knew she had given up resisting his questions. Gavin knew if he asked, she would answer. If he took her, she would...be taken.

Regret for gaining knowledge of her in this manner burned within him. He was doing the same to her, again, that others did. That this time involved words and not flesh made no difference—and he knew it. He could not carry out this task for Orrick. He knew it now.

"Come, lass. Gather up what belongings you wish to take to the keep and come with me." Gavin stepped back and walked away from her. "Orrick has ordered everyone back to the keep until there is a true clearing." He reached up and pulled the leather covering over the window tightly and secured it with a sturdy knot.

"And if I do not wish to return with you? If I wish to remain here and wait out any more storms?"

Her chin rose a bit, showing a hint of defiance. She must not think that showing such to him endangered her. Or did she not know that such defiance shown to other lords in other places would garner a whipping at the least?

He picked up her cloak from the bench and held it out to her. "Even I quake in fear when Orrick wears the expression he did when he ordered everyone who had escaped back into the safety of the yard and keep. He will not be gainsaid in this order, lass."

A different sort of resignation filled her face as she accepted the cloak and threw it over her shoulders. He followed her gaze as it moved over the few furnishings in the cottage and then to the door. He had not realized how empty it was until just then. Did she have need of anything? Was there something he could do to give her ease?

Where had that thought come from? He shook his head and

unlatched the door, holding on to it so it would not slam in the wind. She followed him wordlessly out of the cottage and watched him as he bolted the door with the outside latch. The whole croft had the look that a really strong wind would not force open the door but batter down the whole thing. She needed a home of sturdy stone to protect her from this kind of storm. Another ridiculous thought! Being trapped inside for all these days was making him daft.

"Come, lass, give me your hand."

He thought that holding on to her in the high winds was a good idea. As slight as she was, she could also blow or stumble away. She hesitated only for a moment and then held out her hand to him. Gavin took it in his and began walking toward the keep, tugging her along the path through the trees. When the buffeting of those treacherous winds slowed their pace, he put his arm around her waist, pulled her closer and urged her to move faster. Finally the gate to the yard came into view and he realized that she had dug her heels into a soft place in the frozen mud around them.

"My lord, please go on without me. I need to catch my breath." She twisted to free herself from his grasp and he released her as soon as he realized it. He understood something else, as well.

"Do you fear that others will talk if we are seen together here?"

"Fear it, my lord? Nay. 'Tis a fact already and a topic of gossip throughout Silloth and its people."

"They gossip about us? Why would they do such a thing?" Why would such a thing as speaking to her or having her help with his bath bring them to the center of attention? 'Twas her duties to do so at his request. But he was not so dull witted that he did not know that in the dead of winter, there was not any small bit of activity that went unnoticed or unmentioned in the closeness of living in a keep.

"Was it not your aim, then? You did not intend to stake your claim of me while you are here visiting Lord Orrick? To keep the other men away?"

"Nay," he protested, and it sounded too loud and too fervent to even his own ears. "I did no such thing!"

"I suspect, my lord, that you are the only one in Silloth who missed the intent of your actions. Or is it your intention to simply toy with me until you tire of whatever draws you to me?" She stood with her hands fisted on her hips and let the anger that had obviously been building within her pour forward. "Then you will take your pleasure and move on to the next woman who catches your fancy. So, tell me, my lord, do I resist too much or not enough for your tastes? Tell me so I may get through these games you play with me."

She gasped and a look of horror covered her face as the words escaped her. Gavin knew that even if she had been known as a bold wench, she had just crossed the line to arrogance. And it was a line that should be met with a reprimand or punishment severe enough that she would not think herself better or smarter than those superior to her in standing and in rights. Elizabeth stumbled back a few steps as if she expected him to mete out what her impudence had earned.

And he was horrified, as well, at her words, but not because they insulted his position. Not even because, as a serf tied to this land and to this lord, she had no right to object to anything her lord's guest said or did, whether it was to her or to another.

Gavin was horrified because her words were true.

He could think of nothing to say to her, so he stepped back and walked away, leaving her to remain behind as she had asked—alone to enter the keep by herself. This game of Orrick's had gotten out of hand and he did not know how to bring it back under his control. However, Gavin knew too well that he must.

He trotted toward the gate, but instead of entering the yard, he followed a path to the cliff's edge where he could see the high waves of the sea bashing their fury on the beach. Gavin grasped the rough rock of the outer wall to keep from slipping down the steep trail that led down to the beach. The winds were even stronger here than in the woods and, as he watched, storm clouds darkened and gathered off to the west. The old ones were right—this was but a temporary reprieve in the storm. Knowing that far more important tasks needed to be handled before the storm was back on them, Gavin decided to put his soul-searching aside for another time. He would have words with Orrick and settle this.

Chapter Six

"This game of yours ends now, my friend. I will play no longer and get caught in the web you weave around me."

He slammed the door to Orrick's chamber and stood in front of it, awaiting his friend's reaction. Orrick stood by one of the glazed windows in the wall, looking out. Gavin strode over to his side and watched as the rains began pelting the villagers who had not yet sought cover in the keep. Orrick did not answer him, so Gavin prodded him again.

"I am leaving for home when there is a real break in the weather. I fear I have lost the desire to stay here until Twelfth Night is upon us."

"Did you know that I can see to the southern tree line from this window?"

With a sinking feeling, Gavin pushed to where Orrick stood and looked out. She still stood there, alone, as the rains poured over her. If she felt the cold or wet, he knew not, for she did not move. Her arms were wrapped around herself, but she gave no other indication of being alive. He shifted his stance, calling out to her in his thoughts to get inside and out of the worsening weather. Just as he reached the limit of his patience, she came alive, looking around and then rushing toward the gate. He let out his breath.

"You have learned something disquieting about Elizabeth? Is that what troubles you, Gavin?" Orrick handed him a cup of ale. "Tell me what you've discovered about her."

Gavin swallowed deeply of the brew and thought about the question. He had discovered more about himself and his own limits than he had about the young woman. He had learned that he did not use people as easily as some could—mayhap that was why he was better at battle than at subterfuge and strategy. He learned that he was willing to help a friend, but he could not harm an innocent in carrying out the task. And she was an innocent, he had no doubt.

And Gavin had learned that he could indeed fall in love twice in his life.

The metal cup was crushed in his grasp as the truth of it punched him in the gut. For all that Gavin claimed that Orrick coddled his people, Gavin knew that he had the softer heart. And that Elizabeth, with her ingrained innocence and vulnerability, had claimed it. What the hell did he do now? In love with the village whore? What kind of a lackwit was he?

"Gavin?" Orrick's soft question invaded his thoughts.

"She hails from York, although she has not been there for nigh on two years. I suspect she was gentle or noble born but mayhap on the wrong side of the blanket. And," he added, "I believe she cannot survive the life she is living for much longer."

"Has she threatened to take her life again? She swore to me that she would not pursue that again if I gave her a place here." Orrick's face paled. Suicide was the most grievous sin a soul could commit; even discussing it was uncomfortable.

Gavin considered his options. He could simply ignore what he felt and blame it on his friend's foolish quest. He could stay here and get to know her better and discover if she felt anything at all for him. He could…he shook his head and glared at his friend.

"Did you know I would fall in love with her when you put your plan in motion? Or was I just a respite you thought to offer her during this slow time of the year? An old fool who would never force her to her back?"

"It may surprise you to know that 'twas my ladywife who first suggested that you might be a match for each other."

"Is this some joke, then? Putting together the English whore and Scots outcast?" He slammed the now-empty cup down on the table near the blazing hearth and turned to his host. "Two misfits who have no place in the world and deserve none."

Orrick did not rush to an answer. Instead, he walked to a chair and sat in it, drinking his own ale leisurely. Then he faced Gavin.

"Is that how you see yourself? An outcast? Your clan values your service and…"

"Bah! I am an old man who has outlived his usefulness. My sons fight in my place. My nephew rules as he pleases. There is nothing left for me there." Gavin felt the bile rise in his stomach. He had thought these notions before, but this was the first time he had voiced them to anyone.

"So, should I have the tailor prepare your shroud? Will you lie down and die now or linger until someone puts you out of your misery?" Orrick's sarcasm bit deeply. "You are worse than a woman, bemoaning that which cannot be changed. In all the time that fate has dealt Elizabeth the cruel life it has, never did I hear her complain as you do now."

Gavin grabbed Orrick's tunic and dragged him to stand before forcing him up against the wall. Thumping his head once more against the stone, Gavin growled through clenched jaws.

"How do you dare to say such things to me? I should have taken no pity on you today and crushed you in the dirt as you deserve." He shoved Orrick again and then released him. Pacing away from him, Gavin poured more ale and drank it down. Orrick stayed on the other side of the room.

"It is widely known that no decision is made in the clan MacLeod without your voice being heard. Your nephew credits you with enlarging and protecting the lands under his control. Be at peace about your value to your people."

When he would argue, Orrick held up his hand to stop him. "If you doubt that you still have a place there, then you are welcome here. I would appreciate your help in keeping my lands safe and my properties maintained and successful."

Staying was a choice.

He and Orrick had worked well for many years in various endeavors and they had protected each other's backs more times than he could count. But what would happen to Elizabeth? He wanted her. He wanted her very much, with such a hunger that it made him uneasy.

"And Elizabeth?" he asked. "What would become of her if I stayed here?"

"I have been thinking of sending her to Margaret's niece near Carlisle."

"The nun?" he asked, stunned at the thought. "You would have her enter a convent?"

"The Gilbertines maintain a lay community as well as their religious order. Mayhap Elizabeth could find some measure of peace there."

Orrick's suggestion was a good one. The convent offered protection to women who had no place in the world. She would not need to earn her living on her back.

"I would marry her if she would have me."

Orrick gasped at his declaration and Gavin wondered when the idea had formed in his mind. He could do worse. She was young enough but not so young. He could protect her and offer her a place to live. The glimpses of personality hiding beneath layers of fear would shine through with some encouragement and tolerance. His needs were not the same now as when he had married Nessa, and the love he felt for Elizabeth was very different from the burning, naive passions of youth.

"I fear that would cause some problems. Margaret, as tolerant as she is and as much as she might want to, would never accept her at table or in her company. None of her ladies would. It is something else completely for my ladywife to be asked to ignore the situation when an honored guest has needs and desires, than to be expected to welcome the village harlot into her circle."

Gavin knew this. He knew it well. No matter what Elizabeth's true beginnings were, the past months spent here were lived as a whore and she would be remembered as such. Although he thought himself able to look beyond that as long as it was over, he knew that society's rules were more stringent than that. Everyone had a place, knew it and kept to it. 'Twas the way God ordained it to be.

Only a fool questioned or tried to change that. Only a fool or a man foolishly loving where he should not. Right now, he knew only that he was one of those, but did not have the slightest clue which he was.

"Think on this before you act, friend. Many lives will be changed by whatever path you take." Orrick stood and looked at him with grim eyes. "I fear I made a mistake when I challenged you about her." A soft knock on the door caught their attention. "She comes now at my call."

"And you will tell her what? Of the quest that I began to uncover her secrets?" Gavin knew how closely she guarded anything about herself and her past and the comment she had flung at him outside the gate was so close to the truth that it would hurt her immensely to find out how near. And he did not want to hurt her.

Orrick walked past him to the door and put his hand on the

knob. "I will remind her of the bargain she made with me and make her choices clear once more."

Before he could ask anything else, Orrick pulled open the door, revealing Lady Margaret with Elizabeth standing off to one side and behind her. The women entered and their silent stances told Gavin clearly that he was the outsider here. 'Twas best to retreat and regroup. So, as he bowed courteously to his friend's wife and strode past Elizabeth, he could not help but whisper in her ear, "Come to me, Elizabeth. Please."

His heated breath near her ear sent shivers down and through her and Elizabeth trembled from the ardor in his words and tone. That it caused such a reaction scared her and warned her of the weakness developing in the walls she had laboriously built around herself.

Then she remembered her words to Lord Gavin and realized he and Lord Orrick must have discussed her. She had insulted him, and in doing so, insulted the man before her now, who had shown her only mercy and concern. She must apologize. Dragging her sopping cloak along with her, she waited for Lady Margaret to finish their exchange of words and then she fell to her knees before them both and leaned her head down further in as complete a gesture of obeisance as she could make.

"My lord. My lady. I beg your forgiveness for my actions toward your guest." Elizabeth stayed on her knees with her head bowed, awaiting their words.

"What did you do to Lord Gavin?" Lady Margaret's voice was soft, but in no way less powerful for the gentleness of it.

"I refused his attentions and insulted his honor."

"'Twould be easier to speak to you if your face was not on the floor. Would you stand so I can hear your words?"

Elizabeth gasped and then hurried to comply with the lady's request. She had already left a puddle of water around her from her garments so she placed her cloak on it to soak up some of it. She was about to begin her apology again, when Lord Orrick spoke.

"The reprieve from the storm was not as long as everyone had hoped and you are one of many who was caught by the onslaught of rain. Stand here." He pointed to a place closer to where he stood. "The heat from the hearth cannot reach you there."

If the lady thought it strange for her husband to be offering comfort to a whore, she gave no indication by her expression or manners. Elizabeth knew this was not the way in most noble households. To be given a private interview by the lord and lady, instead of hearing their decisions and orders through several layers of servants and retainers, was quite unusual. She moved to the place he had designated and repeated her words. "I am sorry for refusing and insulting your guest, my lord." She bowed her head and did not meet either of their gazes.

"He most likely deserved the insults," Lady Margaret said.

"And the refusal," Lord Orrick added.

"Did you insult his manners or his place of origin? His manners were probably the safer target. These Scots do not like their customs and families called into question," the lady said.

"As long as you did not insult his fighting abilities, he will not take it seriously." Lord Orrick laughed out loud then, and his wife joined in with him.

Elizabeth looked up in shock. They thought this amusing? She had dared to even speak when not asked something and they were defending her? Even counseling her on how to insult their guest? She knew that her mouth dropped open and she was staring, but she could not stop herself.

"Elizabeth, what think you of Lord Gavin?"

Her breath held in her chest and no words would form in answer to her lord. What did she think of Gavin MacLeod of the Scots? So many things.

He was arrogant and proud and fearless and hard and strong. He was thoughtful and did not let his cock make his decisions, at least not most of the time. He listened to her and showed concern for her safety and comfort. He lusted for her, yet controlled it and did not force her to something she did not want. Well, only the once and she was not certain why he had lost control of himself then. He was…he was….

"Forgive me, my lord, but he is peculiar."

"He is a Scot, after all," Lady Margaret added as though that explained it clearly.

Lord Orrick laughed again and then his expression turned serious. "'Twould seem the time to remind you of our agreement, Elizabeth."

"My lord?" Did he mean to turn her out of Silloth for her transgressions against his friend? Surely not. She tried to search her memories for the words they exchanged when he held her back from stepping off the edge of the cliff that day many months ago.

"I told you that you could remain with us here in Silloth until you were ready to make the choice to live."

She began to shake, the desperation and desolation of that day pouring over her. She had been wandering for days, weeks, with little food or water or shelter or even sleep. Moving from one horror to another to simply survive, Elizabeth had found herself on the road just outside the village. Knowing what most villagers did to itinerant whores, she walked away from the village, drawn by the fresh smell of the nearby ocean. Her steps led her to the cliff wall, not far from the keep.

How long she had stood staring at the powerful waves crashing onto the rocks below her, she knew not. The wind had torn at her thin skirt and threadbare cloak and pulled her hair loose from the kerchief she had wrapped around it. She closed her eyes and took a deep breath.

One step.

Just one step more and all the pain would be gone. She would whore for no one again. She would give up her immortal soul, but the peace of that terrible choice called to her.

But could she? Was she not already being punished for her sins? Was escaping this misery truly worth an eternity of damnation?

One step remained.

She still did not know if she had lifted her foot to take the step or not, but Orrick's strong arm around her waist prevented her from falling. The next thing she remembered was waking up warm and dry for the first time in months. Orrick and Silloth had offered her sanctuary and she had accepted it. But not without paying a price.

"Elizabeth?" His deep voice pierced through her reverie and she blinked several times until the fog of that time cleared.

"Aye, my lord?" She realized that her throat had gone dry, so she swallowed several times to loosen it. "What choice is that?"

"We know not why you have chosen to punish yourself in this way, but 'twas not ours to question. But you have changed now, recovered from your condition when you arrived and grown stronger in these last weeks. 'Tis time to make a choice."

"What choice do I have, my lord. My lady?" she asked. "You are lord here and decide these matters. I owe you much and would do as you say."

"'Tis the season of Our Lord's Birth and a time to reexamine our lives, Elizabeth," the lady said quietly. "Lord Orrick would sponsor you in the spring to live with my niece at the Gilbertine convent near Carlisle if you wish it. You could live and work in their lay community, or, if you feel the Lord's call, take your vows and live with the good sisters there."

"Or you could stay here," Lord Orrick added. "But if you do, you must do other work."

Other work? But she was a whore. What else was she good

enough to do? Good people would not associate with her, afraid that her filth would spread onto them or corrupt them as it had corrupted her. No, she shook her head. Those were her father's words, not hers.

When she began to argue with him, he raised his hand to stop her. "You have told me none of your past, but even I can see that you were raised to another life. I can see the pain and guilt in your eyes every time someone calls you 'whore.'" He paused and took Lady Margaret's hand in his and they met her gaze as one. "But we know the untruth of it, even if you will not admit it to us or to yourself."

Her body began to tremble on its own, violently as the cold and wet clothing enveloped her in their chill. Whether caused by their words or her own fears, she knew not. But once it started, the tremors would not stop. Lady Margaret walked past her to the door and pulled it open, whispering orders to someone outside. Soon a blanket was wrapped around her shoulders and she was being guided from the chamber by one of Lady Margaret's serving women.

"You must change or you will take a chill. Go with Lynna and do as she says."

"But, my lord…" She looked back to Orrick, who stood simply observing his wife's direction of the scene around them. "He has summoned me. Lord Gavin…"

"He invited you as a woman, Elizabeth, not as a whore who answers at his beck and call. Do as you will."

His words did not make any sense to her. What was the difference? Lord Gavin wanted her in a way that made her skin tingle and in a way that tempted her to say yes.

"I do not understand, my lord. My lady?"

Lynna was guiding her out of the room as Lord Orrick answered.

"And neither does he, Elizabeth. Neither does he."

Chapter Seven

It took two days for her to build up her courage and make her decision. Lady Margaret's servant seemed to find things for her to do that gave her time to think and that kept her out of view from most of the keep's inhabitants. Well, if the truth were told, Lady Margaret insured that she did not see Lord Gavin during this time. And that he did not find her. Elizabeth did not know if he even sought her out, but suspected from the fervor in his invitation that he might have.

Her choice to go to the Gilbertine community was not a difficult one at all. Lord Orrick's sponsorship and the word of Lady Margaret was more than enough for her to be permitted to join their community. She did not think she would take vows, for 'twould take much in penance and prayer to cleanse her soul from her many transgressions. If she did decide she heard the call, her mother's jeweled ring, safely hidden in her cottage, would be enough to pay the dowry required.

She felt stronger somehow in making the decision and knowing that she would choose her path. That knowledge did not lessen the gratitude she owed to and felt toward the lord and lady of Silloth. Orrick could have claimed her as a serf and forced her to belong to him as part of his demesne. No one would have or could have challenged his right to that. But he never did. One more extraordinary thing to be thankful for.

Now she walked slowly up the steps and down the corridor that led to Lord Gavin's chamber. Standing quietly outside his door, she thought on this once more. If she was leaving the world behind, she needed to be with him before she did. His embraces and his kisses were the only ones that had ever promised her something and made her want whatever that was. Her body had reacted to the touch of many men, but her heart and soul had stirred only at his. As she reached to knock, she prayed that he would not refuse her this small favor.

Elizabeth heard him moving within the chamber and waited for him to open the door. It shouldn't have, but his appearance surprised her. He opened the door from behind it and she knew from his stance that he was naked and that he held his sword at the ready. His real sword. His eyes widened and then he opened the door to let her enter. As she moved into the room, he tugged on his breeches behind the door before closing it.

"Old habit, I fear," he said, nodding toward the sword that lay on the floor near the door. "I expected no visitors this night."

She had considered what her words should be for hours before she approached his door, but all of the well-practiced ones disappeared as she met his hungry gaze. Were words even necessary? She would not burden someone of his status with words of love. She could not give them and he could not accept them or the promise that was always at the core of them. He would understand the significance of her presence here and her actions in offering herself to him.

They stood several paces apart. Pure terror kept her from taking the first step toward him. So many things were wrong with this; so many things could go wrong. Deep inside, Elizabeth knew he would not let it, and so she made the first movement. 'Twas just a small one, not a step at all, but as she did, he opened his arms to her and she was in his embrace and surrounded by his strength in but a moment.

Not sure what to expect, she waited. Would it be as quick as that other time? Would he linger as some men did, intent on evoking something from her body as he took his pleasure? Would he take her? How could she do this?

She could not breathe. Elizabeth struggled against his hold, trying to pull air into her chest. He did not loosen his grasp and she felt as though the world were going dark. Just before it did, he released her. As her legs gave out, he scooped her up and carried her to the bed. After placing her there, he poured two cups of ale and made her drink some of hers.

"Do not try to talk, lass. Just drink this all. And breathe."

The nervous look on her face had turned to terror just as she reached him and it took only a moment before her struggles became apparent to him. As much as he would have liked to keep her in his arms, just knowing that she was here was enough to give him the courage to let her go. Gavin watched as she emptied the cup and handed it back to him.

"So, I am back to being the terrifying Scots warrior now? You fear my strength and size again?" He tried to keep some measure of levity in his voice and it must have worked, for she gifted him with a soft smile.

"As my grandmam would say," she began.

He laughed. "I am certain not to like what she said, so let us move on to something more pleasant." He sat down next to her so that he did not tower over her and he was pleased beyond measure when she did not move away or cringe from him.

"I…my lord…I…" She began several times and never got past the first word or two. Gavin decided that they did not need words at this time and dipped down and touched his lips to hers, silencing any more attempts to speak. When she opened her mouth and welcomed his tongue, he lost the ability to speak.

Steadying himself with a hand on each side of her, he let her grow accustomed to him before moving forward. She accepted his kisses and even when he pressed for more, she gave it.

She gave it!

Surprised by this realization, he drew back and searched her face, her eyes, for some explanation.

"I have only done this as a whore, my lord. I know not how to do this any other way." Tears glistened in her eyes and his heart hurt as he knew that she was offering him something very precious indeed.

"And I have only done this as a husband for a very long time, lass. Mayhap we can show each other the way?"

His words sank in and a stab of pain pierced him. He had given her a truth that had not been known to him before that moment. Oh, he had lain with other women since Nessa's death, but those times had never involved his heart. Or his soul. This time with Elizabeth did and now they both knew it. When he almost drew back from her to let the pain pass, her soft hands touched his face, holding his cheeks and bringing his mouth back to hers.

That small gesture broke through any hesitation either of them had and he pressed her back onto the pillows as he claimed her mouth with his. He wanted nothing so much as to fill the softness he knew would now welcome him, but he fought to keep his desires under control until she was ready. Until she took him. If she could. He lay on his side and she turned to meet his mouth again.

Gavin tasted her deeply and tugged up the length of her gown and the chemise under it up until he could touch her bare skin. The shudder that went through her simply intensified the arousal he was feeling and he grew harder than he had been. He thought she might be ticklish when she squirmed at his light stroking of her knee and then he moved his hand onto the soft skin of her inner thighs. When her legs opened, he drew back to look into her eyes. If they were empty as before, he would go no further.

She returned his gaze with wide eyes. Not sure if they were wide with fear or anticipation, he slid his hand up until it grazed the silky hair between her legs. Then Gavin parted her woman's flesh and slipped one finger into her heated depths. He did not touch deeper but waited for her reaction. 'Twas swift in coming.

Elizabeth grabbed at his arm and seemed to want to stop him, but she licked her lips and loosened her hold. He leaned down and kissed her once more, sucking gently on her tongue as his fingers moved inside her and found the wetness and heat he desired. She moved restlessly beneath his touch and finally, finally, he felt her hand move from his arm to his chest. He paused and guided her to his hardness, hoping she would, but not forcing her to touch him. And she did.

He did not realize that he had not laced his breeches until her hand slipped inside and grasped his erection. The moan escaped him and filled her mouth before he could stop it. Her small hand and light touch teased his eager flesh and he rocked against her palm in spite of his fear that he would disgrace himself and come too quickly. For a moment, he felt like a youth instead of the aging man he was. When she slid her hand down onto his sac, he knew he must stop her.

"Elizabeth, lass," he whispered as he lifted his mouth from hers. "Can we take this off?" He tugged at her gown. "I would see all of you before we join."

However, before she could comply, she surged against his hand as he spoke and he felt the wetness pour from within her. Not wanting to miss this chance to pleasure her, he slid another finger into her and rubbed from inside out. Elizabeth arched and her eyes grew wider. Her breath had turned to panting and she was trembling next to him.

Gavin moved his other arm beneath her head and pulled her closer, trapping her leg with his thigh. He became relentless in his touch, spreading her woman's wetness over the flesh there until she gifted him with several moans. She tilted her chin and tried to lift her head to his so he lowered his mouth to hers and mimicked the actions of his hand with his tongue. Soon he felt her body tighten and arch and he knew her peak was on her.

"My lord?" She grabbed his arm again and he read the fear in her expression. "I cannot…."

"Let go, lass," he urged. "Trust me and let go."

She closed her eyes and he thought she would refuse to let go of her control and her fear at what he was doing, but a smile tugged the corners of her mouth.

"As you wish, my lord," she murmured after a moment, her eyes now open and meeting his.

"Gavin. My name is Gavin. Say it. Please."

Now she smiled fully as she spoke. "As you wish, Gavin."

"Nay, lass." He shook his head slightly. "'Tis as you wish this time."

He made no move yet to climb on top of her and his words startled her. He sought to pleasure her first, something that had never happened before to her. Not in all the years with Kennard, not in the months and months earning her living on her back. No man had ever put her pleasure before his own.

Elizabeth felt the tightness winding within her until the tension felt too intense, too pleasurable. Even though she recognized the pull to loosen herself from what her body felt, she gave Gavin her trust and stayed with him. And the reward for it made her breathless. When she would usually feel threatened by such a close hold, she now felt cradled and safe. When she would have turned inward and shut off what she felt, she now let the enjoyment of his touch, his kiss, his pleasuring of her fill her.

Aching and throbbing from within, she moved in time with the motion of his fingers until the scream welled in her. Wound beyond tightening, she felt the waves of sensation pour over and through her and this time she let it come. Her flesh, her whole body, tingled and tautened even where he did not touch. And then, when she thought she could feel no more, she fell.

And Gavin caught her.

It took a few minutes for her to catch her breath and in that time he never stopped touching her. His hand glided soothingly over her hip and onto her stomach. He lifted her hair from her face and touched a soft kiss on her swollen lips.

She enjoyed the softer waves that still moved through her and knew that this was the bliss that could happen between a man and woman, something that she'd heard so much about but had never experienced before. She waited for him to say or do something, not sure of what would happen next.

And still he did not take her.

She knew he could, she could feel his hard flesh against her leg as they lay together on the bed. He moved neither closer to nor farther from her. Puzzled, she slid from his side and pushed herself back to sit. She still wore her gown and he his breeches, but the proof of his lack of fulfillment pushed through the gap in the breeches and she wondered if she should pleasure him now.

Before she could do or say anything, he rolled from the bed and handed her the other cup of ale he had poured before and filled the empty one for himself. She drank hers and watched over the rim as he did the same, although he turned slightly from her as he did. Elizabeth choked on the ale as she realized he was covering himself and tying the laces as he drank.

"Was that the first time you…reached your peak?" He said the words, but the wonderful blush that filled his cheeks told of his embarrassment over voicing the subject. "You seemed surprised by it, almost fearful."

How did she answer him without lying or telling him too much? Never in the times with Kennard had her pleasure been important. There were a few times when it was pleasant, but more often than not, it was a hurried affair done in the dark of night and with as little physical exertion as was needed to complete the act.

The first times at the house where she was brought into her trade were too unpleasant to think on and she did not want to ruin this experience with Gavin with memories of those times. He was waiting for an answer, watching her with those piercing blue eyes of his. She gave him the truth.

"Aye, my lord. 'Twas the first time I have felt such things."

"Great God in Heaven! What sort of men are these Sassenachs that they cannot make certain a woman is well-pleasured as they take theirs?"

He slammed down his cup and raked his hands through his hair. Then he looked at her with bleak eyes and she knew he was thinking what had happened between them on this very bed. Before he could speak again, she slid from the bed and walked to him. That had been a mistake; she knew how deeply he regretted taking her that night. He told her with words and by his actions that it had been a misjudgment on his part to do so. No other man had ever regretted his callous taking of her body as his due.

Only this one.

She stepped closer and smiled at him. She wanted to offer him something to show him how much she appreciated his thoughtfulness. She needed to show him how much she cared for him. All she had to give was herself.

Elizabeth loosened the ties on her gown and chemise, bent over and grasped the bottom of the garments and lifted them up. Luckily these were borrowed clothes from someone much bigger than she was so she was able to get them off. Of course, Lord Gavin's hands pulling them over her head helped. She stood naked before him and waited for him to accept.

She followed his hands as they untied his laces and pushed his breeches down over his hips to the floor, exposing his powerful hips and legs to her sight. And his manhood that was still hardened and ready. He reached down and pulled the breeches free and threw them in the corner. Then he stood straight. The fire in his eyes told her he wanted her, but there was something else that reassured her.

When he took her in his arms, her skin sizzled at his touch. Their bodies met and the heat of his warmed her and made her shiver, as well. He turned around and pulled her with him to the side of the bed. Once more he surprised her by sitting on the edge of it and bringing her to stand in front of him. The soft touch of his fingertips on her breasts made her tremble and she felt her eyes close as she concentrated on how her body felt under his touch.

His mouth replaced his fingers and she gasped loudly at how quickly the tension within her built. One and then the other breast received his attentions and her breasts swelled as he suckled on them, tasting them and drawing her nipple into his mouth. When she felt the nip of his teeth against the sensitive buds, she reached out to steady herself. Her hands met his hard chest and she looked at him. Surely he did not mean to pleasure her again? Lord Gavin laughed and Elizabeth realized she'd spoken the words aloud.

"Aye, lass, 'tis my plan. But I would not be opposed if you would like to add to my pleasure." He paused and took her hand, guiding it toward his hardness.

Ah. Elizabeth knew what he wanted. Many men wanted her to take them in her mouth rather than in her body. She didn't understand it, but if it would give him pleasure, she would grant him this service. She began to kneel in front of him when his expression darkened. Something was wrong.

"Nay, Elizabeth. Do not kneel to me." He took her by the

shoulders and lifted her back to her feet. "I but wanted to feel the touch of your hands there."

"Not my mouth?"

"Not if you do not want to. This is not about force now, lass. 'Tis about wanting."

She shook her head. She did not want to do that. It had been forced on her many times, but she never liked it. "I would rather not, my lord." Elizabeth waited for his reaction.

"Then let us discover what you do like to do, lass," he said, and his voice grew deep and warm. "Tell me what you think of this."

His strength amazed her as he lifted her by the hips, brought her onto his lap and slid them both back on the bed. In another moment she found herself sitting over his legs, astride him with his hardness directly under the flesh she now discovered was still quite sensitive. His hands, now freed from supporting his body over hers, explored her body, touching everywhere, making her shiver and shudder as he did.

Elizabeth felt him pulsing beneath her and knew she wanted him inside of her. Surprised that she could feel this desire for a man or for joining with a man, she sat back on his hips and looked at him. Her heart filled with love and tears burned her eyes and throat as she thought of all the years lost in her life and all the unhappiness that had come before. If only they had met before, before she had…before.

He must have noticed the tears, but she was thankful he did not speak of them. Instead he urged her forward to him and brought her to the brink of pleasure with his mouth on her breasts.

"Take me, lass," he whispered to her as he kissed her. "Take me now."

He let her go and she slid back to take him inside her. The thrill of controlling this coupling made her clumsy. "Help me," she whispered as she moved back and tried to guide him into her.

He drew his knees up a bit and supported her bottom with his legs and his hands spread her woman's flesh. With little effort on her part, his hardness entered her and soon she was filled with him. He let out a moan that spoke of his pleasure. He gifted her with a wicked smile, one that foretold of even more gratification to come and then he guided her hips to move as though she were riding a horse.

Elizabeth gasped when he placed his hand between them and began to tease something between her legs. The aching and throbbing increased every time she moved and because of the pleasure she could not stop herself. The tension built even more tightly than before within her and she arched her back and took him in as deeply as she could. Filled with him, she moaned as she reached the edge of something and hesitated for a brief moment, before going over it.

As the core of her began to contract, he reached out and clasped her hands in his. He needed to be even deeper inside of her and so he rolled them over until he covered her. Releasing her hands, he lifted her legs around his hips and plunged his erection in until he met her womb. As tight as the glove he wore for hawking, she fit around him and he could feel every little pulse as it moved through her. Lifting out and then sliding back in, he filled her over and over until she began to cry out her pleasure. Only then did he seek his release, the one that he had held back until assured that she was satisfied. Until she took control.

Until she took him and was not taken.

Until she was given.

Chapter Eight

He knew not how long they slept, only that he awakened to find her on top of him with her hair covering them like a blanket. Although he was hot, her skin felt chilled.

There was no way to get out from under her to stir the embers of the fire or to even pull the covers over them without waking her, so he began to ease her to his side. Although she grumbled, she did not seem to wake. Gavin slipped from the bed and picked up an iron rod to stir the peat in the hearth. Adding a few more blocks of it and a few pieces of wood, Gavin looked back to where she slept.

He still could not believe that she had answered his summons. She'd made him wait for two days and almost lose hope, but then she was there. And she had given herself to him as he'd hoped. Surely they were meant to be together.

He had tried everything he knew to make it good for her, to make the memories of the other times with other men fade and to make her realize what could be between a man and a woman. Especially when deeper feelings were involved. As his were.

Elizabeth began stirring so he finished tending the hearth and returned to the bed. Easing the blankets out from under her, he climbed in and was thrilled when she rolled into his arms and murmured in her sleep. His own body stirred as her softness came into contact with him, but he simply enjoyed holding her close without her fears to get in the way.

"I love ye, lass," he whispered to her, in the Gaelic language of his home. "With all my heart."

She opened her eyes and looked at him. Before she could speak, he touched her lips with his and then smiled. "I am glad that you answered my summons, lass."

"As am I, my…" He stopped her from finishing it.

"Gavin. With all this between us now, we are Elizabeth and Gavin."

Her smile lit his world and she repeated his name in a throaty whisper. "Gavin."

"'Twas the first time you found pleasure in the joining?" he asked, not sure how else to broach the subject without asking it directly.

She looked away, obviously uncomfortable with speaking of it, but he would not let her. Guiding her face back to where he could see it, he kissed her and then asked again.

"Was it?" He was not sure why he asked. Partly male pride, partly curiosity over her past. But he needed to know.

"Not all…joinings have been pleasant, but some have been not unpleasant," she began to explain. "But none have been as was between us."

His arrogance and pride surged as did certain parts of his body at her words. She had gifted him with something precious, as he suspected. And he had been able to make it different and better for her. Did she know now that so much more could be between them? Did she know that more of herself, more than she had buried deep inside her, would be safe with him?

"And will be again, if you wish it so, lass," he said.

She leaned away from him, as far as his arms would allow and searched his face. "You wish me to stay?"

“Aye, lass. I wish you to stay.” He was not about to allow her to leave. He would do whatever he must to convince her to remain with him, until he could speak to her seriously of a possible life together. “Please dinna leave me.” Even he heard the longing in his voice and he offered up a silent prayer that she felt it.

“I will stay with you, Gavin, until you send me away.”

She let him gather her in closer as he tried to show her with his embrace and his body that he would never ask her to leave. Just the opposite, he planned to ask her to stay with him forever.

Two more days and nights passed and still he kept her to himself. He loved her in every way possible and she never refused him. Actually, she became quite the active partner, giving and receiving until they were spent. Gavin arranged for food and a bath to be brought and still did not allow her to leave.

’Twas only when Orrick himself banged on the door, demanding that Elizabeth return to her duties, that Gavin relented in his possession of her and hers of him. Not wishing to cause more trouble or embarrassment for her, Gavin allowed her to answer Orrick’s summons.

But the Elizabeth who left his chambers was a different one than the fearful woman who had entered there a few days before. The tantalizing glimpses of the woman inside confirmed to him his suspicions that there was much more to her than a common whore. She let small clues slip out during their loveplay and in their conversations about her past, before she left York.

And her personality was strong and vibrant! She showed him a keen and sometimes biting sense of humor and an appreciation for learning his culture and heritage. The lass took a passive role in their joinings only the first two times, then she led as much as she followed, to his utter amazement and joy.

There were two things he knew clearly when she walked out of his chambers—that they would suit well and that he did love her. He suspected that she had soft feelings for him, but he did not press for words of love. They would come in time, he was certain. He had only to arrange things with Orrick and then he would ask her to return with him to his home in the Highlands. A short time after she left, he too was summoned to Orrick's presence.

Elizabeth wondered if everyone in Silloth knew what they had been doing for the past two days and nights. She ached in places she did not know existed before his touches and kisses and felt a contentment she did not know before his love.

Aye, she thought as she answered Lord Orrick's call, she knew Gavin thought he was in love with her. And, if truth be told, she would like that very much, but the true situation was not and could not be that simple...or happy. In spite of his words declaring his love, spoken in the Gaelic of her grandmother, nothing could come of it.

Convinced now more than when she went to his chambers of the rightness of her decision to enter the Gilbertines community and her decision to give herself to him before leaving Silloth, she tucked the wonderful memories of their time together into a safe place and made her way down stairs and corridors until she stood before Orrick's chamber. Knocking, she waited to be invited in before opening the door. Lady Margaret's presence was no surprise. Elizabeth knew she had some explaining to do to both lord and lady over her behavior and her plans.

"Elizabeth, are you well?" Lady Margaret asked softly as soon as her servant left them, pulling the door closed behind her. Orrick stood off to one side of the chamber, looking out the window as if not involved. She knew better, though.

Elizabeth curtsied slightly and nodded. "I am well, my lady."

"And you discovered what you went seeking to find?" The lady's gaze missed nothing as did her knowledge of her people.

"I did, my lady."

"And did you and Lord Gavin speak of your lives after this time you spent together? What will you do?"

"I fear we *spoke* of very little, my lady." Lord Orrick choked and coughed a few times at her words, no doubt shocked at her boldness. "I would accept the offer made by you and my lord to sponsor me to the Gilbertines, my lady. I will go there whenever you think it best to go."

Now that she spoke the words, a sense of peace settled over her. This was the right path for her. For she was certain that she could never again offer herself to any man for his pleasure. Now that she had given herself to Gavin, she would not be able to resurrect the barriers that kept her safe and separate.

And she did not want to be with another man if she could not be with him. Elizabeth had given him something that she had shared with no other man and would not betray or dirty that by going back to whoring. She might be placing herself too high, but she knew the truth of it inside her heart and her soul.

"Gavin does not know of your plans?" Lord Orrick asked.

"Nay, my lord." Something was amiss here.

"And he did not speak to you of his plans?" Lord Orrick's tone hinted at something, but she did not know what.

"Nay, my lord. Was there some reason to tell him of my decision?"

"He is a fool, Margaret!" Lord Orrick exclaimed to his wife, apparently ignoring her own presence there and insulting his guest. "I swear he is nothing but a thick-skulled arse."

"My lord, Elizabeth knows not of what you speak. Mayhap Lord Gavin should join us so we may sort this out to everyone's benefit?" Lady Margaret did not wait on her husband's answer, but went to the door and spoke quietly to the servant outside.

A few minutes passed in an uncomfortable silence as they waited for Lord Gavin to arrive. His loud knock startled her and a tremor of nervousness passed through her at what would be their first encounter since…since…so many things had passed between them. Not sure of how he would treat her now, she lowered her head and waited. Lord Orrick did not allow for pleasantries, launching immediately into questions of his guest.

"Gavin, Elizabeth has accepted my offer of sponsorship to the Gilbertines' community. What say you to that?"

She was not certain why he should have anything to say on the matter, but 'twas obvious that Lord Orrick did. Elizabeth clasped her hands in front of her to keep them from shaking. Her nervousness increased as she waited, as they waited on Lord Gavin's reply.

"The convent, Elizabeth? You're to enter the convent?" His voice was gruff and she imagined she could hear pain in it.

"Aye, my lord. Lord Orrick has been more than generous in his offer. 'Twould seem a good place for…me." She did not look at him. She could not.

"I told you of my plan to make that offer, Gavin. You knew it was a possibility."

"Damn you for your meddling ways, Orrick," Gavin said, his voice more threatening for its softness. Elizabeth felt the tension in the room growing and knew that it involved more than simply her decision to leave.

"Do you have nothing to say to Elizabeth, Gavin? No offer to make to her?"

Lord Orrick moved to her side and faced Lord Gavin with the stance that men use when challenging each other. She could wait no longer and cause no more problems for either of these men who had championed her in some way or another for the past year.

Though she knew it was inappropriate, she stepped closer to Lord Gavin and placed her hand on his chest. She had not the courage to meet his gaze. "My lord, I am at peace with this decision. Do not feel that you must make some offer that you do not want to. Or that is not one makes to a wh—"

"Do not call yourself that!" he yelled, making her take a step back. "We both know you are not. There is much more to you than you admit, and I refuse to let you use that word again."

He reached out and took her shoulders in his hands, pulling her closer. Lord Orrick and Lady Margaret did not look away from this wanton display, though Elizabeth was certain they had to be horrified.

"Lass," he said quietly, "look at me."

She slowly tilted her head. Instead of finding the anger in his voice, she found his eyes filled with softness and caring. 'Twould be her downfall now. "My lord?"

"I want you to return to my village with me. Once the weather breaks, I will take you back to my home and my clan."

"As your leman, my lord? To serve as your mistress until you marry again?" Those were her only options. Then what would she do when he married, for she could not stay and would have no place else to go. And she could not watch him marry another, knowing that her love for him would be for naught.

"Nay, Elizabeth. Be my wife."

She laughed out at his words, feeling her control slip away as the pain pierced her heart. Shaking, she could not breathe as she tried to understand why she was punished yet again. Just when she thought she'd found a way to cleanse her soul of the sins it bore and a way to be at peace, he tempted her with the one thing she craved yet could not have. At another time, in another life and place, marrying Gavin MacLeod would have fulfilled all of her dreams. Now the offer simply increased the punishment she would have to bear.

"Elizabeth," he said, squeezing her to bring her attention back to him. "Will you marry me?"

She pulled out of his grasp before she forced out the words that would damn her forever in his eyes. "I fear I cannot marry you, my lord, for I am already married."

"What?" he bellowed as he staggered back from her. "You are married?"

Lord Orrick took his ladywife by her hand and began to walk toward the door when Lord Gavin stopped them. "Oh no, my meddling friend. You put me on the quest to discover her truths, you will stay now and learn them with me."

So, her words to him about being a nobleman amusing himself with a lower woman were true. It had upset him at the time and now she knew why. But encouraging him to use her until he found out about her past was cruel. And not something she would have expected from Lord Orrick. Ah, 'twould seem that all noblemen can turn when their desires are thwarted as she had stymied his in his search for her past. This had all been about finding her weakness and using it to discover that which she would not disclose freely. And Lord Gavin had found it.

"I am married, my lord," she said, trying not to let the despair she felt enter her voice. "And have been since I was ten-and-six." She faced him now.

"Who was your husband?" Gavin asked. "Did he die and leave you unprotected? Have you no family to keep you from wh—?" He did not say the final word.

"My husband *is* a wealthy merchant in York who decided he no longer wanted me as wife. The deal he made with my father did not give him the heir he desperately wanted, so he got rid of me."

"Do you mean he put you aside, Elizabeth? What did the priest say? Or your father? Surely he fought against this?" Lady Margaret asked. The lady stepped to her side and Elizabeth felt some measure of comfort in having a woman nearby. Especially a noblewoman, who understood all of the machinations in a noble marriage.

"My father would not let him put me aside, for he believed it would cast aspersions on his good name. So my husband did what he did best. He made a arrangements with some men to take me in the night and to be certain that I was found by my father with all of them. My father believed, as Kennard had hoped, that I had proved myself a whore and not worthy of his support or his name. A bastard daughter is good for so few things and if I was not worth gold in the match with the merchant, my father wanted nothing to do with me."

Lady Margaret's face drained of all its color and her husband noticed it, too. Lord Orrick took hold of her arm to support her as she stood. After a moment or two, Lady Margaret waved him off. "He did not secure you a place in a convent?"

"Nay, my lady. Kennard sold me to a brothel outside Carlisle and had found a new, fruitful wife when I last saw him. My father refused to see me once Kennard bought his silence in exchange for half my dowry returned to him."

"Half your dowry returned to your father?" the lady asked.

"Kennard would have kept it all since it was my disgrace that brought the marriage to an end, but to smooth things over and to keep my father from meddling, he offered him half of it back. 'Twas a sizable amount, enough to soothe any damages to his name or esteem done by his illegitimate whore of a daughter."

She could still hear the words spewing forth from Kennard and her father. Everything was her fault, for if she had conceived an heir for Kennard, none of this would have happened. If God had not granted her an heir, then 'twas surely a sign that she was sinful. Probably from her whore of a mother, who bore her out of the bonds of marriage, Kennard had said. Blood will tell…blood always tells….

Silence filled the room and she could look at no one, especially not Lord Gavin. Now he knew that she was married, put aside and truly a whore, sleeping with men other than her wedded husband. She could not bear to see the anger and disappointment in his eyes, for she knew he carried some noble idea in his mind that she was more than she truly was.

"So, my lord," she said, finally chancing a look at him, "I am not free to marry you, even if I wished it to be so."

Whatever reaction she expected, she did not receive it. She even thought he might wish her well in her new life of penance and service at the convent, now knowing the sins she must pay for. She thought he might argue with her over the vows she could not break. And part of her hoped he would ask her to go with him anyway, knowing that they each had feelings for the other.

Instead, he nodded at Lord Orrick and Lady Margaret and left the room without ever acknowledging her again. Elizabeth thought her heart had broken, in that moment, but it wasn't until she heard a few hours later that Lord Gavin had left Silloth, with no word on his return, that she knew the true pain of heartbreak.

Chapter Nine

The last day of the year arrived as gray and stormy as the month of days before it, but at least Elizabeth was in her own cottage. She could tolerate no more of the comments being made by the inhabitants of Silloth about her and Lord Gavin. The women took her side, for surely she was not the first woman to give herself in love to a man who then forsook her. The men did not understand how any harlot could have expected more than what she got—a fine tupping by a nobleman whom, they were sure, had left her some trinket to cover the cost of her services.

In spite of the celebrations going on around her, Elizabeth found it difficult not to give in to the desolation she felt inside. The feasting and mummery and joyous marking of Christ's birth and the end of the year all made it worse to be there and not be able to join in with the inhabitants of Lord Orrick's village.

The hostilities between the men and women who took sides over the situation of the Scot and the whore grew until the day after Christ's Mass when she finally sought permission to go to her cottage. Lord Orrick looked as though he might refuse at first, however once Lady Margaret spoke to him, he agreed to her request and even sent one of the stable-boys along with some supplies. Apparently, he and the lady wanted some measure of peace in their household as the year came to an end.

Now ensconced in her own place, with enough food and drink and peat to last for several weeks, Elizabeth decided to take the time to prepare herself for her new life. She understood now that in accepting Lord Gavin's invitation and enjoying those last few nights of bliss with him, she had tempted fate or offended the Almighty. And her punishment had been the awful exposure of her sinful past before the man she loved.

However, when she remembered hearing him speak of his love to her that night or when she woke in the night still feeling his touch on her skin, she was not completely penitent. Nay, she even longed for those nights and days when she had given herself to him. No matter the end they had come to, she would always treasure the memories of those nights with him.

The sun barely stayed up a few hours that day and Elizabeth allowed herself the luxury of a candle until she was finally ready to sleep. The winds howled outside and the ground was now covered with a layer of snow. No one would be going out this night. Somehow the end of the year made her maudlin and she took out her mother's ring and the silken scarf she'd managed to save from her life before.

Holding them, she cried out all of her grief for all she had lost. The tears flowed freely, something that she had never allowed to happen before, not even during her worst and lowest moments. Finally, at some time in the dark of the night she fell asleep.

The rapping on her door startled her awake. No fool would be out at this time in this weather. And she knew that Lord Orrick had announced that she would be leaving for the Gilbertines so that no man in his demesne would bother her. There was no one who needed her so she feared opening the door. Then a voice called out to her.

"Mistress Elizabeth? Are you in there?"

The winds obscured the voice, but she thought it might be the miller's son. What could he want now? She unlatched the door but held on to the leather strap as tightly as she could as she let the door open an inch or two to see for certain. Aye. 'Twas Liam indeed. She let him in and pulled the door closed.

He was wet and stood before her without saying anything. Then he stuttered some words to her in what sounded like Gaelic and held out some wrapped packages to her. He stood silently as she opened them to find a loaf of bread, a jug of ale and a chunk of peat. Just as she was about to ask him the reason for his visit, the door flew open and he was dragged out from behind.

She went to the door, intent on following and finding out what had happened, when her path was blocked by a huge man wrapped in plaid. It took a moment for her to realize that Lord Gavin had returned and stood before her.

"He got the words all wrong, but what should I expect from a scrawny, young Sassenach like that. He was supposed to wish you good luck and prosperity in this new year, but I do not want to tell you what he really said."

Lord Gavin crossed the threshold into her cottage and she backed away to give him room. The cloaks he wore were covered in snow and he pushed them off, dropping them in a pile by the door.

"I would have been here sooner, lass, but I needed to find a dark-haired young man to lead the way in. I did not want to jeopardize your future by being the First Footer this night. Then I had to convince him to accompany me in the storm. It was not a pretty thing to watch."

Elizabeth could not believe her eyes. He stood before her and still she blinked again and again to see if he disappeared. He did not. He had been thoughtful enough to find the right man to step in her door this first night. She could feel tears gathering as she watched him smile and as the heart she thought was broken began to pound in her chest.

"Ah, lass, I have so much to apologize for. Will you hear me out before throwing me back out in the storm?"

"You are welcome, my lord." His expression darkened and he frowned at her. "You are welcome, Gavin."

"May I sit?" he asked, pointing at the small bench. Her cottage did not have the fine furniture he was accustomed to.

"Please. Can I get you something to drink? Or eat? I brought some of Lady Margaret's wassail from the keep if you'd like." She pointed to the small jug near the hearth. Then, Elizabeth reached for the bread Liam had given her. Gavin's hand on hers stopped her.

"First, lass, I have been waiting for weeks to do this."

He pulled her close and kissed the breath right out of her. She was weak—she did not resist the embrace or the heated kisses he touched on her mouth. Indeed, she opened to him and breathed him in as he tasted her over and over again. Then, in too short a time, he released her and stepped back.

"If we keep up with that, I will never tell you what I came to tell you." He began pacing the extent of the cottage. He could only take a few steps before turning back the other way. Finally he looked at her, took a deep breath and let it out, and began the story he hoped would convince her to be with him.

"You gave me quite a surprise that morning, Elizabeth. Of all the answers I could have imagined, you being married was not one of them. Then when I heard your words, I wanted to kill someone." His hands fisted as he remembered the terrible things she had begun to believe about herself. "True men do not blame women for their shortcomings or failures. True men accept their responsibilities."

"But my…but Gavin, I was the one who failed. I was the one who did not give my husband an heir. I was the one…"

"Who did all that she could and still carries the guilt on her shoulders for the ruthless, worthless men who will not accept their part in her downfall." She believed all the wrong things they'd told her. All the filthy names they called her. She did not believe she was worthy of forgiveness, and she had done nothing that needed forgiving. "I went to York to find the slime who you called husband. I needed to find out the truth."

"You went to York? You saw Kennard?" Her voice shook as did her hands. "What did he say?"

"I did not speak to him. I spoke to your father and mother."

"My mother? You spoke to her? How does she fare?" Tears streamed down her face now and his heart was torn by the sadness he saw in her eyes.

The poor lass. She had gone to her father when she'd managed to escape from the whorehouse in Hayton and he threatened to turn out her mother if she tried to seek his help again. Knowing it was her life or her mother's, Elizabeth had walked away and asked for nothing. And the bastard had granted her nothing. His hands tightened again as he remembered wanting to strangle the life from his worthless body at his plain admission of abandonment.

"She is well and being taken care of as your father promised. He is good for that."

"What did he say?"

"I wish I could tell you otherwise, but he is unrepentant for his treatment of you or his desire for what Kennard offered him to betray you."

"And Kennard?"

She looked as though she would pass out, so he gathered her close and sat down with her on the pallet. "Take a few deep breaths, lass." When she had followed his directions and some color had returned to her cheeks, he continued with his story.

"Kennard is dead."

"Dead? Dead? Did you…?"

Perhaps it was his satisfied smile that made her suspect he

played a part in the man's demise. He could not help but be happy that the one who had set out to destroy the woman he loved was dead and rotting in his grave.

"I confess I would have if I had found him alive after seeing the damage done to you for naught but his own greed. But he died of consumption sometime after you arrived here in Silloth. And the brother whom he hated more than he hated you has inherited all that Kennard tried to keep to himself."

Elizabeth leaned back against him in shock from the news, but he savored the feel of her anyway in his arms after these weeks without her. Pure rage had forced his feet out of that room after she spoke of her past. Fury had driven him through storms and over hills and mountains to seek the truth that even she did not know. Anger alone sustained him and gave him the strength to search for the truth so that he could give her something of value.

No one, not even the lowest creature on God's earth, deserved the treatment she described that day and he knew that he must seek out her past. And give her some hope for a future. Even if she did not accept him, he felt content knowing that she had given him a reason for living. Even if for a short time, he was needed again.

"My offer still stands, Elizabeth, although I am sure that you will examine the choices you have now that you are a widow of means."

She sat up and faced him. "What do you mean?"

"Apparently, your marriage agreement provided that half of your dowry would be returned to you if Kennard should die before you. Kennard purposely kept his other deal with your father secret and never changed his will or the marriage settlement papers. So, the other half of your dowry was returned to your father. I confess I had to do some *persuading,* but I have a bag of gold in my cloak that belongs to you now.

There is enough in there for you to go wherever you would like and live well when you get there."

Her mouth dropped open and he reached up and gently closed it. He could only imagine what she was thinking. The questions she must have. The choices she could make now.

"Why? Why did you do this?" She pushed the hair from her face and rubbed her eyes. "You did not know me until just a short time ago. Why would you involve yourself in the cause of a stranger?"

He smiled, knowing he had asked himself the same thing over and over as he traveled across the length and breadth of England searching for her truths. And he knew both of his reasons.

"Part of the reason is nothing more than arrogant selfishness. After months and months of feeling unneeded by anyone, you needed me. You did not know that I would pursue this for you, but you needed to know the truth and I could find it out for you. I was finally needed and it satisfied something within me."

"You foolish man! You are needed. Messages have arrived almost daily asking about your return to your village. Asking for your guidance on matters big and small. Lord Orrick has felt quite put-upon trying to cover for your absence." She touched his cheek and kissed him lightly. "You are needed."

She leaned back into his arms and they stayed just so for several minutes. Was he foolish? Was his arrogant pride standing in the way of accepting his true place in his family? Was there something that an old warrior could offer the new generation of the clan?

"And the other reason you became my champion?" she whispered from within his embrace.

"That should be obvious to anyone who has the Gaelic. As I told you that first night you gave yourself to me—I love you, lass, with all my heart." He laughed now. "And I think you understood my words?"

"My grandmam would say something like that, so I thought I did. But I dared not believe it could be true. A warrior and a whore?"

"A man and a woman," he insisted. "Elizabeth, I know you have the chance to start a new life wherever you'd like, with none of the past following you. I know that I am much older and you probably want a younger man, someone closer to your age. But I would ask you again to be my wife and come home with me to the Highlands."

She climbed to her feet and walked a few paces from him, deep in thought. 'Twas true—she could leave here and begin a new life where no one knew of the things she'd suffered in the past. With the gold in his cloak, she could afford a house of her own, servants, and more. She did not need him now that he had given her the truth. He waited, barely able to breathe, for her decision.

"I cannot give you children," she announced to him. "I am barren."

"I have bairns already, love," he replied. "And they have bairns. I need no more." He meant it. His need for heirs had been fulfilled in his first marriage. He was free to marry for love this time, if she would have him.

"I had thought never to marry again, Gavin. Now, I do not have to and yet I find myself wanting to accept your offer."

"Then accept it, love, and be my wife."

As had happened the first time she came to his chamber to help with his bath, a myriad of emotions passed over her face. He stood watching, knowing that he could do nothing to interfere or it would be as worthless as her first marriage had been. Then a smile filled her face and she gave him the words he needed and wanted and longed to hear.

"Husband and wife?" she asked.

"If you wish it."

"And my past? Can you forget what I have done?" Her

voice shook again as she asked this. He knew this was now the only thing holding her back from moving forward.

"So long as you do not hold mine against me, lass. I am not the saint you believe me to be."

"I suspected as much. But since I love you so much, I will try to overlook that."

"You love me?"

"Aye, Gavin, I love you and want to be your wife."

And, with her first step toward him on the first night of the year of our Lord 1200, Elizabeth gave him everything he wanted.

Epilogue

"You are going to be insufferable now, are you not, my lord?" Margaret whispered to her husband as they sat at table.

The last days of the holiday celebrations continued on around them and everyone took part in the feasting. Pipers and other musicians made merry tunes that brought some to their feet in a dance. Orrick's yule log, now much smaller, burned brightly in the large hearth of the hall, offering its heat and aroma to one and all there. This time of year was special to her husband, and her heart was gladdened to see that her preparations and arrangements had once more proved pleasing to him.

"But my love, you were the one who first gave me the thought that they would suit well together," he whispered back. "And 'twould seem that you were correct again."

Orrick lifted her hand and kissed it. He even turned her hand palm up and touched the sensitive skin of her wrist with his tongue, knowing full well what it would do to her. And she knew that the shivers that ran through her were obvious to him.

"Two more of your wounded creatures will leave you now. Will you search for more?"

He never looked for them, they always discovered him and the sanctuary he offered. And as she learned many years before, when she found him, he never asked anyone to leave.

"I am certain that others will come, my love. Just as long as you are at my side."

He gifted her with the smoldering look that even now, after twenty years together, still set her heart to racing and made her palms sweat and her mouth water. The look that promised so much. The look that foretold of pleasures in the long nights of winter and love in the days.

"I will always be yours, my lord." 'Twas the truth. Nothing would part them. "*Waes hael,* my lord." She lifted a cup to him.

He lifted his to her and replied, "*Drinc hael,* my lady."

They sipped from their cups and she watched as Orrick surveyed the hall and his people, the smile on his face telling of his satisfaction with all he saw. His words but confirmed what she already knew.

"All is well in Silloth. All is well."

* * * * *

Dear Reader,

When I first started writing "A Christmas Secret," I knew Charity had a secret, but I didn't realize that by the time I was finished, everyone would have one. The fun was in the unexpected nature of those secrets, and what Charity would do with the things she learned.

Like Charity, I discovered that not all secrets are bad. Some are generous, loving gifts, given to spare feelings, protect pride, guard privacy, preserve friendships or avoid hurting loved ones. And to quote Sissela Bok, "While all deception requires secrecy, all secrecy is not meant to deceive."

I hope you enjoy the spirit of the season as Charity discovers her own secrets while she's busy uncovering everyone else's.

Cheers!

Gail

A CHRISTMAS SECRET

Gail Ranstrom

For my dear friends Gail and Hank Richardson,
my real-life inspiration for Charity and Drew—
and living proof that opposites attract.
Forty-four years and still going strong!

Love ya, babes.

Chapter One

Oxfordshire, England
December 1819

Andrew "Drew" MacGregor stomped the snow from his boots in the vestibule of Wyecliffe Manor and handed his coat to the butler. He'd arrived in Great Tew, Oxfordshire, earlier in the day and managed to acquire the last remaining room at the local inn before coming to pay his respects to his host for the upcoming festivities. The house would be full of guests, doubled and tripled in what rooms were available, and he was not about to share his bed. He'd even paid the innkeeper double to prevent such a possibility at the inn.

The wide central great hall had been draped with evergreen boughs and the scent of pine permeated the air. Mistletoe and holly had been woven through cedar swags hung from the banisters and a fire crackled merrily on the hearth at the far end of the hall. The sound of laughter echoed from room to room, evidencing the happy, expectant atmosphere. Five days hence would see the long-awaited Christmas wedding of Olivia Fletcher and Edward Mackay.

Though he'd been invited to stay at the manor, Drew had

refused. He was pleased to attend these particular festivities, but he would want a quiet place to retreat. The English were so infernally gregarious and nosy, always meddling in others' business. He usually preferred the quiet of his hunting lodge in the Scottish Highlands and, as soon as the wedding was a fait accompli, he would return to that blissful solitude.

He straightened the lapels of his dark jacket and stepped farther into the hall. With no direction and no host on hand to greet him, he was undecided how to proceed. Right, to a room from which squeals of laughter emitted, or left to a room where the strains of a piano and violin could be heard? If there was a library with a bottle of good malt whiskey, that's where he'd find Edward Mackay. But first he'd take the lay of the land.

He turned left, opting for the less socially demanding music room. He entered and stepped to the side, fancying that he'd made himself nearly invisible against the wall. Glancing around, he found the assembly even less formal than he'd imagined. A violinist occupied the opposite corner, tuning his instrument, and an astonishing blonde sat on the wooden bench, her graceful hands positioned on the keys of the pianoforte as an attentive young man turned the pages of a music book for her. They seemed congenial, almost intimate. Drew suppressed an unexpected twinge of envy.

The man glanced toward the door, then dismissed Drew as inconsequential and returned his attention to the girl. She blushed fetchingly, and Drew realized her companion had likely given her a compliment. And why not—the woman took *his* breath away. Golden hair had been swept to her crown, fastened with a bow of French blue velvet to match her gown, and left to tumble in a cluster of curls down the middle of her back. The swanlike arch of her neck exposed one of the most tempting throats he had ever seen—a throat that begged kisses. *His* kisses.

Lord! How long had it been since he'd been so taken with a woman's appearance? A demure blush? Years? Decades? Ever? He could not look away, even when the man lifted one of her hands from the keys to press a gallant kiss on the smooth back.

Ah, this, then, was a full-blown courtship. Something uncharacteristically possessive shot through him. Too bad.

The woman glanced at an ormolu clock on the mantel near the piano and gave a little start. She withdrew her hand, giving the appearance of reluctance to let go, and stood. Her voice was soft and musical. "I must hurry to Olivia's sitting room for a fitting of my attendant's gown. Will I see you later, Mr. Lingate?"

"Count upon it, Miss Wardlow," the man said.

The lovely Miss Wardlow hurried toward the door. Her gaze met his for a moment and her cupid's-bow mouth curved upward in a fetching smile. She passed him at a near run, leaving a delicate floral scent in her wake. Drew felt as if he'd been punched in the stomach—a little breathless and utterly dismayed at having been caught unaware by the full force of her attention.

Miss Wardlow, he could tell, was not a green ingenue, but a woman with a depth of emotion evident in her soft blue eyes. The smile she had given him was a mixture of surprise and curiosity, and Drew found himself wondering what might have happened if she had not been spoken for.

As he stood there musing the oddities of fate, another woman hurried into the room and joined Miss Wardlow's companion. She also blushed prettily and murmured some apology for being late for their appointment. She was lovely in her own right, but a pale copy next to Miss Wardlow. Mr. Lingate took her hand and pressed an ardent kiss on the back—a trifle more ardent than the one he had given Miss Wardlow. Interesting. Mr. Lingate must be a very popular young man, and not nearly as shy as he appeared. Much to Drew's amusement, the man in question gave him an annoyed glance—a clear invitation to leave. Well, then, all was fair in love and war, and perhaps Miss Wardlow was fair game after all. With nothing further to hold his interest here, Drew decided it was time to explore a little further and find his host.

Charity Wardlow hurried through her fitting and then skipped down the back stairs and along the corridor toward the front of the manor, anxious to rejoin the festivities. There was talk of a skating party at the pond across the meadow tonight. She was a poor skater, but there would be an opportunity for her and Mr. Lingate to have a few minutes alone. Perhaps he would catch her if she contrived to fall.

But best of all, she just *knew* he would propose before they had all gone back to London after Olivia's wedding. She had seen the signs—damp palms when he held her hand or asked her to dance, tongue-twisting nerves when he tried to talk to her, his inability to meet her gaze head-on. Yes, he would blurt out his proposal very soon now. And when he did, she would be ready with her answer. *Yes!* She had been waiting earnestly to say that word for the past three years. Her father would have been so proud, and her mother would simply smile in that vaguely interested way that said she really didn't understand.

As she passed the library, her blue silk shawl slipped from her shoulders. She turned around and knelt to retrieve it. In that moment of hesitation a voice carried from the library.

Lord Edward Mackay, Olivia's intended, was speaking in an angry tone. She was poised to rise and continue on her way when a single word stopped her.

"…baby! What gall," Edward was saying.

"Unquestionably," Edward's brother, Lawrence, agreed. "But the problem remains. You will have to tell Olivia."

"Never!" Edward vowed.

"But the babe's mother is here in Great Tew for the wedding and—"

"Nothing must mar this wedding or—"

"—and is threatening to—"

"—or delay it," Edward finished. "I've waited too long for this. I will not tolerate any interference."

"Interference? Did you hear me, Edward? She is here, and threatening to cause a scandal. She gave me this as a token to prove her claim. I'd say that is more than mere interference."

Charity covered her mouth to stifle a gasp. A baby! Edward Mackay had an illegitimate child. And Olivia did not know. The man was an utter cad! She peeked through the crack of the door to see Edward accept a lace-edged handkerchief from his brother. He glanced down at it, then opened his desk drawer and dropped it inside before turning back to his brother.

"Pay her off," Edward said. "Give her what she wants."

"You know there'll never be an end to it if we submit to blackmail," Lawrence said. "Tell Olivia. She will understand, Edward. Surely you can trust her to understand?"

"I cannot risk it."

"It's the only way. Even illegitimate, this baby is the closest thing the Mackays have to an heir at the moment. Olivia is bound to find out."

"Later. After the wedding," Edward insisted.

"Would she cry off if she knew?"

"She is frayed at the edges from all the planning and arrangements, and now the activity and the guests. Who knows what might set her off?"

"If such a thing could change her mind, perhaps she is not the woman for us." Lawrence sighed.

"*Us?* Have ye gone daft, Lawrence? You are not the one standing before the preacher, are ye? It isn't your heart she holds in her hand, is it? No, it's mine, and I'll be the one to make the decision. Olivia will not be troubled with this bit of ugliness. At least until our vows are said."

Oh, would she not? Charity thought. If the knowledge that her husband had an illegitimate child would make a difference in her decision to marry, then Olivia had a right to know before it was too late and, as her friend, Charity had an obligation to tell her if her fiancé would not.

She stood, her shawl trailing from her hand, and whirled toward the front hall. She nearly fainted when she found that disturbingly intense stranger from the music room leaning one shoulder against the corridor wall, his arms crossed over his chest. Obviously he'd been watching her the whole time.

He gave her a lazy, somewhat cynical smile and said, "Your eavesdropping, Miss Wardlow—is it habitual or occasional?"

He knew her name? She was certain she didn't know *his.* She would have remembered that crooked smile, the sparkling eyes of such a dark blue they could be called midnight, the deep, rich voice with a trace of a Scottish burr. And she certainly would have remembered the width of those shoulders and the dark chestnut hair. But that insulting tone! How dare he speak to her in such a manner?

"I was not eavesdropping, sir," she whispered, glancing over her shoulder to the library door. "I dropped my shawl and stopped to retrieve it."

"And just thought you'd have a peak in the library? Or was it the sound of scandal that drew your interest?"

"Shh! I…I inadvertently heard something mentioned that could be of concern to someone dear to me." She couldn't for the life of her think why she was bothering to defend herself to this stranger.

"Concern, eh?" The man chuckled, a sound both suspicious and genuinely amused. "Now there's an excuse for meddling that I haven't heard before."

"I am *not* meddling," she sniffed.

"From where I am standing, Miss Wardlow, it looks very much as if you are a typical Englishwoman, always meddling in other people's business."

Charity couldn't decide which insult to reply to—the general one to meddling Englishwomen or the more specific one to her. Instead she lifted her nose in the air. He caught her arm as she brushed past him and a frisson of excitement raced through her at the unaccustomed familiarity of his strong fingers circling her forearm. Not even Mr. Lingate took such liberties without her consent.

"If you are not meddling, Miss Wardlow, what do you intend to do with the information you have just acquired?"

"Why, as distasteful as it is, there is only one thing I can do. Tell Olivia, of course."

"I wouldn't, were I you."

Something in the dark tone held a warning, and she was in no mood to let such a thing pass. "Is that a threat?"

"If it were a threat, you would not have to ask." The man leaned closer, intensity in his eyes. "I would simply caution you to consider the consequences of your disclosure before you make it. It could be far-reaching and life altering."

"The same could be said of keeping the secret, sir. Olivia

Fletcher is my friend. What sort of friend would I be if I allowed her to wander into a disastrous circumstance which she had every right to know, but which I had kept from her?"

"You may not know anything. You chanced to overhear a few words that may possibly have sounded worse than—"

"May *possibly?*" she asked. The man was infuriating! "Are you asking me to disregard the evidence of my eyes and ears?"

"Things are not always what they seem, Miss Wardlow. Your eyes and ears can deceive you."

"Things are usually exactly what they seem, sir. Lord Edward has lied."

He dropped his voice and glanced toward the library door. "If you do not want to jeopardize your friend's future, keep your silence."

"If you knew what I overheard, you would not ask that."

"I have excellent hearing. I know precisely what you heard."

"Yet you'd have me betray my friend?"

"I know *my* friend. Edward Mackay would never build his life on a lie. Whatever is afoot, he is blameless."

She shrugged, finding his loyalty admirable if a little naive. "Nevertheless, my obligation is to *my* friend." She glanced down at his restraining grip on her arm.

He released her and stepped back, raising one dark eyebrow in a challenge. "Would you consider a wager, Miss Wardlow?"

Charity frowned. "A wager?"

"Aye. I will give you odds that my friend is not guilty of what you think. My judgment against yours."

Tilting her head to one side, Charity narrowed her eyes and said, "How would you prove such a thing, sir? You cannot simply ask him. He has already damned himself as a liar by keeping the truth from his intended."

"I see your point, although I do not agree that omission constitutes a lie. Very well, then. We shall not ask Mackay. Have you any suggestions for proving your case, Miss Wardlow?"

Charity gave it a moment's thought. "I could investigate the circumstances," she mused. After all, investigations were her forte with her bluestocking friends, the Wednesday League, and they hadn't had a good puzzle for months. "Yes," she said, "a little investigation should get right to the bottom of this."

"Do you swear you will not tell anyone what you've overheard until you can verify it?"

"No. If we have not uncovered proof, one way or the other, by the wedding, we must tell Olivia before she says her vows. That is only fair."

"*We?*" he said, raising a disbelieving eyebrow. "Am I to understand that you expect my assistance in this…this investigation?"

"Of course. We only have five days, and the next is the wedding, and it was your idea."

"How was it my idea?"

"You are the one suggesting the wager and requiring more proof than my eyes and ears. Were it not for you, I would be telling Olivia this very moment."

The stranger heaved a long-suffering sigh. "You could show a little charity in view of the season, Miss Wardlow."

She smiled. "It's a bargain, then. Five days, sir. We had best get busy. I shall catch up to you later this afternoon and we shall plan our strategy."

Strategy? Who *was* this nosy little English miss? Drew watched her walk away, the sway of her blue gown hinting at the curve of her hips. What a delectable morsel she was, all haughty principle and moral high ground. As distasteful as the idea of nosing around Mackay's business was, keeping Miss Wardlow's company could be worth the price.

This gathering had just become more interesting. Yes, indeed. Miss Wardlow had a lot to learn about the "gray" world most of society inhabited, and he was just the man to teach her. Who was more familiar with moral ambiguity than he?

And, if what he suspected was true, Miss Wardlow was about to learn a more devastating lesson than any he could teach her. Her Mr. Lingate *would,* evidently, lie to her—well, mislead her, at the very least. There was trouble brewing there, but damn if he'd interfere—it was none of his business.

As the hem of Miss Wardlow's skirt disappeared around the corner, he had the sudden premonition that he should have made a strategic retreat and allowed Edward Mackay to handle his own business. Good Lord! Had he just become a meddler?

Chapter Two

Charity's mind whirled as she set her teacup aside and stood. Olivia Fletcher, the radiant bride-to-be, smiled and patted the sofa cushion beside her. "Do not run off so soon, Charity. You've barely sat down. We have yet to discuss the Christmas Eve supper. Edward thought it might be fun to have a medieval feast and a Lord of Misrule for the festivities that night. I believe Edward said the Scottish called him the Abbot of Unreason. I know it isn't done anymore, but for just one evening, it cannot hurt. Who do you think we should ask?"

"I—" she glanced around at the other ladies "—I have not met all the guests, so I really have no idea who would make the best jester."

"Someone with a droll humor," Grace Forbush contributed. Ever precise, she whisked the cake crumbs from her skirt to her palm and transferred them to her saucer. "Surely one of your fiancé's friends would meet that criteria, Olivia. Edward himself is wickedly amusing."

Olivia smiled dreamily. "He is, I confess. I can imagine the sort of chaos he would cause. But I believe it is considered bad form for the host to be Lord of Misrule."

Charity did not care if they appointed the devil himself. She simply wanted to find the handkerchief that Edward Mackay had hidden in his desk drawer. At the moment it was her only clue to the identity of the woman Lord Edward had wronged. With more and more people arriving daily in town and at Wyecliffe Manor for the wedding, it might be impossible to locate the woman. She needed to begin her investigation at once.

"I would love to stay and chat, Olivia, but I am deplorably late in my correspondence. Mama will be waiting to hear that I've arrived safely, and I want to make the afternoon post."

"Go on, then, but return to us as soon as possible," Olivia conceded. She squeezed Charity's hand before letting go.

As Charity entered the hallway, she caught sight of Julius Lingate lurking near the doorway. He was holding her heavy shawl and signaled her to follow him outside. She pushed thoughts of the handkerchief aside as excitement raced through her. Was this the moment? Had he finally screwed his courage up to the sticking point? Would he declare for her now? She glanced over her shoulder before following him. Yes, they were quite alone.

A light dusting of snow revealed Julius's footsteps around the side of the house to a small terrace. A stone bench sat between two large arbor vitae, insuring a degree of privacy. Julius must have picked the spot just for its intimacy.

He stepped from behind one shrub and wrapped the woolen shawl around her shoulders. "There you are, my dear Miss Wardlow. I would not have you catching a chill on my account."

She felt a blush heat her cheeks. He really was the most thoughtful of men. They were going to be so very happy. She could almost picture his joy when she informed him, after his proposal, that she was not the pauper he thought her.

"You must be wondering why I drew you out here, eh?"

"Well..." she demurred.

"Deuced difficult to find a private place to talk with all this hubbub going on." He brushed the snow off the bench and indicated that she should sit.

Charity could feel the chill creep through her gown to invade the backs of her thighs and her bottom as she sat. But none of that mattered now. The only thing that mattered was that Julius was about to declare for her! "You wanted to be private, Mr. Lingate?"

"Indeed I do. We have things to discuss. Things you need to know. Er, that I have to ask."

Charity studied her lap, trying to hide the depth of her excitement. "Yes?"

He sat down beside her, his knees brushing hers. Deliberately? He took her right hand between his palms. "You must be aware how I...er, that I...have a certain regard for you, my dear."

"We have been friends for a good many years," she acknowledged. She did not mean to be coy, but neither did she want to put words in his mouth. It was important that Julius should do this in his own way—no matter how convoluted.

"Friends! Exactly!" A wide grin split his face as he seized on her words. "And what better way to begin? It is an admirable foundation, would you not agree?"

Charity nodded. She wished he would just blurt it out. All this dancing around the matter was giving her a serious case of nerves. Ah, but that was not Julius. Julius was ever the gentleman, careful to explain and never give offense, unlike that dreadful man in the hallway.

"But matters cannot go on the same forever, would you not agree? Sooner or later, something must change. I...I would like to see our friendship grow deeper. More...uh, meaningful. Yes, more—" he paused to clear his throat "—more *physical,* one might say."

Physical? Oh, dear! He was not going to discuss the marriage bed, was he? She'd simply die if he asked her thoughts on consummation. Or perhaps he only wanted the liberty of kissing her as he had done on two previous occasions when they'd been private. "I am not certain I understand, sir," she said, tilting her face up to his to grant him access to her lips.

Julius looked bemused. He leaned forward, still holding her hand, and pressed his mouth to hers. His lips were pursed, cool and firm, the same as her father's good-night kisses on her cheek had been. She'd always been slightly disappointed in Julius's kisses, but that was, no doubt, a result of inexperience. *Her* inexperience.

"Gads!" he cursed. "I'm botching this rather badly, but it's deucedly difficult knowing how to ask—"

The scrape of a boot heel alerted them to another presence. Julius released her hand and shifted his knees away from her, assuming an air of casual conversation.

"Oh! Excuse me," the stranger from the hallway said, coming up short. He gave them a devilish smile, as if he'd seen everything that had passed between her and dear Julius. "Am I interrupting?"

Charity prayed that Julius would send the man away, but he stood instead and bowed slightly. It only now occurred to her that she didn't even know the man's name. She glanced at Julius for the introduction.

"Miss Charity Wardlow," he intoned, "may I present Sir Andrew MacGregor. He is one of Mackay's friends come down from Scotland for the festivities."

Charity offered her hand begrudgingly. "Sir Andrew."

He bent over her hand with a courtly flourish, lifting it to lips as soft as Julius's had been firm. Oh, my! The heat of his mouth lingered after he stood.

"Sir Andrew, this is Miss Charity Wardlow, one of the bride's dearest friends and a long-standing acquaintance of mine," Julius continued the introduction.

"Drew," he corrected with a meaningful look at Charity. "My friends call me Drew."

"Sir Andrew was knighted for valor on the battlefield," Julius explained, as if to make the point that Andrew MacGregor was not of noble birth. "Damned French," Julius finished.

"As a matter of fact, Sir Andrew," Charity said, "we were discussing a matter of some import. If you wouldn't mind—"

"No, no," Julius stopped her. "'Tis quite all right, Miss Wardlow. I will catch up to you later. Perhaps at the pond tonight? Take a turn or two about the ice with me?"

She smiled and nodded, trying to hide her resentment of the interruption. Sir Andrew really was the most impossible man! She watched in dismay as Julius made his retreat.

Drew MacGregor grinned down at her as if he knew precisely what he had interrupted—and had taken glee in it. He propped one booted foot on the bench beside her, effectively trapping her between his leg and the arbor vitae. "Oh, *do* save a turn or two for *me,* Miss Wardlow," he mocked. "I should be bereft if I did not have the favor of your company."

"Villain!" she snapped. "How long were you watching?"

"Long enough to see that anemic little kiss."

"How dare you criticize Mr. Lingate! His...his kiss is quite stirring."

He tilted his dark head back and guffawed. "Stirring, was it? Egad, madam! I've seen more passionate kisses between a lad and his mother. I pity you if you call that 'stirring.' Someday you will thank me for my interruption."

"How would you know what stirs me, Sir Andrew?"

"I know what stirs a woman." He looked her up and down and gave her a crooked smile. "You are a woman, are you not?"

That arrogance! That swagger! She longed to bring him down a peg or two, but she suspected he was the sort of man who would have had considerable experience with women. She gave him a haughty lift of her chin and conceded the point. "Last I checked, sir, I did have that distinction."

"Ah, just as I thought," he teased. "For the sake of your education, Miss Wardlow, allow me to demonstrate my meaning."

He held her chin in place with the lightest lift of his index finger as he lowered his mouth to hers. She should turn away! She knew she should, but the heat in his midnight-blue eyes held her hypnotized. His lips parted ever so slightly as they neared hers and he spoke in a sigh. "Open to me, sweet Charity. Let me taste you."

As if she had no mind to control her body, her lips parted and her lashes lowered, inducing a dark, swirling mist. When his mouth molded to hers, it was the sweetest sensation Charity had ever experienced. His lips were soft and cherishing rather than dry and hard. He seemed to drink from her, drawing up all the deepest secrets buried inside her. Dark and erotic things that were completely foreign yet oddly familiar.

Her lips clung as he drew away on a shaky sigh. It was a moment before he spoke—a moment in which Charity prayed his lips would return to her. "That, sweet Charity, was a kiss worthy of a woman like you."

Cold air penetrated her fogged brain and she realized she had allowed her shawl to drop while she was consumed by the kiss. She shivered violently and swept it up, pushing Sir

Andrew's leg aside so that she could stand. "That is a murky talent, Sir Andrew. Is that all you can do?" she asked.

The sound of his laughter followed her down the path and through the door. Trying desperately to remember what it was she was supposed to do, she dropped her shawl on the foyer table, thinking to fetch it later and take it to her room.

The handkerchief! That was it. She had been on her way to the library when Julius had waylaid her. She headed in that direction now, purpose replacing the unsettling feelings Sir Andrew had stirred in her.

She gave a guilty glance toward the drawing room as she hurried along the corridor to the library. Since Lawrence Mackay had said Edward would know the mother by it, the handkerchief must bear an identifying mark. Pray it was something obvious and easy. She wanted this done with quickly. The prospect of working cheek to jowl with Sir Andrew MacGregor did not much appeal to her now. Now that he had kissed her. Now that he seemed to know her better than she knew herself.

Drew wondered if he would spend the next several days watching the hem of Miss Wardlow's gowns disappearing around corners. What was it about her prim self-righteousness that made him want to provoke her? And entice her, enflame her prim little properness. He straightened his jacket and took a deep, bracing breath, the icy air nearly freezing his lungs. Now, if he could just freeze the other heated parts of his body, he might be fit to appear in polite company.

Well, as much as he disliked chasing a skirt, he'd better go after Miss Wardlow. He knew where she was headed and he suspected she would make a blunder of it.

By the time he opened the library door and slipped through,

she had scattered half the contents of the drawer on the desk surface. He shook his head and cleared his throat.

Blond curls tumbled from the crown of her head as she whirled in response to the sound. One delicate hand flew up to cover her heart in a show of fright. The pink in her cheeks deepened when she recognized him. Good. He liked having the advantage. If she only knew how much she affected him, he'd never get the upper hand again.

"Oh! 'Tis *you,*" she gasped. She dismissed him with an airy wave and turned back to her task.

"What do you think you are doing, Miss Wardlow?" he asked.

"I cannot find it. I know it has to be here somewhere. If not, I can scarcely search his…his bedroom."

"I should hope not," Drew laughed. "Are you looking for this, then?" He withdrew a handkerchief from the inside pocket of his jacket and dangled it between a thumb and forefinger.

"Yes!" she cried. "Oh, thank heavens! I wouldn't have known where to start without it."

"Shall we put the desk back to rights, Miss Wardlow, and then discuss the relative importance of this small square of linen?"

She nodded and returned to the task of replacing the contents of the drawer. "How did you…when did you find the handkerchief?"

"Before tea. A simple matter, really. I came in here, ostensibly for a cheroot, opened the desk drawer and liberated the object of your desire."

"You could have told me before I risked coming in here and being caught," she accused.

"I could have if you hadn't run off. Is that your solution to every tense situation, Miss Wardlow? Running away?"

"Tense? I do not know what you mean, sir."

"Shall I show you?" he asked, taking a step closer to her.

"No!" Those incredible blue eyes widened and he recognized a small measure of panic there. She was a true innocent, despite her odd air of worldliness, still uncomfortable with her own sensuality. He would have to keep that in mind.

She surveyed the returned contents of the drawer, nodded her satisfaction and closed the drawer. Free to give him her full attention, she advanced on him, her hand extended to take the hankie.

Drew closed his fist around it and held up his other hand, palm outward, to stop her. "This is your last chance, Miss Wardlow. Leave this alone."

"I cannot. I keep thinking of poor Olivia, about to enter into a deceitful relationship. She loves him so, and he has not been honest with her. She should know."

"She loves him?"

"Deeply, and that may have blinded her to his true nature."

"Come now, Miss Wardlow. I have known Edward all my life. He is a good man. An honest man. And, even were your suspicions true, many wives live in blissful, if not deliberate, ignorance of their husbands' past indiscretions. It is entirely possible that your friend might not care at all."

"Possible," she conceded, "but that does not alter the fact that she has the right to know and make that decision of her own accord. The indiscretion is not the deed. It is the secret. The withholding of the information."

How could he argue that? "Very well, Miss Wardlow." He opened his hand and surrendered the handkerchief. "I hope you will not have reason to regret your choice."

"I shan't, Sir Andrew. Any man who truly loves a woman would not lie or keep secrets from her. I know Ju—Mr. Lingate would never keep secrets from me."

She was so certain. So naive. Drew could almost pity her.

Had he not seen Lingate with another woman, he would have left the little crusader alone, considering her committed to another. Ah, but now he could put his uncertainty aside. Yes, knowing that Lingate was playing her false freed him to explore the lovely mass of contradictions that was Miss Charity Wardlow. What a delightful way to spend Christmas. But he wouldn't tell her what he knew about Lingate. No. That would be meddling.

She glanced up from the handkerchief, her eyes dancing with excitement. "It bears the initial *L.* I shall ask Olivia for the guest list immediately. We will talk to every female with a given or surname beginning with that letter! Oh, I can barely wait to get to the bottom of this!"

Chapter Three

The warm air in the kitchen was humid and heavy with the smell of mincemeat, plum pudding, roasting hens and hams, breads and jams and the spirit of the season. Charity found Olivia and the cook discussing the picnic supper to be delivered to the pond for the skating party. She seized the opportunity to put her plan into action.

Glancing about the busy room, she said, "I have been thinking, Olivia, how remiss I've been in assisting you. It occurred to me that, with all your duties as hostess and all you have to do to prepare for the holiday *and* your wedding, I could be of more assistance to you."

"Do not be silly, Charity. Edward has seen to it that Wyecliffe Manor is generously staffed and provisioned. Aside from planning the menus and coordinating the wedding party, there is little for me to do."

"Yes, but when I could come up with no suggestion in regard to a suitable Lord of Misrule, I realized I do not know fully half your guests. They must think me incredibly rude or self-involved. I suppose I could simply introduce myself to every strange face and hope for the best."

"Oh, dear," Olivia said. "That could be very awkward for you. I should have taken you around with me."

This was not going in the direction Charity had planned. She shook her head. "I would not want to inconvenience you to that degree. I know! If you provide me with a copy of your guest list, I could study the names, then put them with faces. I should be completely familiar with everyone by the wedding."

"Everyone? That is ambitious, Charity. Especially in view of the fact that a good many of our guests are staying in town."

"I will sort it out, Olivia. Do not concern yourself."

"Very well. Cook has a list of everyone with notations on their food preferences. I will have her make you a copy, and you shall have it within the hour."

Charity sighed with relief. "Excellent. Perhaps I shall be able to use it at the skating party tonight." She turned to leave the kitchen, but Olivia called her back.

"Charity, have you had the opportunity of an introduction to one of Edward's friends by the name of Sir Andrew MacGregor?"

Charity's stomach fluttered. Sir Andrew hadn't warned Edward Mackay, had he? "Mr. Lingate introduced us this afternoon. Why?"

"Edward said he has been asking about you. He further said that Sir Andrew seldom asks about a pretty woman. He may have an interest in you, Charity."

Oh, he was interested all right—interested in discrediting her! She shrugged. "He seemed a little rough around the edges, Olivia. Rather forward and plainspoken in that rough Scottish sort of way."

Olivia gave her a sympathetic smile. "Be careful not to pass up a chance to better your prospects, Charity."

Better? Did Olivia think Sir Andrew was better than Julius

Lingate? It was all Charity could do to bite her tongue. But fast on that thought came the memory of his kiss. Oh, if only Julius could kiss like that!

After scanning the names on Olivia's guest list, Charity made note of those beginning or ending with the letter *L.* In all, there were five good possibilities. She knew all but two, and she wondered if it would be too much to hope that Sir Andrew would know them. Of course, it might not be possible for him to ask discreet questions. Anything of a personal nature would be rude coming from a man, especially one as blunt as Sir Andrew.

She tucked the list into the folds of her muff and slung her skates over her shoulder as she fell in step behind a group making their way across the snowy field to the frozen pond. The welcome glow of a bonfire lit the way and the smell of roasting chestnuts and hot cider with cinnamon and cloves greeted them upon their arrival. Cook had sent a wagon laden with sweets and a warm picnic supper.

As she sat on a log to strap her skates to her boots, she caught sight of Julius Lingate skating with Laura Tuxbury. They were laughing and Charity did not care for the way in which Laura was looking up at Julius—almost adoringly. Laura, in fact, was one of the names on her list of possible mothers to Lord Edward's love child.

She spotted Sir Andrew across the pond, standing with a group of men who appeared to be drinking from a small oak cask. They all laughed at something and then slapped Edward on the back with good-natured enthusiasm. Some premarital ribaldry, no doubt. He glanced her way and smiled.

There was something infectious in his boyish charm and she could not help but smile back. He turned to his friends, said a few words and then skated across the pond toward her.

"Ah, Miss Wardlow! I am pleased to see that you have decided to brave the cold. You are so late in arriving that I began to doubt you would come." He bowed and knelt before her. Without asking permission, he cupped her ankle and propped her heel on his knee, taking charge of her skates. "Allow me to assist you with these. They can be tricky."

Gratitude warred with annoyance at his presumption. Gratitude won. Her fingers were stiff with the cold and she longed to put her hands back in her muff. "Thank you, Sir Andrew. I was not aware that I was tardy."

"Perhaps it was my own impatience to see you again." He shifted his attention from her skates and looked up at her. She might have suspected a note of sarcasm in his voice had he not looked so sincere—or been so diabolically handsome.

"I…I was impatient to see you, too," she confessed, then cursed the heat that rose in her cheeks. "I have the list of names."

"Ah. The potential mothers." He nodded and returned his attention to her skates. "Is there nothing I can say to dissuade you from this…investigation?"

"It was your idea, sir," she huffed. "A wager, you said. Your judgment against mine. I was prepared to tell Olivia what I heard at once."

"Hmm. You have me there." He tightened the straps on her skates and stood, looking stern and disappointed. "Then how do you wish to proceed? Shall I take half the names?"

"Investigation takes a certain subtlety, Sir Andrew. You cannot simply ask straight out if someone has given birth to the groom's illegitimate baby."

Now Sir Andrew looked annoyed. "Do tell? I would never have suspected as much." He reached down to cup her elbows and lift her to her feet. "Are you saying you do not think I possess the necessary subtlety or discretion?"

Charity's cheeks burned with the rebuke. "I only meant…well, how *do* you plan to question the women on the list?"

He led her onto the ice and linked arms with her in the traditional couples manner, leaving her hands free to push back into her muff. "I confess I hadn't given it any thought at all. Perhaps I shall employ the services of a female sleuth."

Charity glanced up at him. He wore a solemn expression, but there was a twinkle in his eyes. She tried not to smile. "I may know just the person."

"I thought you might."

She wobbled slightly, her ankles unaccustomed to balancing on the single narrow blades. He quickly slipped one arm around her waist to support her. Snug against his side, she was surrounded by his strength and warmth. She was a little disconcerted by how safe and secure she felt. She began to suspect that Sir Andrew would be a good man to have in a crisis. And almost certainly a good man in a waltz.

"So, how shall I assist you, Miss Wardlow?" he asked, guiding her into the stream of skaters gliding in a wide circuit of the frozen pond.

"There are a few women on the list that I do not know. I was hoping you might be able to tell me something about them."

"Who are they?" he asked.

"Lady Louise Elmhurst," she said, "and Miss Gwendolyn Lindenhouse. I know the others well enough to strike up a conversation and invite confidences, but I do not know those two at all."

"Sorry. I was presented to Lady Louise many years ago, but a duchess is not likely to recall a lowly soldier home on leave."

Charity doubted anyone meeting Sir Andrew would ever

forget him. "She will remember you well enough for you to introduce me, Sir Andrew. I'll make myself agreeable to her, and then—"

"And then, when she has been lulled into trusting you, you will…what, Miss Wardlow?"

"I shall invite her confidences," Charity admitted. "I do not know precisely what I shall say, but I shall lead the conversation toward the topics that will be useful to me."

"Ah, you will use your instincts." Sir Andrew nodded.

She could not tell if he was laughing at her. He looked quite serious. "Do you doubt that I have good instincts, sir?"

"Not at all. In fact, *my* instincts tell me that there is much more to you than anyone knows. Am I right, Miss Wardlow?"

More to her? Charity thought of her own deepest secret. Yes, she supposed he was right. Only one dear friend knew that, through a series of wise investments, she had rebuilt the fortune her father had lost to the debt collectors. For all the ton knew, she and her mother were one step from destitution. And that was the way she wanted it.

She'd had dozens of suitors in the days before her family's financial fall. But when the debt collectors took everything and her father had shot himself in shame, all those suitors had disappeared. Charity had learned her lesson—a woman was nothing without her dowry. That was when she had vowed she would marry only for love, because only love could survive physical or emotional loss. Of all the young men who had declared their undying love, only Julius Lingate remained. And since he believed she was impoverished, when he finally proposed she could be certain it was for love. In her opinion, that was what made him so eminently suitable.

"Miss Wardlow?"

The soft voice recalled her to the present. "Yes, you are

right, Sir Andrew. There is much more to me than one might suspect."

"Blast! Here comes Lingate."

Charity looked around to find Julius skating toward them, having deposited Miss Tuxbury with a group huddling around the bonfire. She smiled a welcome, despite Sir Andrew's obvious dismay. "Never mind," she said, glancing up at him. "Tomorrow morning, sir, you may introduce me to Lady Louise. Once the conversation is underway, excuse yourself. I will find you afterward and tell you what I have discovered."

"Take your time, Miss Wardlow," he murmured, looking toward Julius. "There's a name or two I think *I* shall investigate."

She was about to ask him his meaning when Julius halted before them with a little spray of ice from his blades. "Here you are, Miss Wardlow. I've been looking for you." He bowed stiffly to Sir Andrew and asked, "Do you think you might spare Miss Wardlow for a turn or two with me."

"Miss Wardlow." Sir Andrew offered his own bow and skated toward the bonfire. She found herself annoyed by her feeling of abandonment. She had wanted him to leave her alone with Julius. Hadn't she?

Julius took her hand and skated backward, facing her. He led her into a wide figure eight and Charity suspected he was showing off. Sir Andrew hadn't shown off, despite his confidence on the ice and his quick steadying of her.

"Tell me, Miss Wardlow, are you developing a tendresse for Sir Andrew MacGregor?" Julius teased.

Charity wondered why she hadn't noticed before how sure Julius was of himself. And of her. "He was just telling me how he would…ah, like me to meet his friend, Lady Louise Elmhurst. He thinks wc would be compatible."

Julius looked very pleased. "Such a friendship could be

beneficial to you, Miss Wardlow, and to your family and close associates. A duchess wields considerable influence. You'd have entrée into certain circles currently closed to you. Yes, I think it would be a very good idea to make yourself agreeable to Lady Louise."

Beneficial to family and close associates? Could Julius possibly be referring to himself? And why did that suspicion annoy her? When they were married, she would want to help him advance in society, wouldn't she? And had she not just vowed to "make herself agreeable" mere minutes before? Heavens! What was wrong with her?

Julius released her hand and skated circles around her, finally coming up behind her to take the place beside her that Sir Andrew had vacated. "I can see that you will be an asset to…to anyone you choose to honor…that is…"

Charity's hopes soared. Was this it? Was this finally the moment when Julius would say the words? "Anyone I choose to honor…? Honor how, Mr. Lingate," she led.

"Why, er, in any way you chose, Miss Wardlow."

"Hmm," she replied. Perhaps Julius was right—this was not the moment for a tender proposal. Still, she could execute her little fall so that Julius could catch her in his arms. They could share a blameless moment of intimacy even though they were public.

She saw a twig on the ice just in front of her. Instead of lifting her blade, she skated directly into it. When the tip of the blade caught and held, she lurched forward, dismayed to realize that Julius had let her go the moment she had begun to topple instead of steadying her as Sir Andrew had done. Trying to correct her forward momentum, she threw herself backward and flailed her arms wildly.

Three simultaneous impressions would be forever etched

in her memory. Julius's shocked expression, her sinking feeling of betrayal that he had let her go, and the long helpless fall before the stomach-turning sound of a crack just as the back of her head hit the ice and everything went dark.

Cold. Bone-chilling cold. The world swam back into focus. Charity blinked, trying to make sense of the jumble of faces and sounds. Something had gone dreadfully wrong, but she couldn't remember what.

"Who was supposed to be sweeping the ice?" she heard Edward Mackay shouting in the distance.

"...don't know what happened," Julius was saying, nearer at hand. "When she started to fall, she just pulled away and—"

Lie. That was a blatant lie. He had let go of her. But it wasn't his fault. He hadn't been prepared for her abrupt stop. He'd been as surprised as she. No, *more* surprised. She, at least, had seen it coming, had known she was about to fall.

She moaned and tried to lift her hand to touch her head.

"Charity! Oh, thank God!" Grace Forbush exclaimed. "Say something, dear. Anything."

"Cold," she managed to murmur.

"For the love of God, get her off the ice," Sir Andrew's dark voice snarled. "She's going to freeze. Has anyone looked to see if there's a cut?"

She closed her eyes again and felt slightly nauseous as she was helped into a sitting position. She clenched her jaw as Grace removed her bonnet and examined her head. "No blood, but she has quite a lump."

"That's good, is it not?" Olivia asked, an edge of panic in her voice. "That means the swelling is on the outside and not the inside. Is that not right?"

"Aye. With luck she will not be concussed." Strong arms

lifted her and cradled her against a warm, thickly muscled chest. She turned toward the warmth and buried her face in soft wool scented with a citrus-and-clove sachet. Much nicer than camphor, she thought.

"Here," Julius said. "I can do that, MacGregor."

"I think you've done enough," Sir Andrew said.

"M-my fault," she whispered.

"I think not, Miss Wardlow," Sir Andrew disagreed. "I am taking you back to Wyecliffe. You need a cup of hot cocoa and a good night's sleep. You have much to do tomorrow."

She managed a nod, noting that things were not going precisely as she had planned. In fact, nothing had gone as she planned since running into Sir Andrew MacGregor outside the library door mere hours ago. She prayed this was not a trend.

Chapter Four

Charity's slight headache the following morning was nothing compared to her night of fitful sleep. She'd had dreams, nightmares actually, of Drew MacGregor skating up behind her and sweeping her off her feet and away from Julius. Away from everything she wanted and had worked so hard to win.

She dressed in her finest yellow silk morning gown and brushed her hair gingerly, avoiding the lump on the back of her head. She would like to blame Sir Andrew for that, too, but she knew full well that the fall was her own fault for trying to trick Julius. A gold ribbon embroidered with holly and berries completed her preparations for the day. The memory of the night before did not improve her mood and she was feeling quite foolish when Sir Andrew sought her out after her morning tea.

"How are you, Miss Wardlow?" he asked, a look of deep concern on his face.

"Well enough, thank you," she said, unable to meet his eyes. What would he say if he guessed she'd been tricking Julius into catching her? He'd offer no sympathy and likely laugh at her.

"Well enough to continue with your plan?" he asked with a note of reserve.

"*Our* plan," she corrected. "And yes, I am. I hope you are as committed to finding the truth as I am, Sir Andrew."

He arched one dark eyebrow and gave her a crooked smile. "Do you doubt me?"

"Perhaps a little," she confessed. "I fear your friendship with Lord Mackay could color your opinion."

He took her arm and led her toward the front parlor and the sound of lively conversation. "I wonder what I have done to earn so poor an opinion from you."

Startled, Charity stopped and looked up at him. "I do not have a poor opinion of you, Sir Andrew. Whatever gave you that impression?"

"Your assumption that my judgment could be colored by a personal friendship," he told her. "You must think me a very simple man."

"Simple?" she scoffed. "I would never make that mistake." That was the very last thing she thought of Sir Andrew MacGregor. In fact, she believed he was a very complex man.

"Then perhaps you are still angry that I kissed you yesterday. I will admit that was a bit of a liberty—"

"Bit?" she huffed.

"—but you were just so bloody irresistible that I had to challenge you."

Was that it? A simple challenge to her beliefs? Charity's pride tweaked her. She knew she wasn't irresistible, but she had hoped Sir Andrew…*no!* She had not. He was inferior in every way to Julius Lingate's genteel behavior and faultless manners. What had gotten into her?

"Ah," Sir Andrew said as they entered the parlor. He nodded toward a pretty brunette in a lavender gown. "There is Lady Elmhurst now. Come along and I shall give you your introduction."

Drew watched Charity charm and disarm Lady Louise Elmhurst as he made his retreat. He had little doubt that, if the lady was the mother of a secret illegitimate child, Charity would have it out of her by the time the luncheon bell rang.

And now that he knew she was occupied and unlikely to overhear any more conversations in the library, he headed in that direction. As he suspected, Edward Mackay was ensconced in a large club chair before the fire, a cup of hot coffee between his meaty hands and a sheaf of papers in his lap.

"Drew," he greeted, looking up from the fire, "come sit with me and tell me what you've been doing the last two years."

"Am I interrupting you, Mackay?"

"Nay. Just some last-minute settlements I've been going over. Nothing of much interest."

"Settlements are not of interest?" Drew asked.

"Olivia's family does not have much," Edward explained. "There is not much to settle, but it seems important to Olivia that I understand the extent of the obligation I am accepting when I say my vows to her. Completely unnecessary, since I'd take her with nothing but the clothes on her back."

Drew smiled. "It's a love match, then?"

"Aye."

"That is good to know, Mackay. You deserve every happiness."

"And what of you, Andrew MacGregor? Why do you not have a wife? Is it not time for you to get an heir?"

Laughing, Drew shook his head in denial even as the quick vision of Charity Wardlow flickered across his mind. "I fear the shackles will close around me too soon for my taste."

"I cannot wait," Mackay confessed. "I'd have wed Olivia a year ago, but she'd have none of it. She wanted me to be certain, and there were some loose ends that needed tying up."

"So, you will come to each other with clean slates, eh? Nothing held back? Nothing hidden?"

"She knows all about my misspent youth, if that is what you mean." Mackay tossed the papers on a nearby side table and put his coffee cup down. "God knows she is acquainted with my faults better than most."

Drew suppressed a niggling feeling of betrayal at this line of questioning. Mackay was his friend. He said he'd held nothing back, and Drew believed him. "Then there is nothing left to say," he concluded, dismissing the subject.

"Did you manage an introduction to Miss Wardlow?"

"Aye, I did. She's as waspish as she is lovely."

"Waspish? Miss Wardlow?" Mackay looked surprised. "I've always found her to be the most pleasant and meekest of women. You must provoke it, Drew. Come, tell. What did you do?"

"Nothing unusual," he said.

"For you? Gads! That could mean just about anything. You did not seduce her, did you?"

Drew affected a wounded look. He and Mackay had both been known as cocksmen in their younger days. From tavern wenches to merchant's daughters, the female gender had been generous with their charms to two well-favored lads away from home. He shook his head in denial. "That would be a sore abuse of your hospitality, Mackay. Besides, I haven't indulged in that sort of excess since I was out of Eton."

"You had more tupping at Eton than most men have in a lifetime. The other lads and I marveled that you had time to study at all."

"Well, Miss Wardlow needn't worry on my account, Mackay. She'd set me down if I so much as tried. Besides, I've learned to control my baser impulses." All the same, when he'd seen her in that lovely yellow confection with the lace trimmings this morning, he'd been taxed not to touch her.

Mackay gave him a disbelieving look. "Have a care with her, Drew. She has little but her pristine reputation. If you should compromise her, she wouldn't even have that."

"Poor, is she?"

"As a church mouse. Her father squandered the family fortune, and then put a gun to his head."

Drew's conscience bit him and he vowed he would not take the last thing she had. He'd rather give her everything *he* had. "I'll leave her in peace. You know how I hate meddling. But, um, I'd like to know more about Julius Lingate."

"Lingate? Did the man cross you?"

"Not me, but perhaps a friend of mine. I've met Lingate on one or two occasions when I've been in London, though I know little about his family or background."

"Well, he comes from a well-to-do family. His father is a banker. As a second son, there is an expectation that Julius will marry well and improve the family's financial and social standing."

"He wouldn't be able to accomplish that with Miss Wardlow as a bride, would he?"

"Socially, perhaps. Financially, certainly not." Mackay tilted his head to one side, narrowing his eyes suspiciously.

"Is he the sort to disregard his family and make his own way?"

"So we *are* still talking about Miss Wardlow?"

Drew merely shrugged. He was not prepared to discuss his

feelings for Miss Wardlow, nor was he prepared to speculate on Julius Lingate's intentions yet.

Mackay grinned and slapped his knees. "For someone who everlastingly vows that he doesn't meddle, this sounds mighty like meddling to me, MacGregor."

Charity was not surprised that the duchess was only a few years older than herself. After all, if she had borne Mackay's baby, she could not be a crone. But that she was so lovely and gracious surprised her. She would not be the first well-born woman to hide an embarrassing birth, but she did not seem the sort who would make extortionist threats.

The duchess was married to a man she appeared to adore. She spoke of him frequently and in glowing terms. If ever there was a woman who did not appear to have a secret, it was Lady Louise Elmhurst. Nevertheless, Charity was committed to her course.

As they sat alone by the frosted windowpanes, they watched the men play a game of curling on the frozen pond a short distance from the house. "I know your secret, Lady Louise," she said, keeping her attention on the game as she discreetly withdrew the blackmailer's handkerchief and pretended to dab her forehead with it. No, the duchess showed no signs of recognition.

A slight rustle indicated that Lady Louise had turned toward her. "Indeed? What secret might that be, my dear?"

"The…the one that would devastate your husband."

There was a long silence before she replied. "You will not tell him, will you?"

"That depends upon you, Your Grace. I would like to hear your reasons for keeping it secret." She could not tear her attention from Julius. He could whisk the broom more effectively than any of the others. He glanced up at the window and waved to her, and she was convinced anew that she was quite the luckiest girl in Oxfordshire.

"Why, because you were right. It would devastate Elmhurst. You cannot know the pride he takes in it."

"In…?" What was the woman talking about?

"If he knew I could do it better, he would question our entire marriage. Why, he believes I admire him for it."

Charity frowned. "But, if he knew—"

"Have you ever heard him play, Miss Wardlow? He is passable, but hardly the virtuoso he believes himself to be."

"The…the pianoforte?" she guessed.

"The very first time we met, I gushed like a schoolgirl over his skill and told him how he evoked memories of soft summer nights and daydreams of love. That praise formed the foundation of our friendship. If he knew I was once considered a prodigy and played at the king's request, he…he would be humiliated. He would think I was laughing at him behind his back. I could not bear that."

"For him to know that your skill is greater than his?"

"It seems such a silly thing, I know, but it is his secret vanity. If he knew my skill exceeded his, he'd be so ashamed. I doubt he'd ever trust me again."

Charity's heart twisted. How touching a thing to protect the pride of one you love! "Oh, my dear Lady Louise. Your secret is safe with me. I swear it."

"But how did you find out? I was so careful to cover it. The poor king recalls nothing, and my piano instructor has gone back to France."

"I…I, ah, noted your expression when your husband played the first night you arrived. You looked as if you yearned to touch the keys."

"Oh, I do. I only play when Elmhurst is gone. I shall have to be more careful. Thank you for warning me, Miss Wardlow. I shall be forever grateful."

Charity felt like a complete fraud.

She noted Sir Andrew standing a few feet away. He gave her a little signal and moved toward the door. Clearly he wanted her to follow him. She stood and offered a little curtsy. "I must go now, but I hope we shall have the opportunity to chat again soon."

"I shall make the time, dear Miss Wardlow. It is rare to find someone who understands a wife's deep regard for her husband."

"Your eavesdropping, Sir Andrew. Habitual or…"

A tiny smile twitched the corners of her delicious mouth. The imp was teasing him! No one had done that before and made him like it. "Amusing, Miss Wardlow. I was not eavesdropping. I came to find you."

"Do you have news?"

She took his arm as they walked slowly toward the music room and it occurred to him that he was going to miss her when he returned to Scotland. "I spoke with Mackay," he said. "I am convinced that he is not concealing an illegitimate child. The woman, whoever she is, must think she can extort money from him on the accusation alone."

"I think that is wishful thinking, Sir Andrew, but it does you credit as Mackay's friend. As for me, I had a very enlightening conversation with Lady Louise," she told him. "She has a secret, but it has nothing to do with Mackay."

He had overheard enough to know that, and he admired the way Miss Wardlow—Charity—had handled the situation.

"Who shall we question next?" she asked.

He loved that they could disagree and be at odds yet tease,

laugh and be friends. And, despite that he wanted no part of her meddling scheme, he liked her use of *we.* "Miss Gwendolyn Lindenhouse," he sighed. "I shall introduce you at luncheon."

The music room was, indeed, empty. Charity crossed the large room to the piano, sat down and riffled the keys. "Would it not be glorious to create beauty, whether in music or in art? I am so poorly equipped in both."

He sat beside her, touched by her wistfulness. "Beauty, sweet Charity, is in the eye of the beholder." He lifted her chin with his forefinger until her face was tilted up to his. He searched her expression for any sign that his touch was not welcome and was relieved to find none. He couldn't be certain he could have stopped if he had.

Her smile faded as her lips softened and parted, welcoming his kiss. He knew the moment his mouth met hers that he was in deep trouble. Yesterday, she had been sitting on this very piano bench with Julius Lingate. She had blushed as Lingate kissed her hand, and a prick of envy and regret had tweaked him. He had been taken with her appearance then, but he was captivated by the woman now. He wanted Charity Wardlow. He wanted her modesty, her principles, her strength of character and her quiet determination.

Aye, and he wanted the rest of her, too. He wanted the slender, lithe body naked and twisting against his in the throes of passion. He wanted to watch her breasts grow ripe and her belly round with his baby. He wanted long conversations with her before a crackling fire, and he wanted to know what pleased her, angered her, excited her.

She made a soft little moan when he began to relinquish her mouth. That was all the encouragement he needed to deepen the kiss again. He slid his arms around her and gathered her to his chest, relishing the feel of her soft breasts as they flattened against him, the slender curve of her back and, dear Lord, the graceful arch of her neck when she tilted her head back to meet his mouth.

Wordlessly, instinctively, she turned her head to give him access to her throat. And, just as he'd known she would, she gasped when he lifted the silken blond curls and trailed a line of kisses from her earlobe to the back of her neck. She was so responsive. So ready. Dare he risk more?

As he moved his hand toward the low curve of her décolletage, a clatter of boots in the foyer interrupted them. Blast! It was the overgrown schoolboys returning from their game of curling. He released Charity, noting her look of confused disorientation. Next time he'd lock the damned door.

"Hail Lingate!" the call went up from the hall. "Hail the conquering hero!"

Lingate. That undeserving blighter! Drew couldn't be certain what the man's intentions were, but he knew Charity was prone to favor him. He would have to work closely and quickly if he was to woo her away.

Was Mackay right? Was he meddling in Miss Wardlow's affairs? He glanced at the curve of her flushed cheek as she watched Lingate bask in the glow of her admiration. No. This wasn't meddling. God, no! This was a rescue.

Chapter Five

After the midday meal, Charity went looking for Sir Andrew. They hadn't been placed anywhere near each other for the meal, so the occasion to introduce her to Miss Gwendolyn Lindenhouse had not presented itself. She was anxious for the introduction since time was so short, and she wanted to devote the rest of her afternoon to her investigation. She was not so worried about the women she already knew. She could strike up conversations with them whenever the opportunity to be alone with them arose. After Miss Lindenhouse, there would be four names left on her list. With luck, she would complete her inquiries before Olivia's wedding day.

Masculine voices carried down the corridor from the library. Sensitive to Sir Andrew's accusation that she was a common eavesdropper, Charity walked boldly to the door and stood at the entrance, awaiting Sir Andrew's notice. A dozen or more men were lounging near the fireplace, rum toddies warming their palms. Lord Edward, Julius and Sir Andrew had raised their glasses in a toast.

"To wives and beloveds," Lord Edward declared.

Before they could drink, Julius added, "And may they never cross paths!"

Most of the men laughed and even she smiled, thinking him terribly clever. Sir Andrew, however, shot Julius a nasty look. Only then did it occur to her that perhaps Drew had a finer appreciation of the nature of love. Oh, but surely Julius had only been joking. Julius flushed from Sir Andrew's dark look and Charity realized he was a little afraid of Sir Andrew.

Seeing the two men side by side gave her pause. Though Julius was classically handsome and gracefully built, there was a strong magnetic appeal to Sir Andrew's sheer masculinity and tensile strength that overshadowed Julius. At a distance, she could finally understand why she had been so pliant to Sir Andrew's hypnotic pull. Still, she could not help but be a little chagrined for the liberties she had allowed him—liberties she had never allowed any man, including Julius.

Enough of her silly fickleness! "Psst!" she whispered when Sir Andrew glanced toward the door. She motioned him to join her in the corridor.

Sir Andrew finished his toddy and left his empty glass on the mantel, excusing himself for a moment.

"Miss Wardlow," he said with a polite bow of his head. The grin he gave her when he straightened nearly made her forget why she was there. "Did you wish to speak with me?"

"Um, yes. I wonder if you could introduce me to Miss Lindenhouse now."

"But of course," he said, taking her arm. "Where is our quarry?"

She rather liked the sound of "our." It made her feel as if he were as committed to the investigation as she. "In the sitting room, Sir Andrew. She is conversing with several other ladies at the moment."

“Will we be conspicuous?”

“Conspicuous?” she puzzled. “I cannot think why.”

“I will be entering a female domain, introducing you, and then going away. Would that not look suspicious?”

“Hmm.” How had something so obvious escaped her? “Perhaps you are right. Perhaps I should introduce myself or ask one of the other ladies to do it. I only wanted to avoid the inevitable questions about why I should like to make Miss Lindenhouse’s acquaintance.”

“Ah,” he said. “I see. Well, glad to be of service. I shall stay and take part in the conversation. Then no one shall think it odd that I disappear after the introduction.”

“No!” she gasped. How could she pry into personal matters with Sir Andrew watching her with those unfathomable deep blue eyes? “That is, I do not think Miss Lindenhouse would speak freely in front of a man. And she would certainly think me ill-bred to bring it up in mixed company.”

“Such sensibility never concerned you before,” he murmured.

Was that criticism? “Women are more forthcoming than men, Sir Andrew. We share information with each other more easily,” she said defensively.

“I can see that you’ve given your plan considerable thought, Miss Wardlow. And so have I. Yes, I’ve decided that I will have to stick close to you. How else will I keep you honest? And I would like to hear your conversations for myself. Perhaps some little tidbit will drop that would help point us in the right direction. I am very astute in detecting a lie.”

She was not certain she wanted Sir Andrew witnessing her inquiries. Somehow it seemed a betrayal of the confidences she was encouraging. Before she could express her concern, Sir Andrew took her arm and led her toward the sitting room.

"You can trust my discretion, Miss Wardlow. As you know, I have an abhorrence for meddling and never repeat anything I overhear, by accident or otherwise."

"But would you not rather be with your friends in the library? Surely they provide more compatible entertainments."

"I cannot think of more entertaining company than you, Miss Wardlow." His hand covered hers where it rested on his other arm and a shock of pleasure spiraled up her spine. "And I shall be at hand to discuss the results. I believe it was you who said we would have to work quickly."

She nodded, her skin warming beneath his touch. There seemed no solution but to allow him to come along.

Once the introductions were performed, Drew bowed and excused himself with the reason that he needed to catch up on his correspondence. He took several folded letters from the inside of his jacket and sat in a low overstuffed chair not far away from Misses Wardlow and Lindenhouse. To discourage interruptions, he kept his head down as if in study of the pile of letters in his lap.

Charity—he allowed himself to think of her in that way now that he'd decided to woo her—opened the conversation with a few innocuous observations of the festivities. Indeed, they seemed to agree on almost everything. When they arrived at the point at which men began—friends and acquaintances in common—he had to smile.

"Yes, Lady Auberville is a dear friend of mine. She and I have known each other from the schoolroom," Charity said.

"I was quite surprised when I heard that she and Auberville were married," Miss Lindenhouse admitted. "I knew her from Miss Smythe's Academy for Young Ladies, and she had always sworn that she would never marry. And by special license to one so proper as Auberville—well, you can imagine the amazement that caused!"

Charity laughed. "I can, indeed. Her dearest friends were caught by surprise as well. But the deed is done and she is quite content. More than content, I'd say. Lady Annica admitted it was a love match."

Miss Lindenhouse sighed and glanced down at her hands folded in her lap. "Is that not what we all would like, Miss Wardlow? And yet, how can one trust something so fickle as love?"

Drew saw Charity's chest rise in a deep breath and he knew she had decided that it was time to launch into her inquiry. She leaned closer to her companion and lowered her voice as she offered a handkerchief. Lord! It was the one he'd taken from Mackay's drawer. What a bold ploy. Would Miss Lindenhouse recognize it?

"I know your secret, Miss Lindenhouse. You may speak frankly with me."

"You know?" Miss Lindenhouse looked stricken. "But how?"

Charity shrugged. "People say things when they think no one is listening."

"But that means…he must have been talking about it."

Charity's brow creased in sympathy, as if she regretted causing Miss Lindenhouse distress. "M-more that he was muttering to himself," she said.

"Oh," Miss Lindenhouse sighed. "I suppose you think poorly of me now?"

"Not at all," Charity replied quickly. "We all make mistakes. I have made one very similar to yours."

Miss Lindenhouse's brown eyes grew round as she handed the handkerchief back. "You? With whom, Miss Wardlow?"

Charity's cheeks flushed crimson. To be caught in a lie?

Or because her confession held some truth? And what in heaven's name was she confessing to? Did she even know?

"With…with someone I had known for many years."

"Yes, familiarity is a great danger, is it not? There is something to be said for keeping one's distance and not allowing any familiarities before marriage. Once a door has been opened, it is difficult to shut."

"So you ended it?" Charity asked.

"Oh, yes. Once I realized Mr. Greene had cozened me, I had no choice. The consequences could be too grave."

"What consequences, Miss Lindenhouse?"

"Why, babies, of course."

Charity nodded sagely. "Ah, yes. So you had issue?"

Drew sat forward. Was it going to be this easy? Charity's line of questioning had been so smooth he hadn't seen it coming.

"Heavens, no! I ended it before it could come to that. But I have no doubt it would have. Even so, my innocence and his conscienceless behavior have compromised me beyond redemption. Who will want me now?"

"Now that you are no longer…"

"Precisely. I collect you were not quite so deceived as I and escaped irreparable damage?"

"No," Charity admitted, "I was not so deceived. Even so, Miss Lindenhouse, you must not give up hope. Surely there is a good man somewhere who—"

"No!" Miss Lindenhouse held up one hand in protest. "The experience so damaged my trust in the stronger sex that I want nothing further to do with them."

Drew could not help but admire Charity's ploy. She really was quite adept at questioning, and her instincts were unfailing. Perhaps she had not been boasting when she told him she'd had experience in investigations.

She cast him a covert glance before returning her attention to her companion. "Miss Lindenhouse, if you should ever, ah, require, well, justice, please call upon me back in London and we can discuss this further. For now, simply know that your secret is safe and will never be mentioned again unless you are the one to bring it up."

Charity started to rise, but Miss Lindenhouse took her hand. "Miss Wardlow, what was it that Mr. Greene was murmuring?"

She looked confused for a moment and Drew knew she was weighing her words for possible consequence. If she was smart, she would say nothing to encourage Miss Lindenhouse to renew her relationship with the cad, nor would she unnecessarily hurt the woman.

"Just that he should not have used you so poorly. It may be that he is afraid you will tell someone, for who will trust their daughters to him then? My advice is to say nothing to him and let him stew in his own juices. A fitting form of revenge, eh?"

The smile that spread over Miss Lindenhouse's rather plain face made her radiant. "Yes, indeed. Oh, that makes me feel ever so much better."

The thin winter sun slanted through the sitting-room window as Charity stood, setting a soft glow in her blond tresses and lighting her yellow gown like a torch. There was not a woman in the room who could hold a candle to Charity, and a fierce surprising stab of possessiveness swept over him.

"Well done, Miss Wardlow," Sir Andrew congratulated when he caught up to her in the hallway.

Charity sighed, regretting that there was no other way of collecting the information she needed to help Olivia. "I wish I did not have to resort to trickery."

"Would you rather stand at the dinner table and ask which one of the ladies present gave birth to Mackay's love child?"

The ridiculousness of such a thing made her laugh. "Of course not." Then she smiled at the reversal in Sir Andrew. Just yesterday he had been trying to persuade her to mind her own business, and today he was approving her methods.

He settled his hand at the back of her waist as he guided her toward the music room. The warmth and strength of his touch made her feel absurdly feminine. "Did you mean what you said to Miss Lindenhouse?" he asked.

"Every word," she admitted.

"Then you have had an experience similar to hers?"

"Oh, well, not that. Mr. Lingate would never take such liberties." Good heavens! Had that sounded as prudish as she thought? She looked up to see if Sir Andrew had noticed. He gave her an odd grin and his thumb stoked her spine. Chill bumps raised the fine hair on her neck. Pray he did not realize the devastating effect he had on her. "I, ah, meant that I would never breathe a word of her confidences, and that I did not think any the less of her for having been deceived."

He nodded. "I thought as much. That is very open-minded of you, Miss Wardlow, when the rest of society would condemn her as a loose woman. But I agree with you. Women are given an unfair burden where purity is concerned—an unfortunate result of men's inability to govern their own morally. My gender has little room to judge."

She nodded. "Lately I have begun to think that fewer women than one would suspect are…ah…"

"Virgins?" he supplied with a small smile.

"On their wedding nights," she finished, unable to meet his eyes for the indelicacy of their subject. "Perhaps more matches than one might think are made for expedience."

"And that shocks you?"

"No, Sir Andrew. Nor would I judge them." How could she when she had allowed Sir Andrew to kiss her in a manner so intimate that *she* had almost succumbed? "Indeed, I have recently…that is, I can only guess how deeply those emotions run. My hope is that they do not later regret acting on those feelings, as does Miss Lindenhouse. Such a thing may be of little consequence to a man, but it has life-altering consequences to a woman."

"Yes, regrets would be a great pity," Sir Andrew agreed. "But if such a thing was of little consequence to a man, he would be the wrong man to give such a gift."

Charity glanced up at Sir Andrew and did not miss the sympathy in his smile. For some unaccountable reason, she thought of Julius. Would *he* be the right man to give such a gift? Heaven help her, she had begun to wonder.

The music room was empty and she sighed with relief. She needed a moment to collect herself before making polite conversation again. She heard the click of the door closing as she sat on the piano bench and tickled the keys. Sir Andrew came to sit beside her and lifted her chin with one finger.

"Why so melancholy, Miss Wardlow. Is it Mr. Greene's behavior? Should I have a word with him?"

"That would be meddling, would it not?" she teased. "No, he must have no idea that Miss Lindenhouse has admitted to anything or he might begin to talk. Do not worry. We have ways of dealing with men like Mr. Greene."

"We?"

An unfortunate slip of the tongue. She could hardly admit to being a member of a group of avengers. "Women," she explained.

"I shall trust that," he said, leaning closer.

He was going to kiss her again. Mentally she tried to think where Julius was supposed to be. Not that she did not want him to discover her kissing Drew MacGregor. No, it was that she did not want him interrupting this time. She lifted her face to his, anxious for the bittersweet tingling his mouth evoked.

"Sweet Charity," he murmured against her lips. She shivered. Those two words had preceded both his kisses and she could not help but think of them as harbingers of bliss. She was already tingling with anticipation.

As sweet and evocative as his other kisses had been, this one was deeper, demanding, as if he had taken her measure and knew he could ask more of her. She parted her lips and let him in, meeting his heat with greedy need. She slid her arms upward, wrapping them around his neck and fondling the silky cool curl at his nape.

He sighed, pressing her closer along her spine, and pushed the bench away from the piano to pull her onto his lap. From that vantage, he nibbled at her earlobe, his breath hot and moist in her ear. She shivered again and a little moan slipped from somewhere deep inside her as she dropped her head back to offer her throat. Sir Andrew was coaxing the strangest, most tantalizing feeling from her and she wanted it to go on forever. Why was it that, once he had begun this sweet assault, she forgot everything else in her quest to find…what?

He accepted the invitation of her offered throat, leaving kisses and nibbles in a path to the hollow. There he rested his attention, seeming to savor the pounding of her pulse. Simultaneously, he ran one hand up her side and around. His fingers found the deepest part of her décolletage and worked inward to liberate one breast. She was dimly aware that her nipples had grown taut and ached for his touch, but when his mouth closed around her, she was deliciously shocked. Cupping his head, her fingers tangled in his hair, she tried to pull him closer, though nothing separated them now but their clothing.

As he repositioned her on his lap, she noted a firm pressure against the center of her sex. Oh! She wanted more of that, too. She wiggled to deepen the contact and Sir Andrew gasped. She drew apart from him to see if she had hurt him. His eyes were closed and a grim look hardened his features.

"Charity, if you do that again I will surely disgrace you." He opened his eyes, now as dark and turbulent as a midnight sea. "Go, if you do not want to suffer Miss Lindenhouse's fate."

She hesitated, uncertain if he was teasing her again or perfectly serious. When she did not move, he dropped his head to her breast and circled the nipple with his tongue. He bit lightly at the hardened nub and began to slide her gown up her legs.

Dear Lord! He'd been serious! Even as the sharp yearning returned, the short separation from his mouth had restored enough of her senses to bring her to her feet and propel her to the door. She hesitated there long enough to smooth her bodice and make certain everything was in place before turning the lock to make her escape.

His voice followed her out the door. "If you play with fire, Charity, you are going to get burned."

Chapter Six

Drew watched Charity descend the grand staircase to the sound of the dinner bell. She was wearing a soft pink confection with a puddle of a short train. The neckline was daringly low with a delicate narrow trimming of embroidered lace that barely saved her modesty. He knew Charity well enough by now to know that she had intended her gown to be provocative. It certainly provoked something primal in *him.*

Her hair had been done up to the crown, then fell in spiraling curls down her back, leaving that tempting neck bare. He wished to God she'd dressed for him, but her glance around the hall and her quick smile when her attention lit on Lingate told the tale. He squelched a stab of disappointment.

Perhaps he should not have warned her of his intentions this afternoon. When he'd locked the music-room door behind them, he'd fully intended to introduce Charity to the next level of sensualism, but after their discussion of Miss Lindenhouse, how could he prove himself to be as dishonorable as Mr. Greene? Oh, make no mistake, he wanted Charity Wardlow, and she was ripe and ready despite that she was a novice to real passion, but he would not take advantage of her innocence just to seduce her. She'd come to him fully mindful of what she was surrendering, or he would not take her at all.

Mackay's bride-to-be had shuffled the place cards again tonight, mixing the names to allow the guests to make new acquaintances. Was it coincidence that placed him across from Charity, or a little help from Mackay? She acknowledged him with an aloof nod and a blush. Her friend, Mrs. Forbush, was seated beside him and Julius Lingate was on her other side.

Conversation was innocuous enough with Grace Forbush introducing new topics the moment the current one grew stale. He took a moment to marvel at her social adroitness before he resolved to be difficult.

"Tell me, Miss Wardlow, have you enjoyed making new friends here in Oxfordshire?"

She seemed confused for a moment, then fastened him with a defiant look. "Indeed, Sir Andrew. And I have you to thank for it. You've been ever so accommodating."

He grinned. So, she intended to hold him accountable for her meddling. Very interesting. "And are you finding the… activities to your liking?"

Her color heightened further, but she could only stare at him. Unless he missed his guess, she knew he was referring to their kisses and the sweet little scene in the library mere hours ago. She opened her mouth and the tip of her tongue emerged to wet her lips, but she seemed incapable of speech.

A puzzled frown knit a fine line between Grace Forbush's elegantly arched eyebrows as she glanced between the two of them. "I understand there is to be dancing tonight, Sir Andrew. Will you stay for it, or return to your room in Great Tew?"

"Wouldn't miss it," he said, and grinned.

"And there is to be wassailing tomorrow night," Grace

continued, to cover the awkward pause. "I understand Lord Edward has had to hire sleighs from the town to carry us all. We are to end up on the village green and attend church services afterward."

"Sounds vastly entertaining," he commented blandly.

"Two nights after is the wedding eve."

"Christmas Eve, too, if I am not mistaken."

Grace nodded. She glanced around their immediate vicinity as if seeking help with the conversation. "I believe I've heard rumors that there is to be a Lord or Misrule at the feast. Is that not so, Charity?"

"I...I believe Olivia called it the Abbot of Unreason."

"'Tis the same thing in Scotland, is it not, Sir Andrew?"

He paused for a moment, just to see if Mrs. Forbush would leap into the gap again. Instead, her lips curled into a sly smile. She was on to him. "Aye. The same. Did Miss Fletcher say who would be the Abbot?"

"That is to be a surprise," Mrs. Forbush said. "But now I think I know who I will recommend." She turned to her right and smiled at a confused-looking Julius Lingate. "And you, Mr. Lingate? Are you enjoying yourself here in Great Tew?"

Lingate, immersed in a study of Charity's décolletage, looked as if he'd been caught thieving. "Me? Oh, I see. Yes, I hope to conclude a very important matter whilst I'm here." He gazed at Charity with calf eyes.

Charity smiled and blushed prettily, then looked down at her plate. Drew glowered at Lingate, hoping the man was wise enough to back off, but he doubted it. Men like Lingate were always so full of themselves that they thought everyone shared their own good opinion of them.

Was it true, then? Was Lingate preparing to propose to Charity despite her lack of a fortune? Had he decided her social consequence was enough to compensate for her poverty? Damned discerning of him if he had. And damned unfortunate, too, because Lingate was too late. He'd never have Charity. Drew mentally contemplated pushing the London dandy off the back of a sleigh tomorrow night. If he could wait that long.

Charity was in a fever by the time the orchestra struck the first tune in the upstairs ballroom. She glanced around, hoping to see Julius lurking, but he was already escorting Laura Tuxbury onto the dance floor. Well, she could be patient a little while longer.

Her nerves zinged with excitement. He had as good as announced his intentions at the dinner table. And then she recalled the dark look on Drew MacGregor's face. Her excitement evaporated and confusion set in. She had wanted Julius for what seemed her entire life. She had certainly looked no further than the end of her nose for the past five years. And then a dark-visaged Scot challenged her in a hallway and she was quickly forgetting everything else.

The man was insufferable. He was a rake and a tease. He was certainly a debauchee. But oh, what a debauchee! He could make her heart sing, her pulse throb, her spirits rise and her senses reel. But that was not the stuff of marriage.

Marriage was upbringing and experiences in common—it was being familiar and comfortable in each other's company, wanting the same things from life and knowing what the future would hold. It was being agreeable, safe and sensible. She closed her eyes to picture herself in London, married to Julius, keeping his house and awaiting the birth of his child.

A sharp and surprising stab of regret shot through her. Oh! It couldn't be! There was certainly nothing safe and sensible about her feelings for Drew MacGregor—nothing familiar or comfortable. She'd be insane to entertain the mere idea!

"Such a sultry look, Miss Wardlow. Dare I hope you are thinking of me?" Sir Andrew's deep, mocking voice whispered in her ear.

"Dare anything you please, Sir Andrew," she murmured, glancing around to be certain they were not overheard.

He grinned. "Then I think I shall dare a dance with you." He took her hand and pulled her to the dance floor, making refusal impossible without a scene.

Sir Andrew led her into the strains of a waltz, stepping into the rhythm without missing a step. He held her tight, his hand at the small of her back doing that odd little stroking move he had done that afternoon. She found herself relaxing, becoming fluid with his lead.

"So, has Mr. Lingate bent his knee to you yet?"

She smiled but refused to rise to the bait. "Were you trying to provoke me at dinner, Sir Andrew?" she asked.

"I own it," he admitted. "There you were, all moon-eyed over Lingate, and him such an undeserving lout. I could not help thinking what a waste you would be on one such as he."

She tilted her head back to look at his face. Was he serious? Or was he teasing again? There was no merry twinkle in his eyes, but a self-mocking smile on his lips. "I do not see men lined up for me, Sir Andrew. Am I better wasted wilting on the vine?"

He shook his head and laughed. "Are you really so blind? Or just so focused on Lingate that you cannot see what's in front of your face?"

"You exaggerate," she accused.

His hand tightened on hers and he held her a little closer.

"Close your eyes," he said as he led her into a turn. "Come now, I've got you. This should be interesting."

Unable to refuse his challenge without looking frightened, she closed her eyes. Following his lead when she was unable to see was a lesson in trust for her, and she gained a heightened appreciation of his strength and grace, the sureness of his step and his self-confidence. A man would not have that measure of certainty without good reason.

"Do not peek, Miss Wardlow," he said in a low voice. "Simply tell me what Lingate is wearing tonight."

"His…his green jacket?" she guessed, trying to picture him at the table.

Sir Andrew's laugh was smugly satisfied. "Wrong. Keep your eyes closed and I'll give you another chance. What are the decorations in the ballroom?"

"Potted palms? Um…hothouse flowers? Oh! Holly, of course."

"That was guessing, not recollection. Try telling me what Miss Lindenhouse was wearing this afternoon."

How odd. As vague as her other memories had been, Miss Lindenhouse was etched clearly in her mind. "A burgundy day dress trimmed in white ruching, a small gold heart pendant, a—"

"Exactly," he interrupted. "You see what you want to see, Miss Wardlow, and you stopped seeing Lingate the day you decided he was what you wanted. You have not wasted another moment examining your choice or confirming your original opinion."

Could that be true? Could she have been so single-minded that simple truths had escaped her?

The music grew distant and Sir Andrew stopped abruptly. "Open your eyes and tell me what you see."

She looked about, feeling slightly disoriented. They were no longer in the ballroom but in the gallery overlooking the great hall. "I see the stairway swagged with garlands. I see holly and bows. I see—" she looked up into his eyes "—you."

"Look up, sweet Charity."

Sweet Charity. Her knees grew weak even before she lifted her chin to look toward the ceiling. There, as bold as you please, hung a hoop of evergreens woven with mistletoe, holly and red and white ribbons rippling softly in the air current. Pears, apples and lighted candles encircled the hoop.

"A kissing bough," she whispered.

He smiled. "There may be hope for you after all."

He bent and deposited a kiss so soft and gentle that Charity had the impression it was almost more a thought than a deed. Oh, but when he deepened the kiss she felt his warmth seep downward all the way to her toes. He pressed her close and straightened, lifting her feet off the ground. She relaxed against his surrounding arms, trusting that he would not disgrace her in so public a place. She raised both her arms to circle his neck, afraid she would collapse in a boneless puddle if she did not hold on for dear life.

An amused masculine voice penetrated the fog in her brain. "Well, look who's been caught under the kissing bough."

Sir Andrew released her slowly, allowing her to gain her footing before leaving her unsupported. "You've got the devil's own timing, Mackay," he said.

Their host was grinning at them, Olivia on his arm. "Give someone else a chance," he said with a glance down at his bride-to-be.

Sir Andrew laughed, relinquishing their spot beneath the kissing bough. Before she could escape to the ballroom,

Mackay caught Olivia up in his arms and pressed a heartrending passionate kiss on her. She gave him a shaky sigh when he let her go.

"Only two more days, Edward. Surely you can wait that long," she whispered as a blush stole up her cheeks.

"Do not test me," he teased. He smoothed a tendril of Olivia's hair back from her cheek with exquisite gentleness.

The affection in his gaze nearly broke Charity's heart. His love was so plain to see—and Olivia's return of that love was just as obvious—that she suddenly doubted her mission. How could a man who loved so deeply keep secrets from the woman he worshiped? Could she have been wrong in believing the worst of Lord Edward Mackay?

She found Sir Andrew beside her as she rushed to return to the ballroom. "Were you upset by Miss Fletcher's reference to the wedding night?" he asked.

Terribly upset, she thought, and *envious!* In all her years of waiting for Julius to propose, in all the scenes she had played in her mind about their wedding, she had never once contemplated their wedding night. His kisses had inspired none of the wild longing she felt in Sir Andrew's arms. His cautious, patient wooing was a poor substitute for Sir Andrew's breathtaking seduction. Oh, but she'd eat worms before she'd tell Sir Andrew that. He loved being right far too much.

"Not at all, Sir Andrew. I am, after all, a woman of the world. And I'd prefer you didn't escort me back to the ballroom. I would not want Julius to think I've been up to something shady."

He laughed. "Even if you have? Very well, then. 'Tis time for me to retire to my room in the village. I shall be a little late in coming tomorrow. I have some business matters to conclude and I may have to go to Banbury. Time is short, so please continue without me, Miss Wardlow. You can catch me up on the investigation at luncheon."

He gave her a polite bow and disappeared, leaving her alone and more confused than ever.

"I say, Miss Wardlow, we are having a deuced difficult time finding a private moment together, are we not?" Julius Lingate commented halfway through their dance.

Charity tried without success to muster a measure of her old excitement at the prospect of spending a private moment with Julius. "There are so many activities planned for us, and so many other guests, it is easy to become lost in the crowd," she returned noncommittally.

"Yes, I daresay I have seldom been in such congenial company. With the possible exception of Andrew MacGregor. I've noted the attention he pays you, Miss Wardlow."

"You do not like Sir Andrew?" she asked, her interest piqued.

"I do not know the man well enough to dislike him," Julius admitted. "His reputation is good enough—the fact that he is to stand up with Mackay is proof of that. But he is not a respecter of other men's property."

"Indeed? Has he taken something of yours, Mr. Lingate."

"Would if he could," Julius grumbled.

She was on the verge of asking him what he could possibly have that Sir Andrew would want when the obvious occurred to her. She felt the heat rise in her cheeks and looked toward the sidelines where Grace was regarding her with interest. Good heavens! Had *everyone* seen the byplay?

"Here now, Miss Wardlow, do not overset yourself. No one blames you."

"There is no blame to be had," she snapped.

"Well, never mind, my dear. There's nothing gone on that cannot be remedied," he said with a smile. "And since we seem to be alone for the moment, could you spare me half an hour in Mackay's library?"

This was it, then. The moment that Julius would declare for her. The moment she had planned and waited for. The *Yes, darling Julius,* she had rehearsed for years stuck in her throat and she felt like a hunted animal. "Ah, this would not be a good time, Mr. Lingate. I, um, Grace is waiting for me," she gestured to her friend near the ballroom doors. "Perhaps we shall find a moment tomorrow?"

"Yes. Tomorrow, then. I shall look for you near midday."

Relief flooded through her. By tomorrow she would have had time to think and sort through the confusing jumble of emotions. Surely by tomorrow she'd know what she wanted.

Chapter Seven

Charity seized the opportunity to question Leticia Evans the next morning. She'd known Letty, a pretty dark blonde with huge gray eyes, for years and couldn't picture her having anyone's love child. She was painfully shy, and she simply didn't seem the type. Still, she had disappeared for several months a few years ago, saying she'd been recuperating from an illness in the country. She could have been lying-in for the birth of Mackay's illegitimate issue.

"Letty!" she called after the girl as she hurried along the corridor. "Wait. We haven't had a chance to visit."

The girl turned around and smiled at Charity. "Yes, let's catch up," she agreed. "Come walk with me. I swear I am feeling confined by these walls and the weather. Olivia said the barometer is dropping and yet another storm is coming. I'd like to stretch my legs before another round of confinement."

Charity followed Letty to the cloakroom near the kitchen to retrieve their woolen coats and bonnets.

"I hope the storm will not set in before the wassailing tonight," Charity said as they trudged along a forest path. She tried to ignore the freezing cold seeping through the soles of her satin slippers and wished she'd paused long enough to don her woolen socks and warm boots.

"Oh, so do I! There is nothing more disheartening than to be stuck with yawning bores…oh, I do not mean you, of course," Letty said, looking embarrassed.

"I know just what you mean, Letty." She hastened to put her companion at ease. "Indeed, I think we have more than you might imagine in common."

"Really? That would please me very much indeed. I have long admired you and your bluestocking group—such intelligent ladies. Perhaps someday you will invite me to join you?"

"Perhaps," Charity hedged. But the circumstances would have to be unusual. Otherwise Letty Evans would never know the bluestocking group was really a collection of ladies secretly avenging wrongs done to other women.

"It was so kind of Olivia to include me on her guest list," Letty sighed. "I do so love weddings."

"They are fun, are they not? I have heard that more than marriages are made at weddings," Charity ventured.

"What could that mean?"

"Why…alliances of other kinds, Letty. Discreet alliances."

Letty colored deeply when she realized what Charity was alluding to. "Oh, I see. Well, such alliances are not for me."

Charity allowed the moment to draw out before replying. "I know your secret, Letty."

"My secret? *What* secret?"

"The one about, well, you-know-who. I will not speak his name aloud lest someone overhear."

Letty peered through the trees. "Who would overhear?"

"Never mind, Letty. I only wanted you to know that I know, in the event that you'd like to discuss it."

A long silence ensued. Charity knew there would be a

piece of information forthcoming by the way Letty chewed her lower lip. She had the look of someone making a difficult decision.

"Well, yes. I suppose it might be a relief to say it aloud. But how did you find out?"

"Observation." Charity sighed ruefully, recalling how completely *unobservant* she had been where her own affairs were concerned.

"Has it been so obvious?"

"Only to me, Letty, because I know you."

The girl nodded and pushed her hands into her coat pockets. "I pray *he* does not know. I do not think I could stand that. I have loved him for so long, and Olivia has been so kind to me."

Charity's heartbeat quickened. Here it was at last! Letty loved Mackay and felt as if her love—and her baby—were betrayals of Olivia's trust. That may be why she had threatened to tell.

"Do you really think he does not know?" she asked. How could Mackay not know of his love child, especially if Letty was now blackmailing him?

"I do not see how he could." Letty sighed. "I've told no one. That is the nature of a secret crush, is it not—that it goes forever unknown and unrequited?"

Secret crush? "How long have you loved him, Letty?"

"Since I first lay eyes on him. I must have been ten and one. He came to my father's country house to buy a mare for breeding. He had such a booming, merry laugh that I fell in love instantly. But he does not know I exist. He never has. I knew that someday he would find someone as beautiful and deserving as Olivia, and I am truly happy for them. 'Tis just so…"

"Bittersweet?" Charity guessed.

"Exactly. I wish them both well, but there will be a piece of my heart missing now, and I shall never be whole again."

"Yes, Letty, you will." Charity smiled, understanding at last. "When you finally let go of something that could never have really made you content, you will find your true happiness. After you dance at Lord Edward's wedding and wish him well, something real and infinitely better will come your way."

Letty stopped and threw her arms around Charity in a heartfelt hug. "Oh, Charity. Thank you. That was just what I needed to hear."

A fire was crackling on the hearth in the small sitting room, and Charity sank into the plush overstuffed chair pulled before the fire. She rested her feet on the little footstool and sighed with relief. Her slippers were soaked and her toes were so cold she could scarcely wiggle them.

Though the slippers were ruined, she hadn't had time to change them after returning from her walk with Letty Evans. The luncheon bell had rung as they came in from the cold. Giggling conspiratorially, they'd hurried to find their places before being unforgivably late. She'd glanced around the dining room and felt a prick of disappointment when she'd found no sign of Sir Andrew. His business in Banbury must have delayed him.

Intending to rest just a moment and then go to her room to change her shoes and stockings, she had left the sitting-room door ajar. A timid knock took her by surprise.

"Miss Wardlow? Charity?" Julius whispered, peeking around the panel.

"Come in, Mr. Lingate," she invited, wishing she could delay this interview a little longer. She'd tossed and turned all night, or at least until Grace shook her to interrupt her nightmares.

"Ah, we are alone," Julius observed. "Excellent. At last we can have our little chat."

She smiled wanly. Where was the excitement she felt whenever she thought of this moment? Yesterday she would have said *Yes, yes and yes.* Today she did not know what she would say when he uttered his proposal. She needed more time to think, but she feared she had just run out.

Julius came to prop his elbow on the mantel and affect a posture of bored elegance. "Cozy little room, eh?"

"Yes, indeed," she said, tucking her feet beneath the hem of her gown. She would have to warm her feet later.

"Well, ah, you are aware that I've had something I wish to discuss with you? Yes? Well, I've come to a point in my life where 'tis time to settle my future. The decisions have been extremely difficult and my father has deigned to guide me." He paused to take a deep breath, as if he were in a rush to get the words out. "Though they are not everything I had hoped, they allow for a certain…comfort, if you will. I hope you will consider the offer I am about to make you most seriously, Miss Wardlow, because my affection for you is—"

"Kiss me, Julius," she said impulsively.

"Eh?"

She studied him, aware that she was frowning. Had Julius always been so silly? So superficial? Had Sir Andrew been right, and had she stopped really *seeing* Julius the day she had made up her mind to marry him? "I would like you to kiss me," she repeated. She stood to make the maneuver easier for him.

"Egad," he muttered under his breath. "This is going better than I expected." He advanced on her and drew her into his arms.

She lifted her hands to rest upon his shoulders, aware for the first time of how awkward he seemed with passion. She tilted her head to him and parted her lips slightly, hoping for something more than the quick, almost embarrassed, kisses he was accustomed to giving her.

"Egad," he sighed again before clasping his arms around her. No tight-lipped kiss this time! He opened his mouth and fastened it to hers with such sudden ardor that her inner lip split against her teeth and she tasted a drop of blood. Good heavens! Julius was a clumsy lover!

She applied pressure to his shoulders, trying to ease him away without hurting his feelings. He held her fast, and all the more so as she tried to push him away. She finally turned her head, ending the ill-fated kiss.

"What a tempting little tease you are, Miss Wardlow," he chortled. "When I have you all for myself—"

The sound of someone clearing his throat drew their attention to the door. Sir Andrew stood there, a sardonic expression on his handsome face.

Drew hadn't realized he could be so deeply injured by a kiss. He'd been passing the door when he'd heard Charity inviting Lingate to kiss her. It was all he could do to allow that kiss to happen when every instinct he had demanded that he put his fist through Lingate's face.

And the worst of it was, he knew Charity hadn't responded to Lingate as she responded to him—yet she'd given herself to Lingate without hesitation.

The look on her face when she'd turned to see him in the doorway was one of embarrassment mingled with relief. She appeared so forlorn that he decided to extend an excuse and see if she would use it. "I beg your pardon," he said with every appearance of regret, "I believe we were paired for whist this afternoon, Miss Wardlow. If you've changed your mind about joining the game—"

"No!" she said, stepping away from Lingate. "I have been looking forward to it all day."

Lingate frowned. "But we have not finished our conversation, Miss Wardlow."

Drew smiled. Either she had developed an affection for him or she was deucedly anxious to be rid of Lingate. He suspected the latter.

"Later, Mr. Lingate. I promise," she said. "Certainly by tomorrow we shall find some time to discuss it."

"Very well, then." He bowed and exited the room, brushing by Drew with a hint of challenge.

How amusing. Did the little twit think he could best him? But never mind. He'd attend to Lingate later. Other things were more important at the moment. He leaned back against the door until he heard the soft click of the latch catching, then went forward, studying Charity's face. Her lower lip was swollen and she looked a little bewildered. If Lingate had damaged her...

"There is no game of whist, is there?" she asked.

He grinned. "Shall we drum one up?"

"I'd rather sit by the fire. I haven't been warm since my walk with Miss Evans this morning." She returned to the chair by the fire and put her feet on the footstool. "Did you conclude your business in town, Sir Andrew?"

He nodded, thinking of the little trinket he'd had to go to Banbury to purchase, there being no jeweler in Great Tew. "So you talked with Leticia Evans this morning? Did she have a secret?"

"Yes." Charity bowed her head and studied her fingernails. "But it did not involve a love child."

There was something interesting here. "And?"

"Do you think there is any harm in a crush, Sir Andrew?"

He came around her chair and added more wood to the fire. "None, unless someone would be hurt by it."

"What if no one knew?"

"Then who could it harm?"

She nodded pensively. "I agree, but I have begun to doubt my own judgment."

Now this *was* interesting. He sat on an edge of the footstool and frowned. "When did that happen, Miss Wardlow?"

"When..." She looked at him and a pretty pink stained her cheeks. "When I left the house this morning without my boots."

He smiled at her discomfort. If he knew her at all, she'd begun to doubt herself when he'd challenged her last night beneath the kissing bough. Still, he looked down at her feet and was surprised to see that her slippers were sodden. Without asking permission, he unbuttoned the tiny pearls that secured the straps, pulled the shoes off and placed them by the fire. "Being dry should help, sweet Charity."

She blinked but her focus did not waver. He lifted one foot to rest on his knee and ran his hand up her leg beneath her gown. She caught her breath but said nothing. When he found the ribbon of her garter, he tugged until it gave way, then ran his hand slowly around her inner thigh to find the rear garter and do the same. He clenched his jaw to resist the temptation to allow his hand to linger at the heat between her thighs and perhaps wander just a little higher. Her breasts rose and fell rapidly as her breathing sped with her pulse. Lord, but she was responsive.

Slowly, savoring the experience, he rolled the freed stocking down her thigh, over her slender calf, and off her chilled foot. He dropped it on the hearth beside her slipper and began chafing her foot to warm it. Her feet were small and perfectly formed, with high arches and well-shaped toes. "Pretty feet," he commented evenly.

She blinked again and cleared her throat. "I…I should go to my room, Sir Andrew."

"Half-shod?" He shook his head. "And can you not learn to call me Drew?"

Her lips parted as if she would say his name, but she caught her breath again as he removed her other shoe and began the exquisite journey up her leg. Her eyes did not leave him, and there was something wildly erotic about watching each other while his hand made that agonizingly long, slow journey.

He grew uncomfortably hard. Lord, how he wanted to watch her every expression, her every reaction, as he took her and taught her to surrender to the pleasure. But not yet. Not here. He unfastened the front garter and slid his hand between her thighs again. Her muscles quivered beneath his fingers and her eyelashes fluttered.

Bracing his knee on the footstool, he rose to cover her mouth with his, hoping to forestall her protest. He ran his tongue along the seam of her lips, and slid his hand the rest of the way up her leg. When he stroked his thumb up the cleft that shielded her sex, she gasped and her eyelids flew open wide.

"Shh," he urged. "I'll be done in a moment." But he had no intention of hurrying this. She was ready—more than ready—for this. He took intense satisfaction in the feel of her, the slick heat at the entrance of her passage and the little mewling sounds she made when aroused.

She swallowed hard, her gaze holding his again.

With his thumb, he found the hard little nub that was the core of her arousal. Simultaneously, he slipped his middle finger to her opening. He made a shallow entry and pressed lightly upward.

"Oh!" Charity gasped.

Her knuckles turned white where they grasped the arms of

the chair. Lord, how he longed to be inside her, watch her cheeks flush from his lovemaking, feel her warmth close around his shaft as he buried himself inside her. *Soon,* he promised himself. *Soon.*

Her eyes had grown dark as her pupils dilated with passion. Her tongue wet her lips and Drew could not tell if that was a nervous reaction or an invitation. If it was an invitation, he dared not take it. He was already on edge. The least little provocation would destroy his self-control and he was painfully aware that the door was closed but not locked.

He continued his rhythmic stroking, increasing the depth of his entry in small measures. When her breathing became ragged and erratic, he deepened the pressure of his thumb. She arched her throat and moaned as pleasure swept over her, her muscles convulsing around his fingers. He kissed her and murmured endearments, stroking lightly now, ever slower, until her gasps softened to sighs.

With profound regret, he withdrew his hand, unfastened her rear garter, and began to roll her stocking downward. Charity sat mute and limp, her hands in her lap, as he chafed her foot to restore the circulation.

Not trusting himself not to ravish her, he stood and stepped back. "Warm enough yet, sweet Charity?" he asked with a grin as he retreated to the door.

Would she be angry with him and declare that she hated him or swear that she loved only Lingate? Would she call him well-deserved names and accuse him of being a libertine?

She covered her mouth to muffle a giggle. "Quite warm, thank you."

What an unexpectedly saucy wench she was! It was all he could do to close that door and keep walking.

Chapter Eight

A footman helped Charity and Grace down from the sleigh at their first stop at the Lord Mayor's house. Charity had worn her red wool coat trimmed in white fur and carried her white fur muff. She also wore her warmest stockings and boots. There would be no repeat of this afternoon. Just the thought of that had her aching for Drew's touch again. Was he some wizard who had cast a spell on her? Everything was so confused in her mind that she vowed to stay away from him until she could think clearly.

She glanced around as the other sleighs arrived and deposited their occupants. Julius waved to her from a small group of his friends and she gave a listless acknowledgment. Oh, dear. What was she going to do about him? She used to live in happy expectation of his declaration, and she now lived in dread. She was finding it nearly impossible to let go of her dream. She was not at all sure she could.

And there, stepping down from yet another sleigh was Andrew MacGregor. No boyish wave, just a slow, knowing smile that started a burning deep inside her. He looked as if he were going to come over to their group, but Lord Edward shouted and gestured him over to a small circle of men. He gave her a regretful smile that said he would look for her later. She sighed. And what, dear heavens, was she going to do about *him?*

How could things that had been so clear mere days ago be so muddy now? She couldn't believe the change just three days had wrought in her life. She had arrived at Wyecliffe Manor a rather prim little miss with her heart on her sleeve for a young man she'd known half her life. But since Drew MacGregor's arrival, she was considerably wiser and close to surrendering herself to a man she'd known two and a half days all told. And all without mention of love, a future or a commitment.

Make no mistake—he was seducing her, conditioning her to respond with no more than two simple words. All he needed to say was *Sweet Charity* and she was pulsating for his touch. She was mortified that he had such power over her, and that he knew it. It was a dark, erotic secret between them, and it was almost unbearably intimate.

Seeking to break her brooding mood, she glanced around to get her bearings. A group of women who had been among the first to arrive were standing in a tight little circle speaking in whispered tones and looking toward Edward Mackay's group. A moment later, a peel of laughter rose from their circle. They had turned their backs on Miss Foley, a sweet-natured, soft-spoken young woman with a pleasant but plain face. There had been something deliberately exclusive about the way the other women had turned their backs on Miss Foley that angered Charity. She and Grace started forward as if of one mind, but before they could arrive, Andrew MacGregor called out.

"Miss Foley," he said in a raised voice, gesturing her over to his group of mostly men. "Will you consent to lend your voice to ours? Without you I fear we shall all sing off-key."

Grace opened her mouth to issue her own invitation, but Charity silenced her with a wave. "No, Grace. 'Tis better this way," she said, fighting down a twinge of jealousy. "Now Miss Foley will be the envy of all."

"Very generous of you, Charity, given that I collect you are growing fonder of Sir Andrew by the moment." Grace smiled and winked. "Shall we join Olivia's group?"

"Go on without me. I shall be along in a few moments."

She watched Sir Andrew a little longer, noting how kindly he treated Miss Foley and how deliberately he flaunted her before her peers. The girl glowed with shy pleasure. Charity knew how it felt to fall outside the bounds of society. Oh, she was accepted by virtue of her good birth, but when her father's fortune failed, she learned very quickly who her friends were and how such a thing could taint acceptability.

She sighed, squared her shoulders and went to stand beside Miss Lucinda Matthews. "We have not found time to chat since you arrived, Miss Matthews. When was the last time we talked?"

"Last spring?" Miss Matthews ventured. "We discussed the virtues of waltzing over a reel, if I recall."

Charity laughed. "I hope I did not shock you, but it is ever so much easier to talk to your partner when not separated by other dancers."

"I quite agree." Miss Matthews smiled. "And it would take much more than that to shock me."

"Yes, I would imagine." Charity affected a look of world-weary sophistication. "We are both too wise for our years, I think. That is why I can tell you that I know your secret."

"Ah," she said with a sage nod. "And I know yours."

Charity thought nothing could surprise her after the past few days, but this left her speechless. "Mine?"

"'Tis fairly plain to anyone with eyes in their head."

What could the woman be talking about? "You must tell me how I betrayed myself, Miss Matthews."

"It is not something you can control, Miss Wardlow. Love shines out."

Love, was it? Had Miss Matthews seen the way she looked at Julius? How she found occasions to meet with him, talk to him, touch him? And if she had seen it, who else might have seen it? She groaned. "Am I a laughingstock? Are people talking?"

"Not at all. 'Tis so recent that I do not imagine many have had the opportunity to notice."

"Recent?"

"Yes, and I must say I am glad. I never thought Julius Lingate was the man for you. Not enough depth, my dear."

Heavens! Miss Matthews was talking about Sir Andrew MacGregor! "I am an absolute idiot," she muttered.

Miss Matthews laughed. "Never say so. 'Twas *coup de foudre,* my dear. The thunderbolt. It often takes the brain several days to catch up to the body."

Yes, she'd agree that her body was well ahead of her mind. It was true, then—that niggling suspicion that she'd have to refuse Julius.

"I wonder, Miss Wardlow, what you will do with *my* secret."

"Oh, um, that depends, Miss Matthews." On whatever the secret was. She liked Miss Matthews, and she hoped the girl was not the mother of Mackay's baby. She withdrew the handkerchief from her muff and pretended to dab at the corner of her eye, but she could not discern any flicker of recognition.

"How did you discover what I'd done? Did you see me putting it outside his door?"

Heavens, had she left the baby outside Mackay's door?

There was nothing for it but to bluff. "Yes. I must say that I was quite surprised."

"I hope you will consider keeping the secret. The world would not end if you told, but I'd prefer to remain anonymous."

"Anonymous?" she repeated.

"Certainly. Mr. Fredrickson would consider it charity, and I would not embarrass him for all the world. If he should see pity in my gesture or some implied criticism, it would make our friendship very awkward. The same could be said if he misread my intent as affection."

Completely bewildered, Charity nodded. "M-may I ask what it was?"

"A new cravat along with the latest book on stylish knots. He is always fiddling with his cravat, especially after a spirited dance, and his knots are…shall we say abominable? I hope the instructions will help."

"But why Mr. Fredrickson, if you have no particular affection for him?"

"He is a very kind man, Miss Wardlow. He does not have a valet to attend these matters for him, and he deserves better than to be laughed at behind his back."

Charity smiled and squeezed Miss Matthew's arm as the sound of voices raised in a carol beckoned them to the task. "I shall never say a word," she promised.

"How long have you known?" Charity asked Grace the next morning.

Grace continued brushing her glossy dark hair. "I think from the day he arrived. There was an excitement to your step that I hadn't seen before, and a saucy lift to your chin. I must say, dear, love becomes you."

"But I love Julius."

"You are infatuated with the *idea* of Julius," Grace contradicted. "I wonder how much longer you will allow him to waste your time."

"I hate it when you are so right," she complained. "Why did you not tell me?"

"Would you have listened?"

"No, but that is beside the point."

Grace stood from the dressing table and tightened the sash of her dressing gown. "More importantly, Charity, what will you do about it now?"

Charity slipped her willow-green gown over her head and turned her back for Grace to button. "What *can* I do? It isn't as if Sir Andrew has declared himself. I sometimes think he barely suffers me. We are at odds on so many things, and even our friendship, if you can call it that, began with an argument and a challenge."

"Yes. I am glad you finally told me what you've been up to. I was beginning to wonder what was taking so much of your time. And time is growing short. There is only today and tomorrow, then the wedding day. How many women do you still have to interview?"

"Two. Laura Tuxbury and Lydia Foley."

"Lydia? The same Lydia that Sir Andrew befriended last night? Can you be serious?"

"Her name begins with *L* and there is no one else left that we have not investigated. I cannot believe it is either of them, but who else remains?"

"Someone unknown to you. Someone not on the guest list. Have you taken the handkerchief to the linen merchant in the village to see if he recognizes it? The Mackays have made their home here for many years. It is not beyond imagining that Edward might have dallied with one of the local girls."

"That is an excellent idea, Grace. I shall walk to the village to make inquiries directly after lunch."

"Leave Lydia Foley to me, Charity. Now that I know what you're up to, I want to help. Oh, and dress warm, dear. The temperature is dropping."

Charity glanced helplessly up and down the deserted street. All her careful plans were falling apart. She had been almost to the village when great huge flakes of snow began to fall in such a thick curtain that she could scarcely see her hand in front of her face.

The villagers were saying it was the worst storm they had seen this early in the season. Most merchants closed shop early and hurried home for the day, including the linen dealer. She'd made the long walk for nothing. There was no place she could take refuge in such a small village, and the last wagon that passed Wyecliffe Manor had departed hours ago. Unless the snow relented, she was stuck.

There were no rooms available at the local inn, the Falkland Arms. The innkeeper had doubled and tripled guests, and there was simply no more space. He sent inquiries to a local family requesting lodgings, but they responded that their homes were full to bursting. The innkeeper told her she could spend the night in the public room, though he recommended against it. The crowd would be mostly male and very rough, he warned.

There was nothing for it but to trudge back to Wyecliffe Manor in the storm. In all the confusion of guests and activities, only Grace would miss her, and she would be beside herself if Charity was not home by dark. She was heading into the storm this time, and she fastened her bonnet tightly and tucked her hands as deeply as she could inside her muff.

She had to be back by morning. Tomorrow she had the final fitting for her bridesmaid gown, the arrangement of the hothouse flowers and the preparation of the Christmas Eve feast that night. In addition, it would be her last opportunity to interview Laura Tuxbury.

Depending on her findings, she would need to have a long talk with Olivia and disclose the information she'd been able to gather thus far. Once disclosed, she would still urge Olivia to go through with the marriage. She could not doubt Mackay's love for Olivia after seeing them beneath the kissing bough.

Not half a mile outside the village, she knew she'd made a mistake. Better the hearth at the Falkland Arms than frozen on the road. The large, heavy flakes turned to water when they melted against her face and clothing, and she was beginning to feel the chill all the way to the bone.

As she debated the wisdom of turning back, she heard the sound of hooves muffled by the blanket of snow. A moment later, a huge chestnut stallion reared before her and she lost her footing, tumbling to the side of the road as she tried to scurry out of the way. She was still brushing the snow off her face when a strong arm lifted her to her feet.

"Well met, Miss Wardlow. I thought I'd have to knock on doors to find you. What are you doing out here? Have you not the good sense to come in out of the weather?"

Relief made her weak and she sagged against him. "Sir Andrew, thank heavens. I feared you might be a highwayman."

He laughed. "Even highwaymen respect the weather. When Mrs. Forbush told me you'd gone to town, I was appalled. She assured me you did not know how severe the storm would be."

"Oh, dear. Is she worried?"

He brushed the snow from her cloak and righted her fur-trimmed bonnet. "I promised her I would find lodgings for you."

"A premature promise," she said. "There are no lodgings to be had, save for the public room at the Falkland Arms. That is why you find me on the road. I could not even find anyone I knew to prevail upon. Could you take me back to Wyecliffe Manor or lend me your horse?"

"You're daft," he said, lifting her off her feet. "It took me an hour and a half to come this far. We would both freeze before we could get to Wyecliffe. No, it's back to Great Tew for us."

"Very well," she consented as he put her in the saddle and swung up behind her. "But I shan't be responsible if I come away swearing like a soldier and smelling like stale ale."

"And you're mad if you think I'd leave you in the common room," he grumbled. "I have comfortable accommodations."

The horse set off at slow but steady pace and Charity relaxed against the broad, warm chest at her back. "The innkeeper said he had doubled and tripled the guests."

"Not me, Miss Wardlow, unless you count doubling my rate."

"Do you propose to sneak me up the back stairs?"

"There's only one staircase. We shall have to brazen it out."

Chapter Nine

"Why in blazes did you not think to ask for me by name?" Sir Andrew asked Charity as the innkeeper stood by.

Unprepared for this tactic, Charity batted her eyelashes. "I did not think of it, sir."

"Women." He exchanged a telling glance with the innkeeper.

She was not going to let him get away with making her look like a simpleton. "Why did *you* not tell the innkeeper you were expecting your wife? Last time you did not leave word for me, I found a tart in your bed. How was I to know—"

"Never mind. I've found you now and I think you will thaw satisfactorily." He grinned and turned back to the innkeeper. "Could you send up some bread, cheese and wine for me? A little eggnog for the wife, if you wouldn't mind, along with a hot bath and fresh towels."

He dropped a few coins on the counter—more than the items cost, Charity was certain—and took her by the arm. He led her up the narrow winding staircase and to the end of the second-floor hall. She should have been shocked to the core, but all she could do was try to muffle her laughter. When he unlocked his door, she hesitated.

"Come now, Miss Wardlow. You'll find no tart in my bed. Too late for maidenly modesty now. And if we do not get you out of that sodden stuff and warm soon, you'll have pneumonia."

A gentle nudge at the small of her back propelled her across the threshold into a charming little room with a canopy bed and a fire on the hearth. The room smelled of spice and citrus, like Sir Andrew's coat. A heavy mound of snow had piled against the panes of a mullioned window with heavy draperies that looked out on the green where the snowfall deepened. A single chair sat in front of a side table, where a tiny box wrapped in gaily colored paper sat. Everything was quite charming—and tantalizingly indecent.

"It is unseemly of me to be here, Sir Andrew." She dropped her muff on a chair and turned to face him.

"What a difficult choice. Unseemly or dead? Hmm? Which would I choose?"

The wretch was making light of her dilemma. "I should go downstairs."

"And be raped in your sleep? Or have your throat slit for your purse?"

He was exaggerating, of course, but he had a point. She glanced at the small straight-backed chair where she'd dropped her muff. Perhaps she could sleep sitting up if she rested her head on the little table beside it. Perhaps not. She looked up and smiled. "Then *you* should go downstairs."

He laughed. "Not a chance, sweet Charity. I am enjoying this too much."

Sweet Charity? Warning bells went off in her head and she began to tingle all over. "I can see that," she said. "But why?"

"Secrets, m'dear. Now you and I have one, don't we? What lengths might you go to in order to keep such a secret? Will you lie to your Julius?"

Her Julius? Then he hadn't guessed? Before she could reply, a soft knock announced the innkeeper, who brought in a small hip bath and two large towels. His wife followed, carrying two large buckets of steaming water.

"You can cool it with snow from the ledge," he told them as he shut the door.

Sir Andrew lifted her cloak and bonnet away and hung them on a peg behind the door. "Better hurry if you want warm water," he said.

Then the obvious occurred to her. "This is absurd. I cannot disrobe. What will I wear until my things dry?"

He took a deep maroon velvet robe from the clothes press and dropped it on the foot of the bed, then crossed his arms and grinned at her.

"Will...will you wait downstairs?"

"You are determined to ruin my fun. Are you certain you do not need help?" he asked.

"Positive," she vowed.

How bloody long did a woman need to take a bath, Drew wondered. Longer than two glasses of port? He intercepted the innkeeper's wife heading for the staircase with the tray of food he'd requested. She'd added a pear and an apple to his order and he gave her an extra coin. He took the tray—with instructions that they did not want to be disturbed.

After a soft knock, he unlocked the door and let himself in. Charity was standing by the window draped in his deep maroon dressing robe and her clothing was hung from various pegs and hooks to dry. She was so swaddled that all he could make out were those slender ankles and feet on one end and the mass of blond hair pinned to the top of her head on the other. Ah, but she'd left that slender neck bare and vulnerable.

He was seized of a possessiveness so fierce that it hit him like a blow to his gut. He placed the tray on the table and carried her eggnog to her. "Hungry, Miss Wardlow?"

She turned to him and he drew in a long breath. Free of the artifice of fashion and society, she was even more stunning. Her eyes were soft and luminous. Only her fingertips peeked out from the sleeves of his robe, and she smelled of his soap instead of her own sweet perfume. Having her in his room, seeing her like this, was so *right* that he realized he would stop at nothing to have her.

She gave him a shy smile and took the offered cup. "Thank you, Sir Andrew." She sipped and then sat on the narrow window seat, cupping the mug between her hands. "I've been thinking of a likely story to hide our secret. I shall tell anyone who asks that I passed the night in the common room."

"As long as we are lying, can we not make *me* sound more chivalrous? Shall we say *I* spent the night in the common room?"

She giggled. Drew usually had little patience for gigglers. But when Charity giggled, it was not of nervousness, a social affectation or silliness. It was an expression of sheer enjoyment. The little minx was having fun in spite of herself.

He sat beside her and rolled her sleeves up several times until her hands were completely exposed. "I had hoped I would make a better fit for you, Charity."

"I think you fit quite well," she said in a low murmur.

Fit quite well? He grew hard when he thought precisely how she would fit him. He prayed he would have enough self-control to go slowly and do this right. "Drew," he supplied. "Call me Drew." He did not want her calling him by anything but his given name. He would loathe any formality between them now.

"Drew," she repeated, looking down to cover a blush.

Yes, she knew what was about to happen here. He prayed she would not change her mind, because that would certainly leave him a ruined man.

Unable to resist any longer, he lifted her chin on the edge of his hand and lowered his mouth to hers. Her shy hunger, as if she were embarrassed by it, was deeply arousing.

"I believe I am about to get burned," she sighed.

He removed the pins from her hair and let it fall like liquid silk around them. "If I do it right," he murmured against her throat.

A flash of fear raced through Charity. How could she do this? Could she trust she was not just another entertainment for Drew? Would he still want her once he had conquered her? Oh, but how could she *not* do this? Every part of her being cried out for it—every instinct screamed that it was right. And if she never had him again, at least she would have him tonight.

Drew stood, dragging her up with him. When she steadied on her feet, he released her and lifted her chin. He held her with his gaze as he pulled the sash and let the robe fall open, then slid it over her shoulders to puddle at her feet. He drew in a long breath and she stood still as his eyes swept over her. The room, which had seemed suffocatingly close a moment before, was suddenly cold. Chill bumps rose on her arms, and her breasts puckered and firmed.

He cleared his throat. "Sorry," he murmured, lifting her to carry her to the bed and place her beneath a thick eiderdown quilt. When it seemed as if he would rise, she caught his arm and dragged him back down to her. He kissed her deeply, drawing up a sweetness from her very core. Impatient, she fumbled with his buttons, desperate to have him next to her. He aided her clumsy attempts by simply ripping his shirt off, scattering buttons everywhere, then shed his boots and stockings.

He was magnificent. She wasn't certain how a man should look, but he exceeded her expectations. His chest, lightly matted with dark hair, was strongly muscled and broad. His waist and abdomen were narrow and firm, and then courage failed her as he pushed his trousers down his narrow hips. She lifted her eyes to his again—those remarkable midnight eyes. They sparkled with humor and understanding.

"Easy, sweet," he said. "Nothing to be frightened of. You are its master."

He must be jesting. How could she command such a thing?

He slipped beneath the eiderdown to join her and brushed her hair back to cup her face. "If I do something you do not like, anything that makes you uncomfortable, tell me."

She could not even imagine him doing something she would not like. Indeed, his kisses immediately drew her deeper into some sweet abyss—she was drowning in them, consumed by them. His hands worked their way down her spine to cup her buttocks and hitch her higher. Then he lifted her outer leg and drew it up his thigh, leaving her cleft vulnerable.

She remembered this from yesterday in the small sitting room. Her breathing deepened in anticipation of his touch and that bliss, but it did not come. Long, teasing caresses accustomed her to his touch on her thigh well before he found the soft, vulnerable center of her sex. He stroked and whispered praise in a low purring voice until she writhed with anticipation. Was she a wanton to want him so much? Would he think her bold and wicked if she demanded more?

"Drew…" she moaned.

"Patience," he whispered, moving lower, leaving a hot trail

with his tongue from her throat to her breast. "I'm discovering you," he explained. "I want to know all your secrets."

Oh! What sweet torture when he bit lightly and swirled his tongue over the tender pink tip, nibbling and kissing until she thought she'd go mad. She tangled her fingers through his hair and wrapped her legs around him.

"You make me wild," he groaned. As if to reward her, he slipped his finger inside her—stroking the inner folds with a sure touch over and over again until she thought she'd go mad.

"Please, Drew. I cannot stand any more. Just…just do it." She writhed beneath his hand and finally squealed with impatience when he stroked lightly at that breathtaking spot he had found yesterday. "Oh, my!"

He kissed her deeply, swallowing her cries of ecstasy. "There," he whispered when she quieted, "now you are ready."

"I am done," she moaned.

He laughed. "Oh, no, sweet Charity. We've just begun. You're hot and wet and ready for me."

He moved over the top of her and drew her legs up on either side of his. She guessed how they must fit and she lifted her hips to him. Shc wanted him, wanted him inside her desperately, but she'd heard there would be pain. She took a deep breath and prepared herself, trying to remember what she had heard of such events. He kissed her as he pressed downward, forcing a snug, shallow entry.

"Relax," he urged. "Breathe."

His voice was hoarse, hot and moist in her ear, sending little vibrations along her nerve endings and a shiver of delight up her spine.

"Inhale," he whispered, and waited for her to follow his instructions. "Exhale…inhale…."

When she inhaled the second time, he thrust downward. A

sudden sharp pain ripped through her and she twitched, trying to adjust to the thickness of him, stronger, deeper, more intimate than his hand had been.

"Exhale, Charity. You cannot hold your breath all night."

How had she forgotten to breathe? She let her breath out in a long shudder. She glanced up at Drew. He was watching her with a hint of concern. He smiled, and the warmth that surged through her with that simple gesture reassured her. Drew would never hurt her, never let her down, never let her go. She was safe with him. She'd never felt that with Julius.

He kissed her, keeping his mouth on hers as he began moving, and a slow fire kindled in her center again. The burning and heat built with the intensity of Drew's thrusts, and she was gasping again, reaching a new pinnacle, ever higher until, at last, she cried out with him and stilled as the tremors swept through them.

"Oh, Charity," she heard him moan as she fell into a languid swoon. "Sweet, sweet Charity."

Near morning, when the inn was quiet and she thought all her passion had been spent, he slipped his arms around her. He pulled her back against his chest, nesting his thighs behind hers, and his arms around her, one hand intimately resting on her breast. She felt the shape and weight of his sex under her. A sudden hunger kindled inside her and she wanted him again.

"Drew, could we do that again?" she whispered into the dark.

"My God, but you are a bawdy wench!" He laughed and pulled the comforter over their heads as he answered her soft plea.

Chapter Ten

Charity stretched and yawned, turning toward the light. She squinted into a clear blue dawn and sparkling icicles dripping steadily from the eaves. The storm was over. It was time to reckon with her waywardness.

Memories of the night brought heat to her cheeks and she turned back over to look at Drew. Dark stubble covered his jaw and his absurdly thick lashes lay against his cheeks. He was so handsome that she wanted to wake him and tell him so, but the temptation to lie abed another day would be too great to resist. How would they keep their secret then?

She traced his lips with her fingertip, remembering how they had felt on every part of her, and she shuddered with the sweetness of it. But no wonder he was so deep in slumber. He'd been very athletic last night—and ever so much more fun than a silly game of curling. Drew, not Julius, was the conquering hero.

He muttered something unintelligible in his sleep and reached out to throw an arm around her waist. A smile curved his lips and Charity resisted the impulse to kiss him awake.

Instead, she eased from the bed and hurried to dress. She

needed to be back at Wyecliffe Manor before the guests stirred. She certainly did not want to start gossip by arriving with Drew as an escort.

She wanted to ask Drew to meet her later, to tell him she loved him, to thank him for discovering her secrets last night, and for answering her prayers. She looked for a sheet of paper in the drawer of the tiny escritoire in one corner, but could find nothing to leave him a note. Well, no matter. He would come to Wyecliffe when he'd bathed and dressed, and they would talk.

Her head whirled with a list of the things she had to accomplish today. There was still the matter of Mackay's baby to settle, an interview with Laura Tuxbury and her unfinished business with Julius Lingate. Though she had no idea what her future held, she hoped she would be strong enough to face him and apologize for leading him on for the past three years.

Drew rapped solidly on the door of the last cottage in a back lane. Tucked safely inside his coat pocket was the linen hankie that had started this strange journey. 'This was the delivery address the linen merchant had given him this morning when he found Drew waiting for him to open.

He waited impatiently for the door to open, anxious to be done with this. His unfinished business with Miss Wardlow was much more pressing than this bit of meddling. She'd woken and left without a word. No note, no kiss goodbye, no maidenly tears of remorse for last night, no recriminations. 'Twas as if nothing had happened between them. Oh, but it had, and he wasn't about to let her forget. He and the headstrong miss would come to a fast understanding or his name wasn't—

"Drew MacGregor!"

He blinked. Ah, this explained everything. "Why if it isn't Miss Lavinia Corbin," he said. "How long has it been?"

She pulled her paisley shawl a little closer around her and stepped aside for him to enter. "Years, Sir Andrew. I believe I was still…with Madame Fifi at the time. But what brings you to Great Tew? Oh, the wedding, of course."

He removed his hat and ducked beneath the low door lintel. "Aye. Edward has fallen victim to Cupid. But what are *you* doing here?"

She gestured to a straight-back chair near the fire as an invitation to sit. He didn't. "I've come to visit my cousin. But then, you know that since you have found me here. And why, may I ask? I always suspected I was not a favorite of yours."

Drew did not deny it. Lavinia Corbin had been taken out of a brothel to be mistress to a duke. After he had tired of her, she had taken lover after lover. Apparently, she had decided that bearing a lover's child would secure her future.

And now that Drew knew with whom he was dealing, this would not take long. He withdrew the handkerchief from his pocket and dropped it on the chair. Lavinia's attention went to the piece of cloth, then back up to him. A cunning smile lit her face.

"Did they send you to deal with me?"

"They have no idea I am here. The last I heard, Edward refused to traffic with you at all."

"They must. If I do not receive a package from them by tonight, I shall be at the wedding tomorrow. I would be loath to cast a pall…."

"But you would do it, just the same," he finished.

She sighed and waved one hand in a helpless gesture. "I have no other options, Sir Andrew."

"What will it take?"

She sighed to indicate a difficult decision. "Ten thousand would keep me quite well."

He laughed at her audacity.

She gave him a coy smile. "Of course, this will not relieve him of his obligations to little Lawrence."

"Lawrence? You named his baby after his brother?" That was a twisted logic even for Lavinia.

Lavinia laughed, a melodic trill that had captured many of her lovers. "You think Lord Edward is little Lawrence's sire? La! That is amusing. No, *Lawrence* is the father."

He hid his surprise. Even though he'd had faith in his friend, the conversation he and Charity overheard had been sufficiently vague as to create doubt. But no matter the baby's parentage, Mackay had not wanted his bride upset or their wedding day marred by scandal. Drew shrugged. A joyous day to celebrate and remember was the least he could give them. He removed a large wad of banknotes from the inside pocket of his vest and held them up.

A greedy light flared in Lavinia's dark eyes. She reached for the notes but he pulled them out of reach. "You'll keep quiet?"

She evaluated the size of the wad and shook her head. "They cannot buy me off so cheaply."

"They refused to buy you off at all. *I* am your only option. And believe me, Lavinia, it is nothing to me if you starve in a gutter or take yet another lover. I only want your assurance that you will leave Great Tew this afternoon and not return for a full month or more."

"Done!" she agreed, lunging for the banknotes.

Charity hurried down the back stairs and turned along the corridor toward the small ladies' retiring room that had been converted to the sewing room. The day was speeding by with all the preparations for the medieval feast being set up in the great hall and the final preparations for the wedding tomorrow.

When she'd arrived back at Wyecliffe Manor this morning, all out of breath for running half the way, Grace was just stirring. She had sized Charity up with a knowing smile but asked no questions—bless her for her discretion—and reported that her interview with Lydia Foley revealed that the secret she held was a contribution to the Sailor's Widows and Orphans Fund.

Charity was relieved to realize that all that remained to be done was to have the hem marked on her bridesmaid gown, find Miss Tuxbury and quiz her about any secrets she might have—and she was certain to have one since everyone at Wyecliffe Manor did. Perhaps everyone in Great Tew. Now that everyone else had been eliminated, Miss Tuxbury was the last remaining candidate.

Then she could wait for Drew to arrive from the village. She could not wait to see him again, and yet she was afraid. Heavens! The man had seen her naked! He'd...no! She couldn't think of that or she'd collapse in a quivering puddle.

"Miss Wardlow!" a voice called from behind her in the corridor. "Could you spare me a moment?"

Her heart fell. "Not at the moment, Mr. Lingate. I am already tardy for an appointment. Later perhaps."

"That is what you said yesterday."

His voice was petulant and she wondered why she had never noticed before how peevish Julius could be. "The...the chill quite did me in, Mr. Lingate. I stayed abed," she said, proudly realizing she was not, strictly speaking, lying.

"Sorry to hear that, my dear," he said, looking properly chagrined. "But I must speak with you. Now."

"Now? But what can be so urgent that it cannot wait until after my appointment?"

"It concerns us. You and me, dear...Charity."

Gads! Here it was—and at the worst possible moment! The tall grandfather clock at the end of the hall struck half past three. "I really must go, Mr. Lingate. Olivia's seamstress is so busy that I will be tripping over my hem tomorrow if I miss this appointment."

"When—"

"Before the feast," she promised, already rounding a corner. "I will find you, Mr. Lingate."

And, half an hour later, as she left the seamstress, she ran directly into Miss Tuxbury. Before the woman knew what had happened, Charity linked arms with her and led her toward a quiet corner of the great hall where they could sit and watch the harried preparations for the medieval feast. Even more garlands of evergreen were being draped from every available surface. A yule log was laid on the hearth and fresh white candles were being placed on the table and in the chandeliers above. Everywhere she looked, there were kissing boughs and mistletoe. No maid would escape unkissed tonight.

After a few preliminary pleasantries, Charity sprang her trap. "I must say, Miss Tuxbury, that I was amazed when I learned your secret. I never would have thought it."

"You…know?" she asked, wide-eyed. "Oh, I suppose Mr. Lingate told you. He has always said what a dear friend you have been. I used to be quite jealous, you know."

"Jealous? Whatever for?" Charity asked.

"How you two always have your heads together and seem to be having such a merry time. I thought he might have more special feelings for you than mere friendship. I feared his only interest in me was my dowry."

Charity blinked. What had she missed? Why had Miss Tuxbury thought she had any right to be jealous? And why had

Julius told her their relationship was "mere friendship"? He'd kissed her, for heaven's sake, and had been trying to propose.

"But now, of course, I know better," Miss Tuxbury continued, "and I hope you and I can be friends, too."

"Certainly," Charity responded, more confused than ever. "If your secret does not make that impossible."

"I cannot think why it would. Within the next month, everyone will know. I believe it is my father's intent to begin by announcing it to this assemblage tonight."

A cool draft from the foyer claimed Charity's attention. Drew walked in, scanning the hall. When he saw her, he gave her a slow smile that made her mind go blank. When she gathered her wits again, Miss Tuxbury was smiling, too.

"But I collect you will be making your own announcement soon," she said.

"A-announcement, Miss Tuxbury? About what?"

"Why, your own betrothal, of course. I have seen the way you look at Sir Andrew. It is love, is it not?"

"Mmm," she sighed, unable to tear her gaze away from him.

Miss Tuxbury laughed. "Yes, I can see that it is."

Charity came back to herself with a start. Betrothal? Miss Tuxbury was betrothed to Julius? Absurdly, she giggled. So *that* was what he'd been trying to tell her. How droll. And what a relief.

Poor Julius, how he must be dreading to tell her that he'd fallen in love with someone else. And that explained his urgency—he wanted to tell her before Mr. Tuxbury made the announcement tonight. But she would not make it easy for that rascal! He deserved to suffer just a little for leading her on for the past years when he likely had no intention of ever proposing. Oh, this was going to be fun! She would find Julius at once and allow him to "break her heart" with the announcement.

* * *

Drew waited impatiently for Charity to finish with Miss Tuxbury. By now she would know that none of the women on her list were the mother of Mackay's baby and would be preparing to tell Olivia of Edward's deceit. Thank heavens, he had arrived in time to prevent that.

Miss Tuxbury looked his way and smiled. Charity stood and started across the room toward him, a luminous glow in her eyes. She looked different today. Her hips had a soft sway and there was something less girlish in her bearing. His blood rose just watching her move.

He'd taken no more than two steps before Grace Forbush entered the hall, seized Charity by the arm and pulled her down the corridor. She glanced over her shoulder, shrugged and mouthed the word *soon.* He would have to be patient. Not his strong suit.

A clock chimed six times and Drew realized Mrs. Forbush had found Charity to dress for the feast. The guests had decided to dress in makeshift costumes. Mackay had told him not to worry—that he would provide something for Drew. He'd better find Mackay and change so he could catch Charity before the feast began, and before she could talk to Olivia.

Charity was scandalized by her costume. Grace dressed her in a long white nightgown, twined a golden cord with tassels around her waist and topped her unbound hair with a wreath that looked suspiciously like a kissing bough without candles. She was supposed to be the Christmas angel. She felt more like the Christmas tart.

She left her room in search of Drew as the guests began to gather for dinner. She hoped he would be waiting for her in the great hall. They needed to discuss what they should do about Olivia. If Drew could take Lord Edward aside and persuade him to confess all to Olivia, then there was a chance Olivia would understand and forgive him. But Olivia must know. And if Edward would not tell her, Charity would.

The moment she entered the great hall, she saw Julius Lingate pacing in front of the fire. He was dressed a tunic made from an old tapestry and long green hose. The moment he saw her he cut through the gathering crowd and hurried to her.

"Miss Wardlow! Thank heavens you are here. You promised to find me."

There was something of an accusation in his words. Charity felt a guilty twinge. She *had* forgot all about him. Oh, well, how long could it take him to break her heart? She allowed him to take her arm and pull her into the music room.

"We really must speak, Miss Wardlow. There is something I must tell you, and a very important question to ask."

She tried to look innocent. She knew she wouldn't be able to muster tears, but she certainly knew how to pout, and his rejection would give her the perfect opportunity to storm out.

She sat in the middle of the hard piano bench, making sure there would be no room for him. He would have to pace or stand uncomfortably in front of her.

He paced. Looking down at his feet, he cleared his throat. "I regret having left this until the last minute, but I did try to speak with you several times, and—"

"Yes, I know, Mr. Lingate. I must bear a part of the blame," she volunteered, hoping to speed him along.

"No!" He turned to her and fastened her with a worshipful gaze. "You are too kind, Miss Wardlow. The blame is all mine. I have been a cad, an absolute blighter, whilst you have been a perfect angel."

Oh, dear. He really *was* trying to soften the blow.

"And when you hear what I have to say, you will, no doubt, despise me."

"Come now, sir. It cannot be that bad. Tell me what has you so troubled."

"How…long have we known each other, Miss Wardlow?"

"Nine years, I think. I met you in my first season. I was ten and six, if I recall."

"Ah, yes. I was taken with you even then. On the verge of making an offer when your father…that is, when you withdrew from society in mourning."

That surprised Charity. She had only noted Julius's interest in the past five years.

He began pacing again. "Such a tragedy, that. Had I known the implications, I might have pressed my suit anyway. But when my father found out about…"

"My father's insolvency?" she supplied, growing impatient.

"Yes," he nodded. "Yes, precisely. At any rate, my father would have none of it. Still, I couldn't abandon hope. Had it not been for money, I might have persuaded him."

Yes, she had suspected that money was the culprit. But she always believed that Julius would overcome that obstacle. That he would find some way to make his father listen, or find the courage to defy him. She had sadly overestimated him.

Then another thought occurred to her. Laura Tuxbury. She would never know that Julius had chosen her because of her dowry while Charity would be left to wonder if Julius, had he known about her money, would have wed her as much for that money as herself. And just how much could he love her if he was not willing to stand up to his father?

"Such is the uncertainty of life, Miss Wardlow," he was saying. "And now…"

"Now?" she encouraged, preparing to look heartbroken.

He dropped to his knees in front of her. "Now I must inform you that I am engaged to marry Miss Tuxbury."

She tried to cover her sigh of relief with a gasp and a pout. "*That* is what you have been trying to tell me, Mr. Lingate? That you are going to marry someone else?"

"Yes," he cried. He dropped his head to rest on her knees. "But I cannot give you up. I cannot!"

"What!" She was astonished as he continued to weep into her lap. She tried to stand, but he wrapped his arms around her legs. "Mr. Lingate! Collect yourself."

"Not until you say you do not hate me."

"I do not. I swear it. I am…ah, disappointed. But I understand. Your father wants what is best for you."

"You! You are best for me, Miss Wardlow. I cannot—I *will* not—relinquish you! I must have you for my own."

The door clicked as the latch was turned and she looked up, trying to unfasten Julius's arms. Sir Andrew MacGregor stood there in a costume as strange as her own, looking for all the world like a thundercloud while Julius kept his face in her lap, oblivious to the interruption.

"I knew it," he cried. "I *knew* you loved me."

Drew's jaw tightened and he gave her such a dark look that said she would answer for this little tableau. He pulled the door shut and she was alone with Julius again.

"It is too late for us, Mr. Lingate," she said as gently as she could. "Release me while I yet have my pride."

"No, it is not too late," he said, looking up at her at last. Hope lit his eyes. "I only ask this, Charity, because I know your poverty will preclude any good offers for your hand. Be my mistress. Once I am wed to Miss Tuxbury, I will have enough money to set you up in a cottage of your own in Saint Albans. We could be together every weekend."

"Mistress?" Her pity turned to anger in a flash. "You want me to be your *mistress?*" What kind of man would use his wife's money to support his mistress? This was appalling!

"Yes, my love. If you truly love me—"

Truly loved? She pushed Julius away and stood, no longer concerned for his feelings. In fact, she could only think of the look on Drew's face. She needed to talk to him at once.

"Miss Wardlow! Charity! Come back," Julius called.

Chapter Eleven

Good God! Could he trust his ears? Had Charity declared her love for Lingate? Fresh from *his* arms, had she—no! He refused to believe that. It had given him a nasty turn to see Charity in her nightgown with Lingate's face in her lap. Something odd was afoot or Lingate would find himself with a blackened eye and a hell of a headache.

As he entered the great hall, he noted the amused stares of several guests. What could Mackay be thinking to dress him in a harlequin's outfit? All he needed was the belled cap and he'd be a complete fool. He advanced on Mackay, making no attempt to hide his disgust.

"What's got under your skin, MacGregor?" he asked.

"Hard to know," he answered. "It could be Miss Wardlow. It could be Lingate. It could even be this damned outfit you've put me in."

Mackay grinned. "I'd vote for Miss Wardlow."

"Maybe. Where's your bride-to-be?"

"She's around here somewhere. Saw her a moment ago."

"Well, find her and do not let her out of your sight. Most

importantly, do not let her speak with Miss Wardlow until I've had a chance to talk to her."

Edward scratched his head. "Olivia or Miss Wardlow?"

"Miss Wardlow. She knows about the baby, Mackay, but she has her facts twisted. She thinks you are the father, and she intends to tell Olivia."

"How the deuce—"

"Later," Drew interrupted. "I spoke with Lavinia this morning. She left Great Tew and will not be back for a month or more. My wedding gift to you and your bride."

Edward stared at him in disbelief and then guffawed. "Did you meddle in my business, MacGregor? Well, this is an interesting turn of events. The imperturbable, aloof Drew MacGregor turned meddler. Faith, I was feeling bad for what I am about to do to you, but now I'll have a clean conscience."

The fine hair on the back of Drew's neck stood up on end. "Do? What are you going to do, Mackay?"

He went to his place at the head of the table and hit a small brass gong to quiet the gathering crowd. "Honored guests," he began, motioning Drew to his side, "please take your seats and meet your host for tonight, MacGregor, Lord of Misrule." He turned and bowed to Drew as he passed him the leather-wrapped mallet and a belled cap.

Drew was still standing there with the mallet and cap in his hand when Charity rushed into the hall. Her eyes widened as she looked at him and covered her mouth to hide her laughter. He wanted her instantly, his body firming with no more than her smile. He could not wait to get her private later tonight.

She took a place beside Mrs. Forbush halfway down the table as servants dressed in costume carried in a roasted pig complete with an apple in its mouth. Other servants bearing all manner of delicacies and footmen dispensing an endless supply of wine, cider and hot buttered rum followed them. A moment later Lingate entered and sat with a group of his friends. Drew hit the gong once to signal the beginning of the feast and then sat beside Mackay.

"I haven't the faintest notion what I am supposed to do," he muttered to his friend.

"Preside over the feast and the merriment aftcr. Everyone must do as you tell them," Mackay grinned.

That was a heady notion, and he planned to have fun with that before the night was over. But there was still the matter with Charity to take care of. Pray she had not yet found Olivia. He had to find a way to make her understand that all was well with the bride and groom. He glanced down the length of the table to see her rising from her seat, her attention fastened on Olivia, who was just entering the hall.

He stood and rang the gong. "You!" he said, pointing to Olivia. "Yes, you coming late to my table! Come sit by me."

Mackay grinned as he made a place for her between them. "You are taking to this quite well, MacGregor."

Drew shot him a disgruntled look. He could not think of a way to let Charity know that her concerns for Olivia were unfounded. And if he called her to his side, she might say something to Mackay or Olivia over the roast pork. No, he would have to speak publicly, couching his words in a game.

He tossed his buttered rum down his throat and stood. "Time to sing for your supper," he announced. "We shall have a game of discovery—each of us must tell what we've learned during our stay at Wyecliffe Manor." He paused for only a moment. "What? No one rushing to be first? Very well, I shall—"

"Me! I will go first," Charity stood. She wanted him to understand that she knew he'd been right all along. Not all secrets were bad. Some were worth keeping. And omission was not a lie. She needed him to know she would not expose his friend.

"No, Miss Nightgown. Sit down or I shall banish you from your supper."

"I shall not, my lord. Not until I've told what I've learned." She cleared her throat as her gaze swept the guests. "I have learned many secrets over the past few days, and that things are not always what they seem." She wondered if he would recognize his own words from the first time they'd met.

A collective gasp seemed to suck the air from the room. Drew groaned. How many people here lived in fear of her knowledge? The time had come to reassure them all.

"I have learned that not all secrets are bad."

"Miss Nightgown, I'd advise you—"

"I've learned that some secrets are generous, loving gifts, given to spare feelings, or to protect pride, preserve friendships, or avoid hurting loved ones. Some—" she glanced toward Miss Foley "—are even kept for the sake of modesty.

"I had thought that all secrets were bad and that, if something could not stand up to scrutiny, it was wrong. But *I* was wrong. And I will never reveal anyone's secrets."

Sighs of relief exhaled around the room. Would Drew recognize that her little speech was her way of telling him that she would keep Mackay's secret? He nodded to her and waved his gong. "Very well, Miss Nightgown. You may sit."

"I am not done, Lord MacGregor." She moistened her lips, gone dry with anxiety. "I have learned secrets about myself, as well. I learned that I did not want what I thought I wanted. And that I want what I denied myself for the past five days. So, you see, what I've really learned is that the worst secrets, the most damaging lies, are the ones we tell ourselves."

Drew stared at her as she dropped her napkin on her chair, curtsied and hurried from the great hall. She did not care in the least what sort of scandal this would cause with the meddling gossipmongers of the ton.

Drew caught up to her in the hallway and pulled her into the library, locking the door behind them.

She backed away, uncertain what his intentions were. "Are you angry, Sir Andrew?"

"Angry does not half describe it," he said.

"But I swear I will not tell Olivia. I do not even know who the mother is."

"I do, but we will get to that later."

Her sparkling eyes widened. "Who?"

He advanced on her. "Later, Charity. For now I only want to know about what you said out there." He gestured toward the great hall. "Did you mean it?"

She nodded. The calves of her legs hit Lord Edward's desk and halted her backward progress. "Every word. I will never breathe a single syllable of anyone's secret."

"Not that, Charity," he said in a low, throaty voice.

She licked her lips as he came closer. She could not catch her breath for the heat in his eyes. "You mean about the secrets I kept from myself?"

He nodded, bending her slightly backward to place his hands flat on the desk on either side of her. "Tell me," he demanded.

"I…I thought I wanted Julius. I thought I loved him and that he loved me." She wanted to look away, to preserve her modesty, her pride, but his scrutiny held her as firmly as his arms. "But that was an illusion—a lie I told myself so that I would not feel so alone."

"What is real, Charity?"

He bent closer, his thighs pressing along hers, and she felt herself melting. Breathless, she managed to gasp, "You. You are real."

He smiled and nuzzled her ear. "And what have you denied for the past five days?"

"That I want you," she confessed. "But you knew that before I did."

"A man likes to hear these things, Charity. Is there anything more?"

"I love you, Andrew MacGregor." She could feel the heat rising in her cheeks. She'd never told a man that—not even Julius. Would Drew laugh at her? Say he'd only been teaching her a lesson?

He took a tiny box from the folds inside his harlequin tunic and set it on the desk. "No more meddling?" he asked.

She shook her head.

"And no more secrets?"

She thought of her bank account in London and the investments she had made. If she told him, would he want her for her fortune? Would she be just like Laura Tuxbury, always wondering if love or money had wooed her hand? But after all her fine principles and moral indignation on Olivia's behalf, how could she lie to Drew now?

"Well, perhaps just one. You see—"

"Hush, sweet Charity. Whatever it is, 'twill make no difference. Just say you will be my wife and you will learn *my* secret."

"Yes," she sighed, tears filling her eyes. "Yes…" She felt the tiny box being pressed into her palm. She lifted the lid and found a band encrusted all around with dazzling diamonds nesting in black velvet. She gasped and tears obscured her vision. Drew's secret had been a ring for her.

He took the ring and slipped it on her finger, then brought

her hand to his lips and smiled. She had finally gotten everything she never knew she wanted.

His mouth descended to hers. He nibbled her lower lip until she opened hers. "I love you, sweet Charity, and I love your little secrets and your meddling ways."

* * * * *